Eric Wilder

River Road

Gondwana Press

Edmond, Oklahoma

Other books by Eric Wilder

Ghost of a Chance
Murder Etouffee
Name of the Game
A Gathering of Diamonds
Over the Rainbow
Big Easy
Just East of Eden
Lily's Little Cajun Cookbook
Of Love and Magic
Bones of Skeleton Creek
City of Spirits
Primal Creatures
Black Magic Woman

This book is a work of fiction. Names, characters, places, and incidents either are products of the author's imagination or are used fictitiously. Any resemblance to actual events or locales or persons, living or dead, is entirely coincidental.

Gondwana Press LLC
1802 Canyon Park Cir. Ste C
Edmond, OK 73013

For information on books by Eric Wilder
www.ericwilder.com

Front Cover by Higgins & Ross Photography/Design

ISBN: 978-0-9791165-9-9

Acknowledgments

I would like to thank Donald Yaw for helping me edit the book, and providing valuable input involving timeline and character development. Thanks to Higgins and Ross for their evocative cover. Lastly, thanks to all the wonderful people that love Louisiana and New Orleans.

For Marilyn

River Road

A novel by
Eric Wilder

Chapter 1

It was one of those days, rain falling in a gentle mist as I glanced down Canal Street. When thunder shook the windowpanes, I stopped gawking and hurried up the sidewalk.

Late afternoon streets were empty as I reached the Saenger Theater. The old auditorium had occupied the corner of Canal and N. Rampart for as long as I could remember. My parents liked their liquor. They could buy cocktails at the balcony bar and get drunk as they watched the latest Hollywood flick. They loved the Saenger.

Flooded and damaged during Katrina, the theater had recently undergone renovation. With work finally completed, the facility is a destination for music and touring acts. The marvelous new sign over the front entrance greeted me, flashing crimson neon as I entered the lobby.

I wasn't the only one that had braved summer

rain, dozens of other people filing into the main amphitheater with me. Music from an old pipe organ flooded the auditorium as I entered the ongoing festivities. The occasion was a wake, the atmosphere anything but somber. As I gazed at the crowd, I spotted someone I knew.

Rafael Romanov smiled and worked his way toward me. The tall man with thinning hair seemed as dark and mysterious as his hooked nose and Eastern European face. He'd grown a tiny goatee on his pointed chin since the last time I'd seen him.

"Wyatt," he said, grasping my hand. "You're looking dapper."

"Don't hold a candle to you, Rafael," I said.

He brushed an imaginary flake off his cashmere sports coat. His expensive jacket complimented the military crease of his dark pants and the gleam of his spit-polished shoes. His light blue silk shirt splayed open enough to draw attention to a hairy chest and the heavy gold chain around his neck.

"I didn't know you knew Jeribeth," he said.

Jeribeth Briggs was a recently deceased New Orleans socialite. Unlike most wakes, Jeribeth wasn't in a coffin. Her corpse, dressed to the nines in a red designer dress and audacious hat, sat on a wrought-iron bench. Her signature feather boa draped her shoulders. As in life, she had a cigarette with a long filter in one hand, a glass of Jack Daniels in the other. Garlands of flowers and lush potted shrubs surrounded her almost as if she were enjoying cocktails in her garden.

"Didn't know her," I said.

"Just gawking?"

"I have reasons for being here."

"Such as?"

"A new client. He requested I meet him at the wake."

"Strange place to meet a client," he said.

"His call, not mine. Did you know her?"

"You mean Jeribeth? Saw her many times at Madeline's when I was a child. Like you, someone is paying me to be here."

"Oh?"

"My usual gig. Comforting family and friends of the bereaved. From the quantity of alcohol everyone is consuming, I'd say my services will go unneeded."

Rafael was a defrocked priest; defrocked because his mother Madeline is a witch. As the saying goes, once a priest always a priest. Since leaving the church, he'd served as a rent a priest aboard a cruise ship sailing out of New Orleans. Like most of the other guests crowding the auditorium, he had a drink in hand and a smile on his face.

The Saenger Theater auditorium is large, its walls decorated to mimic an Italian villa. Priceless chandeliers hang from the ceiling. The crowd included actors, politicians, musicians, and many of the city's richest people. Human chatter didn't begin to overwhelm the background music. The acoustics were so acute you could hear every musical instrument while eavesdropping on your neighbor's conversation.

"Now this is the way to have a wake," Rafael said.

"Wildest thing I've ever seen."

"It's the Big Easy, Cowboy, not the real world."

His smile disappeared when I said, "Not sad like Kimmi's wake."

My ex-wife Kimmi had married Rafael. When she died, we'd met at her wake and had maintained a friendship ever since.

"Mind if I change the subject?" he said, sipping his whiskey. "See the attractive woman by the punch bowl?"

3

"Gorgeous. How do I know her?"

"Lucy Diamond. A reporter for Fox. National, not local."

"Bet she gets lots of jokes about her name."

"From her frown, I don't think I'd ask," he said. "Want to meet her?"

"You know her?"

"We met on one of my cruises, and we've kept in touch."

Rafael waved, catching the reporter's gaze. Smiling, she made her way through the noisy throng.

"Rafael," she said, on her tiptoes to plant a sensuous kiss on his lips.

"Lucy, this is my friend Wyatt Thomas."

She nodded, acknowledging my presence with only a frown.

"Got to rush, Rafe. Can we do lunch while I'm in town?"

"Love it, beautiful lady," he said.

"I'll call you," she said, kissing him before disappearing back into the crowd.

"Rafe?" I said.

Rafael grinned. "What can I say? She has a thing for tall, dark, and mysterious men."

"I'm jealous. What's she doing in New Orleans?"

"Working on a sensational story; something to do with Jeribeth and Dr. Mary Taggert."

"Oh?"

"The old lady had a few skeletons in her closet. She was best friends with Dr. Taggert."

"How do I know that name?"

"A prominent surgeon murdered fifty years ago. The case was never solved."

"I wasn't alive, but remember hearing about it. Doing cancer research, wasn't she?"

"Along with Dr. Louis Hollingsworth, the founder of the Hollingsworth Clinic. Someone wrote a book saying the C.I.A. had a hand in the murder," he said.

"What interest did they have in her?"

"Not sure, my friend. Something to do with the Kennedy assassination."

I must have rolled my eyes because Raphael held up a palm, smiled and shook his head.

"It's hard to separate fact from fiction because there are so many conspiracy theories floating around out there," I said.

"Don't know about that. What I do know is Madeline used to hold séances at our house when I was young. Jeribeth and Doctor Mary often attended."

"What's your mother's told you about it?"

"Madeline never discusses her clients, even with me. If you want to know something about Dr. Mary, Lucy is the person to ask."

As with Rafael, the Catholic Church had also expelled Madeline. Her heresy was being a witch. She has a shop in the Quarter called Madeline's Magic Potions. By all accounts, she is a witch. When Rafael grabbed another drink from a passing waiter, I glanced at the punchbowl.

"I'll keep that in mind. Has Ms. Diamond told you anything?" I asked.

"Not much, even though we had drinks last night at the Carousel Bar."

"Sweet."

"I wish. Lucy's there every night, usually drinking alone."

"Not even with her crew?"

"Hardly. They're staying at the Sheraton."

"Because?"

"Lucy's a bitch!"

"I see," I said.

"Razor tongued, and she uses her words like blunt instruments. Her producers have an impossible task enticing celebs and politicians.

She has rough edges, but her viewers love it when she unloads on her guests."

"So she's . . ."

"Bitch personified," he said, finishing my question.

Jazz music had grown louder. I glanced at the punchbowl again, realizing I was the only one without a drink.

"Excuse me a moment?" I said. "I need to visit the punchbowl."

"I'll be here when you return."

"I think you're right about having no consoling to do."

He nodded, hoisting his whiskey glass in a salute. "I ain't complaining, boss."

The crowd had grown. As I inched toward the punch bowl, a young woman in front of me caught a heel and almost fell. When I grabbed her shoulders, she nodded before moving away into the throng.

From the spread on the table, some lucky caterer had earned a fat payday for this gig. They weren't the only ones. Local florists had also made out like bandits. I noticed as I sidestepped a potted peace lily.

Smelling the gumbo, I remembered I hadn't eaten since breakfast. Piles of shrimp and crawfish rested on sheets of yesterday's Picayune. In deference to my white jacket, I decided to pass on the food.

No one had touched the grape punch. Likely because it wasn't yet spiked with alcohol. Since I have a low tolerance for anything alcoholic, I took a sip first to make sure. When I turned, I bumped the person standing behind me. Grape punch splattered the woman's silk blouse, the growing stain spreading across her chest like a bloody wound. It was the Fox reporter Lucy Diamond.

"You idiot!" she said.

6

"I'm so sorry."

"Back off, you moron. Do you have any idea how much this blouse cost me?"

"Is there anything I can do?" I said as she pushed away through the crowd.

"Yeah, drop dead!" she said, showing me her middle finger.

People were staring at me as if I were a serial killer. I slunk away in shame to a corner of the amphitheater vacant of guests. When I backed against a potted tree, someone tapped my shoulder.

"Don't turn around," a man's voice said. "I told you to come alone."

"I did. I bumped into a friend."

"Nothing we can do about it now."

"You're the person that asked me to meet them here?"

"Yes," he said. "I got a job for you."

"What exactly are you hiring me to do?"

"You've heard of Mary Taggert?" When I nodded, he said, "My mother. Everybody in New Orleans knows someone murdered her. I want you to find the killer, and then make sure everyone in town knows his name."

"The case is fifty years old. It's not just cold; it's frozen solid."

He placed an envelope in my hand. "You're my last hope. There's information in the envelope and a large retainer. Can I trust you?"

"Yes."

"Hope so. Not much I can do about it now."

The man turned me until I faced the potted palms, my mind blocking sounds of the noisy wake.

"At least tell me something to get me started," I said.

"Check the envelope and you'll know everything I know. Now, give me five minutes

7

before turning around."

"Wait . . ."

"Don't turn. Trust me; it's for your own good."

I wheeled around the moment I heard his feet begin to shuffle. He was too busy elbowing his way through the crowd to notice. I followed the balding little man in white socks and old checkered sports coat. It was dark outside as he hurried through the doorway. He broke into a run when he reached the sidewalk. It didn't take me long to realize why.

A black sedan waited on the street outside the Saenger. It pulled away from the curb when he exited the front doors. Seeing the vehicle, he dodged traffic and sprinted across Canal Street. The sedan did a sliding u-turn, barely avoiding a streetcar returning from the cemeteries. When it screeched to a halt two Hispanic looking men exited, chasing my client up the sidewalk.

Both men wore black sports coats and khaki pants. One of them tackled my new customer, sending him sliding across the concrete. The second pursuer tapped the back of his neck with a club. I raced across the street, dodging traffic as they dragged him into the awaiting car.

"Hey, stop right there!" I yelled as they shoved him into the backseat.

One of the men had a pistol, people on the sidewalk ducking as he pulled the trigger. Two muffled pops were the only thing I heard, and it was the last thing I remembered for a while.

Chapter 2

I awoke in a strange bed, two people dressed in medical scrubs staring down at me. If that wasn't enough to send my alarms blaring, a mule inside my head was trying to kick its way out. It was then I noticed the numbness in my left arm. The IV hanging above me was dripping fluid into my veins.

"How you doing?" the young man asked.

"Where am I?"

"Hospital. Gunshot wound to your left shoulder. Luckily, the bullet didn't strike bone. How's your head?"

"About to explode."

"You banged it on the sidewalk when you fell. Mild concussion. You'll feel better in a few days. I'll be back to check on you tomorrow."

Though the doctor's blond hair was thin, he didn't look old enough to shave. He had yet to smile. The nurse watched, flashing a silver-toothed grin as he disappeared into the darkened hallway.

"I'm Claytee," she said. "He's is such a baby. It makes me feel like spanking him sometimes." When I glanced at the bandage on my shoulder, she said, "Don't worry. It's the Big Easy, and you're not his first gunshot victim. You making it okay,

9

hon?"

I massaged my temple with my free hand. "I can't feel my arm and there's an angry mule inside my head."

She grinned, her silver tooth catching the dim light cast by the medical instruments. "Time for a dose of cloud nine. You'll feel better in a minute."

"How long have I been here?"

"Don't matter none. You alive, nothing broken or missing. Lots of my patients can't say that."

After injecting me, she turned off the lights and left me alone in the hospital room.

The only words I'd understood were "gunshot victim."

I needed to use the facilities and wheeled the IV cart with me. Before the bathroom door shut, a ruckus in the hall disturbed me. The commotion continued as I exited the bathroom. Cracking the door, I peeked down the darkened hallway.

Something I'd heard piqued my curiosity. Familiar voices resonated down the hall. The same two men who were responsible for the bullet hole in my shoulder. They were asking the night nurse directions to my room. Shutting the door, I hurried to the bed.

I plumped pillows under the covers to resemble a sleeping man. The needle didn't even hurt when I jerked it out of my arm, sticking it into the mattress. My clothes were hanging in a bathroom recess. Scooping them up, I rushed into the hallway, and then to a tiny break area across from my room.

The smell of burned coffee hit me as I hid in the supply closet. Men entered my room, two muffled pops shaking my already fragile consciousness. I backed against the wall behind a rubber apron, my heart racing as I held my breath.

Shuffling feet entered the break room. Someone opened the door to the supply closet, peering in. It was then the alarm on my abandoned instruments began to blare. The door shut as night nurses and emergency doctors descended on my room. I pulled on my clothes, glanced down the empty hallway and hurried to the elevator.

Nurse Claytee's cloud nine had rendered me numb. I noticed as I floated down the hall, my sense of well-being worrying me. Though feeling no pain, I realized the seriousness of two men trying to kill me. Emerging from the hospital, I almost expected to take a bullet in the back. It didn't seem to matter.

Outside, the sky was dark. I recognized the well-lighted area as the New Orleans hospital district. A cabbie waiting in front opened the back door when he saw me looking.

"Where too, bub?" he asked

"Bertram's bar on Chartres," I said, ducking as I saw the two men exit the hospital.

They didn't see me.

The French Quarter wasn't far. As I exited the cab, music from a brass band wafted up from the direction of Bourbon Street. It was summer in the Quarter and business slow at Bertram's. The Cajun bartender wasn't happy, and his dark eyes showed it. He didn't bother removing his trapper's hat as he mopped his brow with a red-checkered handkerchief.

During the day, large windows flooded the open room with ambient light. It leaped off polished wood floors and an ornate bar that had to be two-hundred years old. Tonight, only flashing neon reflected through the windows. Panties, bras, and other undergarments hung from the ceiling over the bar. They were a testament to the consumption of gallons of alcohol resulting in lost inhibitions. What happens in Vegas stays in Vegas, they say. Unlike Vegas, visitors celebrate what happens to them in the Big Easy.

Bertram had no permanent help, preferring to do everything himself. It didn't seem to matter because the bar rarely closed. Sometimes, there were so many customers that beer flowed like water. I realized he must have been making a fortune. You'd never know it from looking at him. He still drove the same old truck, and he'd never spent a dime remodeling the bar.

"Tourists like it like this," he always said.

Yes, they did and so did I.

"Where the hell you been?" he asked when I came through the door. "The N.O.P.D. was here earlier and tore up your room looking for something."

"Did they have a search warrant?"

"Didn't ask," he said.

Sensing something was amiss he locked the front door and flipped his closed sign.

"You let them in my room without a search warrant?" I asked.

"Hell, Cowboy, since when does the N.O.P.D. need a search warrant?"

I didn't bother answering his question. "What were they looking for?"

"Don't know, but your room's a mess. What the hell's going on?"

"Too much to explain and not enough time. No sense in calling the police now."

"What happened to your arm and why are you slurring your words?"

"Someone's trying to kill me. Can you take care of my cat for a few days?"

"You ain't told me what happened to you, yet."

Before I could answer, someone began banging on the door. Bertram nodded for me to get out of sight. A door behind the liquor cabinet led to the suite of rooms where he lived. I called to him before I slipped through it.

"Bertram, alert Tony. Tell him I'll meet him at

Culotta's tomorrow, about noon. Ask him to dig up anything he can on the Mary Taggert murder. And Bertram, tell him to come alone."

He nodded as he hurried across the empty bar to check on the disturbance at the front door. Slipping into his apartment, I looked to see if it was my two new companions. It was.

A back door to Bertram's apartment led to the tiny garage where he kept his old beater. Another door exited into an alleyway. I stepped into the darkness, disturbing a stray cat pawing through the trash. If I weren't already paranoid, I was now. Someone was trying to kill me, and the New Orleans cops were somehow involved. I needed answers and headed to the only place I knew where I might get some.

I had no idea what time it was as I hurried to the Carousel Bar, hoping it was still open. Lucy Diamond, according to Rafael Romanov, might be there. I wanted to see her.

The rain had ended, moving east to Mississippi. Water, glistening from reflected streetlight, flooded the streets. A few late-night party people were still prowling the Quarter. I hurried past them as I entered the majestic Monteleone. I didn't have time to admire the chandeliers, ducking into the Carousel Bar instead.

The intimate setting featured a circular bar that rotated like a circus carousel. It had a top, shaped like a crown, and decorated with carved Mardi Gras faces. A single person, the reporter Lucy Diamond, sat alone at the bar. Her eyes widened when I joined her.

"You! Are you stalking me?"

"I assure you I'm not, but I do need to talk to you."

"You ruined my new silk blouse, you asshole."

"We met before that. I'm Rafael Romanov's friend. Remember?"

As she glared at me, it was my first real look at her. She was a knockout with striking green eyes and ash blond hair. Her pouty lips required no lipstick, nor did her Nordic complexion need any makeup. She sounded tipsy, and the punch stain formed a rose bloom on her silk blouse.

"Fred, would you please call security and have this man removed?"

During my drinking years, I'd spent many hours rotating at the Carousel. I didn't recognize Fred, the bartender, but put up a hand as he reached for the phone.

"Please, wait. What I have to say to Ms. Diamond is important."

"He's a stalker. I've dealt with your kind before."

"I'm not a stalker. Won't you at least give me a minute to explain why I'm here?"

Lucy nodded to Fred, giving him permission to replace the phone. With arms clasped to her chest, she gave me a quick look.

"Okay, buster, this better be good."

"Doctor Mary Taggert," I said.

"What about her?"

"I'm a private investigator. A new client who said he was Mary Taggert's son hired me earlier tonight."

"Impossible. Mary Taggert had no son. She was a confirmed lesbian."

"Sure about that?"

Lucy Diamond didn't answer, sipping her martini instead. "Your jacket." she finally said. "What happened to you?"

My bandage had failed, blood oozing from the bullet hole in my linen sports coat.

"My client. Someone kidnapped him in front of the Saenger. They shot me when I tried to stop them."

"You kidding me?"

14

"I met him for the first time at the wake. He hired me to find his mother's murderer, and make sure everyone knew their name."

By now, I had Lucy Diamond's complete attention.

"What's all this got to do with kidnapping and getting shot at?" she asked.

"He gave me a package. Told me not to turn around until he was gone. I ignored his instructions, tailing him out to Canal."

"And?"

"Men in a black sedan were waiting outside for him. He tried to run away. They chased him down and threw him into the backseat of the car. They shot me. When I fell, I hit my head on the sidewalk, unconscious until I came to in a hospital."

"You expect me to believe that crazy story?"

"I didn't make up this bullet hole in my shoulder."

"Then why aren't you still in the hospital?"

"Because the two goons that shot me returned to finish the job. I managed to escape and came to the Carousel because Rafael told me I could find you here."

"Why didn't you call the police?"

"Because they're somehow in on it. They trashed my apartment looking for something."

"This tale is growing a little too tall," she said, glancing at a bottle of gin on a rack above the bar.

Fred was polishing a glass as he listened to our conversation.

"Want me to make that call?" he asked.

"Wait," I said. "I have something important to show you."

"Like what?"

"This," I said, dropping an object into her hand.

"A Mardi Gras doubloon?"

"1948 Krewe of Rex. a rarity, I'd guess

15

"Oh my!" she said. "This is so heavy it must be . . ."

"Solid gold."

She fingered the Carnival coin, holding it up to the light for a better view.

"There's a strange symbol on the back. What does it mean?"

"No idea," I said. "It was the only thing my client gave me, except for twenty thousand dollars."

"You have to be making this up," she said. "What the hell am I supposed to make of an old Mardi Gras doubloon?"

"My client seemed to think it was all I needed to solve the case."

"What did you say his name was?"

"He didn't tell me."

When I grabbed my head, the bartender reacted by handing me two aspirins and a glass of water.

"You don't look too good," he said. "Want me to call an ambulance?"

"A sinking spell. I'm okay now."

"Finish your story," Lucy said.

"That's about it. Two goons in black sports coats are trying to kill me. I can't go to the police, and my head's about to split."

"Charge my room, Fred," Lucy said. "Buy this pest anything he wants. I'm out of here."

"Thanks for the aspirins, Fred," I said, following her out the door.

I caught up with her at the elevator.

"Your story reeks, but Fred seemed a little too interested. Everything I have on the Taggert murder is in my room. We can have a little privacy there. I'm too drunk to worry about whether you're going to rape and kill me."

Her remark made me grin. "I've never raped or killed anyone. My shoulder is killing me. Right now,

I'd have trouble arm wrestling a bunny rabbit."

She stopped in her tracks and stared at me.

"That's the first thing you've said all night I believe."

Chapter 3

Late night had left the lobby of the Monteleone deserted as we took the elevator to Lucy Diamond's room. Approaching her doorway down the long hallway, we noticed something was amiss, the door standing wide open.

"Someone's been here," she said, starting for the door.

I grabbed her elbow. "Wait. There may be someone still in there."

"Then I'm calling the police," she said, removing her cell phone from her purse.

"First, let's have a look."

"But why?"

"Once the cops get here it'll be a crime scene. If you have something you need to retrieve, better get it now."

"It's probably just a simple break and enter."

"Let me look. It'll only take a minute."

I crept to the open door and glanced inside. The place was a mess, clothes scattered across the floor. Nothing was moving. Whoever rolled Lucy's room had already found what they were looking for and left. She pushed past me, rushing to the opened closet.

"My laptop's gone, and my briefcase."

She nodded when I said, "Your Mary Taggert notes?"

"Now, I am calling the police."

"Don't think you'll need to. From the sound of sirens, they just pulled up in front. I'm leaving now. Coming with me?"

"You're crazy. I'm waiting here and telling your story to the authorities."

"Have it your way," I said, heading for the hallway.

"Wait! Where will you be if I need you?"

"Nowhere for long."

"At least give me an hour."

"I'll wait until midnight at Café du Monde. If I don't hear from you by then, I'm history."

She frowned as I hurried out the door. Afraid to take the elevator, I walked the stairs, exiting on Royal Street through a service entrance and alleyway. The street was empty, my white jacket easy to spot by the driver of the black sedan racing past. Seeing me, he wheeled around on the one-way street, racing after me in a screech of burning rubber. When I tried to run, I realized how bad my head and shoulder ached.

After living in New Orleans for most of my adult life, I knew the location of every darkened alleyway in the Quarter. Ducking into one, I headed toward Café du Monde, wondering if I dared stay there an hour even if I managed to shake the goons in the black sedan. When I exited on Chartres and found them waiting on the corner, I jumped back into the shadows.

Cell phone, I thought. They're tracking my cell phone. I started to throw it into a trash dumpster behind a restaurant. Thinking better of it, I returned it to my pocket, hurrying to the moonwalk by the river. The streetcar was running, and I made it to the stop in time, jumping on board before the driver pulled away. I didn't bother

19

sitting, immediately pulling the cable to signal I needed to get off.

"Sorry," I said. "Made a mistake. Can you let me off here."

"You know I can't let passengers on or off between stops."

"It's late, and I'm the only one on board. Make an exception?"

When the streetcar rattled to a halt, I handed the driver a twenty and hurried to the sidewalk bordering the riverfront. With any luck, my phone would make it to the far end of the line before the goons chasing me realized I didn't have it anymore. By then I would be long gone from Café du Monde and holed up for the night someplace safe. When I got there, Lucy Diamond was alone at a table, waiting for me.

"How did you beat me here?"

"Long story."

"Tell me."

"The police were rude, treating me as if I was the one that had wrecked my room. I thought they were going to cuff me."

"They didn't?"

"I showed them my credentials and told them who I was. When they said I had to go with them to the station, I panicked, invoked a local Federal judge's name and told them I'd follow in my car. When a cop tried to join me in the front seat, I hit the lock button and slammed on the gas. That's my rental car across the street."

"I hear sirens. Leave your cell phone on the table and let's get the hell out of here."

"How will I access the internet?"

"Give it to me," I said, taking it from her and tossing it toward the levee.

"You asshole! Why did you do that?"

"Just trying to save your life," I said, grabbing her wrist.

"I didn't get my beignets yet."

"We have to leave. Now, unless you want to go with the cops."

As we watched from the shadows, three patrol cars descended on the rental car, cops surrounding it, pistols ready.

"My God!" she said."

I didn't wait around, dragging her deeper into the darkness and away from the unfolding scene at Cafe du Monde.

"Where are we going?"

"Someplace to spend the night and get off the street. There's a flophouse on N. Rampart."

"I'm not going to a flophouse. Don't know about you, but I'll use my credit card and stay someplace nice."

"Might as well send up a smoke signal. I have twenty grand in twenties and hundreds. Where we're going, cash is all we'll need."

"Let go of my wrist," she said. "My feet hurt, and I need to pee."

"Ditch the heels. There's an alley. I won't watch."

Lucy was drunk and wobbling when she emerged from the darkened alleyway. Her heels were gone, only nylon pantyhose covering her feet.

"How far is this flophouse?"

"Quite a ways yet. There's a cab at the streetlight. I'll try to flag it down."

The cab saw us but didn't slow when it passed us. We kept walking, Lucy starting to sober and whimpering long before we neared N. Rampart.

"Take my shoes," I said, slipping them off and handing them to her.

"I'm not wearing your stinky shoes," she said.

"Suit yourself. All I can do is offer."

"They won't fit me."

"Put them on and lace them tight. We don't have that much further to go."

21

Lucy glanced up at a bat, diving in the light of a street lamp as it chased Big Easy insects.

"How much further?"

"Couple of blocks," I said. "Four at the most."

"You're an asshole," she said.

"I'd carry you, but my shoulder's starting to ache," I said.

"Fine, asshole. I can walk."

We were both exhausted when we reached N. Rampart. It was still dark, but not as dark as the street from where we'd come. Though traffic was light, we slunk into the shadows every time we heard an approaching vehicle. We finally reached the flophouse, a destination for pimps and prostitutes. A man named Alligator took our twenty bucks through a slotted grill, and I had no doubt he had a loaded shotgun waiting beside him.

"This is just gross," Lucy said as we walked down a dampened hallway to our room.

"It's not the Monteleone," I said.

"You're not serious about spending the night here, are you?"

"Not much night left," I said as I opened the door, the smell of mold and must sweeping over us.

Lucy shrieked when a spider descended from its web and crawled on her shoulder. A single bare light bulb hung from the drab ceiling, filling the room with dim illumination when I turned it on.

"Smells like a toilet in here," she said.

"A bit earthy," I said.

"Like an opened grave ten days after burial."

"At least we have a bed."

"You have to be kidding? I'm not sleeping on that thing. I'll bet it's the same sheets from the last person that slept here."

"Last ten customers more than likely," I said.

"I feel dirty."

"Take a shower. It'll make you feel better, even if you have to put on the same clothes afterward."

Lucy screamed when she went into the bathroom. I rushed in to see her staring at the toilet.

"Oh my God! There's a rat in the shower stall."

The rodent stared up at us with dead eyes. "I'll get it," I said. "Turn on the air conditioner. I'll call you when I finish."

After cleaning up the bathroom as best I could, I returned to find her sitting on the floor by the bed. She was crying.

"It's okay," I said, sitting beside her and putting my arm around her shoulders. "This is just for one night, and not forever."

"Then keep your creepy hands off me," she said."

"No problem," I said, sliding away from her. "There aren't many pay phones left in town, but I know where they all are. Tomorrow, call your producer. Your people will get you. You'll be okay because no one would dare harm a Fox reporter."

Lucy cracked a smile for the first time since I'd known her. "

"And you?"

"A client paid me lots of money to solve a murder. I'm going to give it my best shot."

By now, the air conditioning was gasping out a steady stream of fetid air. At least it was cooling the little room. Lucy didn't even jump when another spider dropped from the ceiling and scurried across the ratty carpeting.

"You don't have a clue where to begin."

"Oh yes," I said, showing her the doubloon. "All my answers are right here. I just have to figure out what it's trying to tell me."

Lucy gave the bed a pat, kicked my shoes off and sprawled on the covers.

"Midnight at the Roach Motel," she said as I removed my sports coat, turned off the lights and joined her.

Chapter 4

Lucy was standing in front of a grimy window, drying her hair with a ratty towel when I awoke. I grinned when she sensed me staring at her and wheeled around.

"What are you laughing at?" she said.

"Sorry. You had a smile on your face, and I can see by your damp hair you had a shower. I thought you were afraid of the critters roaming around in there."

"Not as much as smelling like a dirty bedspread," she said. "The water never got hot, and a roach kept trying to crawl up my leg."

"Glad you're feeling better."

"Except for this fleabag room and having to put my dirty underwear back on."

"Since you've chased away all the roaches and spiders, I'll try the shower."

"Then you'll have to drip dry because this is the only towel."

I struggled to get out of bed, the pain in my shoulder more than I cared to confide in Lucy. For a moment, I thought I was going to faint.

"You kept me awake all night moaning and groaning," she said. "I seriously considered moving to another room."

"Why didn't you?"

"No cash and I doubt this fine establishment takes American Express."

"Oh, they'd take it all right, but you'd have had to cancel the card."

"I stuck it out," she said.

"I'll say. You were sawing logs five minutes after you hit the covers."

"Excuse me? I don't snore."

"Whatever," I said. "The painkiller they gave me at the hospital wore off somewhere between here and the Carousel Lounge. At least my headache is gone."

"Don't pull my chains. I can't imagine how obnoxious you'd be if you were totally healthy."

Ignoring her sarcasm, I said, "You wouldn't have a couple of aspirins, would you?"

"Take them," she said, tossing a bottle to me.

Blood had soaked through my jacket, leaving a crimson stain on the faded bedspread. I realized how weak I was when I padded to the bathroom. As Lucy had said, the water never got hot. Didn't matter because it felt wonderful as I leaned against the shower wall, letting lukewarm water pour over my shoulders. Lucy gave me a glance when I returned shirtless to the tiny room.

"Take it," she said, throwing me her damp towel. "Now what?"

"An old voodoo woman I know lives in Faubourg Marigny. Her daughter will have something to help me with my shoulder pain. First, we need to get out of here and buy some new clothes. There's a thrift store down the street."

"You're kidding."

"About the thrift store or the voodoo woman?"

"Both."

"Neither. We'll stand out like sore thumbs in what we're wearing. I'm sure the town is swarming with cops and whoever else is looking for us. If you can stay with me until I get something for the pain, I'll take you to a pay phone so you can call your producer."

"Good, because I can't take much more of this amusement," she said.

"You trust him, your producer I mean?"

"You're kidding! Sandy Jennings is as powerful as they come at the network."

"Power and trust aren't always reciprocal."

"Whatever's going down in this town is nothing more than local. My network covers situations around the world."

"You didn't have to be here with me, you know."

"Believe me; I had no other choice. The sooner I get to a phone and get out of here, the better I'll like it."

"You haven't exactly been a barrel of laughs."

Lucy shot me the finger, turned her back to the bed and proceeded to ignore me. Taking a deep breath, I almost choked on the dust in the musty little room. When my coughing jag subsided, I finished dressing. A fat roach scurried past my foot as we walked down the hall to the lobby. The attendant didn't bother glancing up from his men's magazine.

"See you later, Alligator," I said.

"I thought you were in pain," Lucy said as we exited to the sidewalk.

"I am, but I'm not dead."

She just shook her head, not bothering to crack a smile. We were less than a block from a thrift store. I didn't realize she had never been inside one. Like a kid in a candy store, she browsed old paperbacks, thumbed through computer parts and fingered candles, picture frames, and souvenir cups.

"Enough," I finally said. "Let's get some clothes. You can come back later and get your rocks off."

"I'm not wearing someone else's dirty old clothes," she said.

"They may be old, but they're not dirty so stop whining and try these on," I said, throwing her a shirt and pair of shorts.

"You're kidding," she said, sticking her head out of the tiny dressing cubicle and throwing the clothes back at me. "Get me something nicer to wear."

"This is a thrift store, not Saks," I said.

"Just do it," she said.

After twenty minutes of grumbling, Lucy finally gave up trying to find something stylish. We left the store dressed in Hawaiian shirts, Bermuda shorts, flip-flops, straw hats and cheap sunglasses. I tossed our dirty clothes into an alleyway dumpster as she glared at me.

"That dress and blouse cost me fifteen hundred dollars," she said.

"Quit carping. You're rich and famous. You can buy plenty more where those came from."

"We look like idiots," she said. "Are you taking me to a phone now?"

"Not until we visit Madam Aja and her daughter Senora in Faubourg Marigny. If we're lucky, we can catch a cab and won't have to walk."

"These flip-flops are practically useless. At least you have a pair of real shoes."

"They looked good on you last night."

"I'd like to pop you with one," she said.

We weren't in a good part of town, and our clothes spoke volumes about the money we likely had to pay for a cab ride. A desperate cabbie finally stopped, taking us to Madam Aja's French cottage, surprised when I gave him a dollar tip after he counted out change.

28

"Last of the big time spenders," Lucy said as the cab drove away in a screech of rubber.

"Don't want to cause attention," I said.

Madam Aja and Senora were sitting on their front porch and didn't immediately recognize me. When I pulled off my straw hat and sunglasses, the old woman smiled, stood from her wheelchair and gave me a hug.

Madam Aja seemed as old as time; facial skin pulled tight around her prominent cheekbones. Her hair was black, though I suspect the color came from a bottle. Senora was a foot taller, her hair snowy white. Although supposedly Madam Aja's daughter, I failed to see that as a real possibility as Senora was probably not yet fifty.

Mama Mulate, my sometimes business partner, had introduced me to the women when I'd had a problem with a ghost. Madam Aja practiced voodoo, or more correctly French Quarter hoodoo. Senora sold a wide array of plants, herbs and other concoctions that had both magical and medicinal powers.

"You're hurt," the old woman said when I winced. "Senora, take him in the house and see what's wrong."

Looking concerned, Senora took my hand and led me to the kitchen table where she pulled up a chair for me. Without asking, she began removing my shirt. Lucy had wheeled Madam Aja in behind us. Backing against a kitchen cabinet, she folded her arms tightly against her chest.

"Madam Aja and Senora, this is Lucy Diamond."

Senora stopped what she was doing and glanced up at Lucy. "Oh my God! You are Lucy Diamond. Are you on assignment?"

"Yes. You watch my show?" Lucy said.

"Never miss it," Madam Aja said as she began heating water on the stove. "We love it when you trash one of them, crooked senators."

"I do my best," Lucy said, obviously pleased.

Senora and Madam Aja had little time to talk television, my old bandage soon removed, wound cleaned and a new dressing, complete with herbal potions, applied.

"What's your pain level on a scale of one to ten?" Senora asked.

"Twelve," I said.

She smiled and gave me something from an unmarked bottle.

"This will help, but it'll take a while to start working," she said. "Once it does, though, you'll feel much better."

"Mr. Macho here says you practice voodoo," Lucy said.

"Heavens, child, everyone in New Orleans knows that."

"Really? You have a shop in the Quarter?"

Madam Aja chuckled. "My people know where we live."

"How do tourists find you?"

"Madam Aja's a national treasure but she isn't a tourist attraction," I said.

Lucy persisted. "What do you do, poke needles in voodoo dolls and things like that?"

The old woman cackled, not taking offense. "Haven't hexed anyone in years."

Senora wasn't smiling. "Madam Aja is the community connection to the spirit world. Believers in New Orleans trust her guidance."

Even Lucy could feel the sudden chill. "I didn't mean to be rude. The studio pays me lots of money to ask blunt questions. Sometimes, I forget I'm not on the air."

Madam Aja shook her head and grinned. "It's all right, child. There are many more doubters in the world than true believers."

"Show her the doubloon," Lucy said, changing the subject.

Madam Aja joined me at the kitchen table, and so did Lucy. The old woman's eyes grew wide as she turned the Mardi Gras coin in her hand.

"Ever seen anything like it?" I asked.

"Especially the engraving on the back," Lucy said.

"Senora, please get me my Old Crow."

Senora retrieved a bottle from a cabinet, filling a glass with straight whiskey.

"Is it a voodoo vever?" I asked.

Madam Aja drained the glass before answering. "Ain't got nothing to do with voodoo, child."

"Then what?" Lucy asked.

"Mark of the Beast," the old woman said.

Chapter 5

Madam Aja shook her head when Lucy pressed her to expound on her ominous proclamation.

"You are in grave danger, but I think you already knew that."

"Thanks for doctoring my shoulder and giving me the pain medicine. We have to go now. We'll be okay."

"I know you will," Madam Aja said, hugging me. "You're a traveler. Not many places you ain't been."

"Maybe," I said, but I don't remember hurting quite as much as I am now."

"You're relief will kick in directly," Senora said. "Here's more when that wears off."

She gave me a packet of pills to help with the pain, and then she and Madam Aja followed us outside, watching as we hailed a cab in front of their French cottage.

"Where to?" the cabbie asked.

"Culotta's, on the river," I said.

"Aren't you afraid of being spotted in a public place?" Lucy asked as we drove away.

"It's off the beaten path. Mostly locals. We're meeting someone there."

"Who?"

"Tony Nicosia. A former homicide detective with the N.O.P.D. He's bringing me a police file on the Mary Taggert murder."

"Good luck with that," she said.

"What?"

"Just that the N.O.P.D. has never been very forthcoming when it comes to the Mary Taggert case. You trust this man?"

"With my life," I said.

Lucy wasn't smiling when the cabbie let us out on the riverfront by Culotta's. The tiny restaurant sat alone near the western terminus of the Riverfront Streetcar. Though close to the Esplanade Avenue Wharf, it featured an unmatched view of the river and lots of repeat customers. We found Tony reading a newspaper as he waited alone in a corner booth.

"Help you?" he said when we scooted in beside him.

I removed my straw hat and dark glasses. "It's me, Tony, and this is Lucy Diamond."

Tony didn't bother shaking hands, raking his fingers through thinning hair instead. A tuft of dark hair protruded from the open button of his flowered Hawaiian shirt, the sports coat and tie he used to wear as a homicide detective a distant memory.

"Ma'am, you two are in a whole lot of trouble."

"For what?" she asked.

"Murder," he said.

"Whose murder?" I asked.

"Timothy Taggert, and you're the number one suspect."

"That's crazy."

"Maybe, but the cops have evidence."

"Such as?"

"A bloody handkerchief."

"I don't carry handkerchiefs."

"This one has your monogram on it. Mama Mulate gave it to you last Christmas. You showed it to me. Remember?"

It took me a moment to realize what Tony was saying. Before I could respond, a frazzled waitress arrived with coffee and menus. Extra makeup failed to cover her black eye, and I tried not to stare.

"What's your special today?" I asked.

"Monday," the little woman said. "Red beans and rice."

"That's what I'll have," I said.

"Make it two," Tony said.

Lucy handed the woman her menu. "Why not?" she said.

I dropped a fork on the floor, and it rattled beneath my feet.

"Don't worry about it. I'll bring you another," the waitress said when I bent down to retrieve it.

"Bertram said the police searched my room while I was in the hospital. They must have taken the handkerchief."

Tony's eyes rolled. "You accusing the police now?"

"It was in a drawer in my apartment. How else would they have it?"

"They found Taggert's body in a ditch near St. Johns Bayou, your bloody handkerchief in the bushes nearby. They're saying you stabbed him to death, and then used the handkerchief to wipe off the blood."

"And then tossed it in the bushes nearby? Yeah, right! I'm dumb, but not that dumb."

"Does sound pretty lame, but it don't take much to convince a jury when you got a badass D.A. calling you every dirty name in the book. Hey, and the handkerchief also has your blood on it."

"What else do they have?"

34

"The murder weapon. They found it on the closet floor in your hospital room. Traces of Taggert's blood on the blade."

"This is beginning to reek. I suppose they're saying Taggert shot me when I stabbed him."

Tony crossed his arms as the waitress returned with my new fork and our beans and rice, not answering until she'd refilled our coffee cups and had left the table.

"Pretty smart, Cowboy. Now you're thinking like a defense attorney again, and not a private dick."

"You're an attorney?" Lucy said.

"Past tense. Disbarred years ago. Don't ask."

Lucy brushed the back of her hand against her nose. "I knew there was something about you I didn't like."

"Lots of people hate lawyers," I said.

"I know," she said. "I quit telling people years ago that I have a law degree."

"Hmm!" was all I could muster.

Tony doctored his beans with a liberal dose of Louisiana hot sauce before taking a bite.

"You were in the hospital. What happened?"

"One of the goons that kidnapped Taggert shot me when I chased after him. I must have passed out because I woke up in the hospital."

"Why did you leave?"

"The goons returned to kill me. I escaped before they could finish the job. Now what?"

"Don't know, but I wouldn't give myself up if I was you. To me, Mexico sounds better than life in solitary confinement up Angola way. Whatever, I'd think about finding a way to get out of town."

"You have to help me, Tony."

"Hell, Cowboy, you royally pissed off someone that's got more stroke than I ever had. What's your deal with Taggert?"

"He hired me to find his mother's murderer."

35

"Why was you meeting him at the wake?"

"His call. He didn't want me to see his face. When I followed him out to the street, the goons shot me."

"You need a material witness. Anyone else see you at the wake?"

"I was there," Lucy said. "That's where we met."

"You're in trouble yourself, miss," Tony said.

"How so?"

"The bartender at the Carousel Lounge reported to the police that you two were drinking together last night. You're with him now. The authorities think maybe you colluded in Taggert's death."

"Total bullshit! I never met this man before last night, and I've never laid eyes on Taggert. Why in God's name would I have any reason to kill him?"

"Doesn't matter," I said. "We're the primary suspects in the Taggert case. The police are laying out their evidence, albeit manufactured, against us."

"This is just crazy. I'm not believing such a thing can happen in modern society," Lucy said.

"Happens all the time. Why do you think so many innocent people get convicted of murder?"

Tony didn't let her answer. "Anyone else at the wake who can verify your presence?" he asked.

"No."

When Lucy's mouth opened to say something, I grabbed her hand and squeezed. Tony finished his beans and rice. Lucy had pushed hers aside. Mine had a metallic taste, and I stopped eating after a single bite.

"Did you bring us anything on the Mary Taggert murder?" I asked.

"Not much. I set off a shit storm down at the precinct when I asked Tommy to get me what he could on the case."

"Tommy O'Rear was Tony's N.O.P.D. partner. A good cop," I said.

"Not good enough to get me a file. He got a look at it, but all I have is what he could remember to tell me."

Our booth sat beside a picture window fronting the river, a tugboat's wake lapping against the bank as the vessel moved slowly back to the dock. Lucy glanced at the boat before returning her gaze to Tony.

"Did you get anything?"

"Mostly just stuff you've already read in the papers. There was a statement by a rookie detective that was first on the scene. I remember her because she was retiring from the force about the time I started."

"Is she still alive?" I asked.

"Yes. Her name is Edna Callahan." He handed me a business card. "Her address and phone number are on the back."

"Anything else?"

"That's about it. Something strange, though."

"Like what?"

"The lead detective assigned to the case was the precinct chief."

"Is that unusual?" Lucy asked.

Tony and I exchanged a glance. "Detective work isn't part of the job description for a precinct chief," I said.

"Then why did it happen in the Taggert investigation?"

"I only seen it a time or two during my years as a cop," he said.

"Because?" she asked.

Tony glanced at the tugboat before answering. "Cover up," he said.

Chapter 6

On a path near the river, a group of cyclists raced past a lone jogger bent at the waist, trying to catch his breath. We'd pushed our plates aside, and the mousy waitress with the black eye frowned when she saw my food was untouched.

"Something wrong with the beans?" she asked.

"Been sick. Shouldn't have tried eating anything so soon."

"Want a doggie bag?"

"Sure," I said. "Maybe I'll feel better later tonight."

She was smiling when she returned with a sack for my beans and rice.

"I brought you extra French bread and a side of hot sauce."

"Thanks, Verna," I said, seeing her name tag.

"I think she likes you, Cowboy," Tony said when the woman walked away with a smile on her face.

"Don't doubt it," Lucy said. "From that shiner she's sporting, she obviously has poor taste in men."

Tony snickered and I just shook my head. "What now?" he asked.

"I'm taking Lucy to a pay phone so she can call her boss. He'll get her, and at least she'll be out of the line of fire."

"And you?"

"I'm going to see Edna Callahan."

Tony finished his coffee and motioned Verna to bring us more. Lucy frowned, and Tony grinned when she winked at me before leaving the table.

"Maybe you ought to give her your number, Cowboy."

"I think she has enough trouble in her life already without taking on mine," I said.

"You are so full of yourself," Lucy said.

I stuck two twenties on top of the tab. "Cut me some slack."

"Gonna leave a fifty cent tip, big spender?" Lucy said.

Tony cracked another grin. "You two sound like an old married couple."

"Precisely why I hate that particular institution," Lucy said.

"Hey, once was enough for me," I said.

Tony made a T with his hands, calling for time out. "Stop it, you two. You ain't gonna get much out of Edna, Cowboy. She's a tough old bird and will probably shoot you if you show up on her doorstep dressed the way you are."

"I'll take my chances."

"I'll go with you. She always liked me."

"No use getting involved more than you already are."

"Not much to worry about if we work it right. I'll leave first. You two take the Riverfront Streetcar to the aquarium. I'll wait in the parking lot for you."

"I have to get Lucy to a pay phone," I said.

"I'll wait," Tony said

"Just a minute," Lucy said. "I need to interview Ms. Callahan every bit as much as you two clowns. I'll call my boss afterwards."

"You better fly back to New York while you have the chance."

"Don't tell me what to do," she said.

"You're looking for a sound bite. I'm trying to find a killer."

"You have no idea what I'm trying to do, and you got into the mess you're in with no help from anyone. You're getting no sympathy from me," she said.

Tony gave Lucy a look, and then glanced back at me. "I see what you mean about ex-wives," he said.

Verna returned for the tab and glowed when I told her to keep the change. Lucy's eyes rolled when Verna kissed my forehead, and then hurried away into the kitchen before I changed my mind.

"Am I supposed to be impressed?" she asked.

Tony shook his head and glanced at the ceiling. "I'm leaving you two lovebirds. Give me ten minutes, and then take the streetcar. I'll be waiting in the parking lot."

"Hold it," I said, pulling the cash from my coat. "Taggert gave me twenty grand to solve his mother's murder. Here's half. You're now officially on the payroll."

"You know I'll help you any way I can. You don't have to pay me."

"I promised the man I'd do my best. If I weren't on the run, I'd keep the money and do the job myself. You'll earn every penny I'm giving you."

"Just don't feel right," Tony said.

"Are you helping me or not?"

"Hell, Cowboy," he said. "You had me at hello."

Heat and humidity of July in the Big Easy accosted us the moment we left the little cafe. Gone was the morning's mild temperature, replaced by a damp slap in the face. Lucy wasn't smiling as I tossed my doggie bag into a dumpster.

We had a long walk to the streetcar terminus. When we reached it, I realized the pain in my shoulder was gone, replaced by only a dull ache. Senora's painkiller was working.

A bright red streetcar moved toward us as we reached the terminal and we were soon rumbling along the riverfront toward Canal Street and the aquarium. Lucy leaned against the window, her arms and legs again tightly crossed.

"You okay?" I asked.

"How do you live in this place? I've never been anywhere this hot and humid."

"How about Houston in August?"

"At least their mass transit system is air conditioned."

Reaching across her, I opened the window.

"Bet their buses can't do this."

A gentle breeze wafted through the window. It didn't change her frown into a smile, or cause her to uncross her arms. I pointed to a spot across the river.

"It's hazy, but you can see all the way to Algiers Point." The riverboat Natchez was heading toward port, happy tourists hanging on the rail. "If we get out of this alive, I'll take you on a midnight cruise on that old paddle wheeler."

"The only place you're taking me is to a pay phone, soon as I get my interview," she said.

The lone passenger on the streetcar other than us pulled the cable, standing at the exit until we screeched to a halt. Lucy looked no happier as he disappeared behind us.

"Cut me some slack. We're searching for the same answers here. We could help each other."

"You're just a private dick with a useless law degree. I have the best research team in the business. You have nothing I need."

"Did your research team tell you Dr. Mary and Jeribeth Briggs were part of a group that attended séances regularly?"

"What's that supposed to mean?"

"Something you apparently haven't thought about."

"Such as?"

"Dr. Mary's personal life."

Lucy flashed me an especially dirty look. "We're working on that aspect."

"You and your team are out of your league. This is the Big Easy. Everyone wears a mask. If they didn't tell you about the séances, what else don't you know?"

"Like I said, you're full of yourself."

"I know this town."

"Then why do you need my help?"

We'd caught up to the Natchez and some joggers that waved as we rumbled past.

"Two men are trying to kill me, the N.O.P.D. likely complicit. I don't need much. Doesn't matter because I'll be dead before I get up to speed without your help."

Lucy continued frowning as she slowly uncrossed her arms.

"This goes back to the Kennedy assassination. Doctor Taggert taught at Tulane. She also ran a covert research laboratory that apparently had a dual purpose."

"Such as?"

"Studying viruses in primates with the aim of curing cancer. That was the politically correct reason for the lab."

"What else?"

"Using viruses they created as weapons, ostensibly for the purpose of assassinating Fidel Castro."

"Who called the shots?"

"C.I.A."

"You know that for a fact?"

"It's public information. Our government funded several of these research facilities. The C.I.A. pulled the strings, including at the local lab run by Doctor Taggert."

"How does this tie with Kennedy's assassination?"

"David Ferrie worked there. According to the case filed by D.A. Jim Garrison, Ferrie knew Clay Shaw and Lee Harvey Oswald."

"Shaw was acquitted. The jury found no connection between he, David Ferrie, and the assassination," I said.

"Garrison was stonewalled and many of his witnesses, including Ferrie, died mysteriously. Other potential witnesses also met mysterious and untimely deaths. I'm talking about Dr. Taggert."

"How was Dr. Taggert murdered?" I asked.

"Horribly burned, one arm totally missing."

"How do they know it was murder and not an accident? If it was murder, where did it occur and what was the motive?"

"They found the body in her apartment, on the floor beside her bed. Someone in the building had reported a fire. When firefighters arrived, they found the body."

"If the fire was hot enough to burn her arm off, what kept the apartment from burning to the ground?"

Lucy gave me a look as if I'd showed a little too much prescience for the idiot she thought I was.

"Her bed was barely scorched. Someone had piled undergarments on her naked body and set them on fire. It was barely burning when the firefighters arrived."

"Sounds like a stretch to me."

"Me too," Lucy said. "Dr. Taggert likely died somewhere else, her body returned to her

43

apartment so the police would believe an intruder had killed her, during a robbery, maybe."

I gazed out the window at a river barge. We were approaching the end of the line, and I still had more questions than answers.

"No evidence of a break-in? Broken window, maybe?"

"Nothing like that," she said. "To me, her killer must have known her. Maybe even had a key to her apartment."

"What did the police report say?"

"Like your friend Tony said, What police report? That's why I want to talk to the first officer on the scene."

"Lots of unanswered questions here. Why is the Taggert murder so important to you?"

Lucy glanced across the river toward Algiers Point. "There's volumes of information out there about the Kennedy killing. Maybe too much information."

"And?"

"So many facts, you don't know what to believe. The story itself has become a giant smokescreen."

"The Taggert murder can't be more than a blip on that screen," I said.

Lucy glanced out the window as we approached the terminal, a dozen tourists waiting to go in the other direction.

"Every lock has a key," she said. "Dr. Taggert was murdered for a reason. If I can determine that single cause, maybe it'll unlock the mystery of the Kennedy assassination."

Chapter 7

When we exited the streetcar, we found Tony waiting in the parking lot. Tourists crowded the area, lined up and waiting their turn to enter the Aquarium of the Americas. We climbed into Tony's red Mustang convertible, Lucy pointing to the back seat.

"Stop for a nooner? I was starting to worry," Tony said.

"Fat chance of that ever happening," Lucy said.

"Streetcars aren't exactly speed mobiles," I said. "How far to Edna's."

"Around the corner. She lives in a shotgun in Uptown."

"Didn't know cops made so much money."

"Don't," Tony said. "She inherited the place from her grandparents. Probably doesn't even know how much it's worth."

"What's a shotgun house?" Lucy asked.

"Pull the trigger at the front door," Tony explained, "The shot would travel through the back door without hitting anything."

"Uptown's a hot area. House flippers are buying shotguns like crazy," I said. "Remodeling and putting them back on the market for twice the price."

We found Edna's house close to the river, towboat whistles sounding as we parked on the street. Though not remodeled it had lots of character.

"Let me go first and tell her who you are," Tony said.

Lucy's frown told me all I needed to know about what she thought of Tony taking charge.

"I've been interviewing people for years. Don't you think I'm capable of dealing with an old woman?"

"Her nickname is Dirty Edna. I know you're good at what you do, but you need to trust me on this one."

Lucy continued to frown but acquiesced, and Tony was soon hugging a woman on the front porch, motioning us to join him.

Edna Callahan wasn't what I expected, her hair dark, and she was anything but frail. Though she looked somewhere south of sixty, she was probably older.

"Nice to see you, Tony. My age, I don't have many friends left."

"You ain't that old, Edna. I brought someone with me. Wyatt and Lucy."

Like Tony had said, she probably wouldn't have let Lucy and me into her house looking the way we did. Her stare proclaimed as much. Lucy didn't care and proceeded to plow right in.

"Tony told us you were the first officer on the premises at the Mary Taggert murder."

"Did he now?" she said, casting Tony an unmistakable look.

"Can you tell me about it?" Lucy asked.

"Let's sit in the living room," Edna said. "I got a pitcher of ice tea in the refrigerator."

Edna's remark brought a smile to Tony's face. "You gotta be kidding me, Edna. I never knew you to drink anything but hooch."

"Things change," she said.

When Edna went into the kitchen, Tony glared at Lucy and shook his head in a signal for her to keep her mouth shut. Lucy shot him the finger.

Though located in the booming Uptown District, the house had seen few renovations. It didn't matter because her tiny back porch had a gorgeous view of the river. If she'd wanted to sell it, she could have done so in a heartbeat.

An old couch, two side chairs, a dated coffee table and little else occupied the living room. There was also a fake fireplace with no family photos, only a cheesy picture of Elvis Presley painted on black velvet. Edna noticed me staring when she returned from the kitchen with the pitcher of tea.

"You like Elvis?" she asked.

"I like his music but never had the pleasure of seeing him in person."

"You're too young," she said. "We lost the King years ago."

"Ms. Callahan, I'm on a tight schedule," Lucy said. "We're here for answers concerning the Mary Taggert murder."

Edna ignored her, pouring tea instead before sitting beside Tony on the threadbare couch. A boat whistle from the river rattled the back of the house, prompting a neighbor's dog to start howling. Edna smiled as she glanced at Elvis's picture.

Lucy glared at me when I said, "You saw him in person?"

"Many times. The greatest performer ever. My girlfriend Holly and I caught his act every chance we got." She smiled again. "We went to Vegas so many times the Chief asked me if I was taking kickbacks from the mob." She sipped her tea before saying, "We even saw his last performance."

"You're kidding?" I said.

"Summer of '77 at the Pershing Municipal Auditorium in Lincoln, Nebraska."

Edna wiped away a tear and then sipped her tea trying to hide it.

"They have airports in Nebraska?" Tony quipped.

"Didn't need a plane. Holly and me drove all the way in my '67 GTO convertible." She chuckled. "Never once raised the top the whole way."

By now, Lucy was seething, her arms and legs crossed tightly. Lost in memory, Edna didn't notice.

"Is that a picture of the car on your mantle?" I asked.

Edna beamed and retrieved the pewter-framed picture of two young women in a shiny black GTO. She handed it to me.

"Never had so much fun in my life," she said. "They may not have many airports in Nebraska, but the people are grand, partying and drinking like there's no tomorrow."

"You drove all the way to Nebraska just to see Elvis Presley?" Tony asked.

"If you loved Elvis, you'd go anywhere to see him. I'd fly to the moon if he was still alive."

"Tell us about the concert," I said.

"Holly and I had the best seats in the house. Right on the front row. Elvis even blew me a kiss."

"He remembered you?" I said.

Edna grinned. "Doubt it. He'd gained lots of weight since the last time we'd seen him, sweating and slurring his words. I didn't know if he'd be able to sing."

"Did he?" I asked.

She nodded. "He mumbled that he'd recorded Unchained Melody on his last album. He was so wobbly someone had to help him the few steps to an ivory white piano. He cracked a joke about hoping he didn't flub the lyrics. I was afraid he would, and I'm sure everyone in the audience was worried as well."

Edna hesitated, staring at the black velvet Elvis on the mantle as if remembering something so poignant that she found it hard to continue her story. In a sudden change of mood, Lucy sat beside her and took her hand.

"Please, Edna," she said. "I want to hear."

Edna smiled and nodded. "He started playing the piano. I didn't even know he could play piano. Then he began to sing."

The old woman gazed at the ceiling and drew silent.

"And?" I said.

"His slurred words were suddenly gone, replaced by this silky voice that made me want to cream my pants. I'm sure every female in the audience felt the same way. He kept flashing his famous grin as he sang. When he finished, knowing everyone in the audience was hanging on his every word, he blew a kiss and just stood there smiling, soaking up the applause and their standing ovation."

Edna put her face in her hands and began to cry. Lucy took her in her arms, rocking her like a baby.

"It's okay," she said.

"It'll never be okay again. He died twenty-eight days later."

I refilled Edna's glass, and Lucy held it to her lips until she began drinking and stopped blubbering. I glanced at Tony and caught him rolling his eyes. When Edna's crying ceased, she gave Lucy a hug.

"I'm just a silly old woman," she said.

"You're not," Lucy said. "I'm only sorry I never had a chance to see the King in person."

"Edna squeezed her hand. "Thanks, baby. You made my day listening to my story."

"You've made our day," Lucy said. "We probably need to get out of your hair now."

"Wait," Edna said. "Don't you want to hear about the Taggert crime scene?"

"Only if you want to tell us," Lucy said.

Edna nodded. "Though it happened so long ago it's still seared in my memory."

"Come on," Tony said. "You must have investigated hundreds of murder scenes. Why does this one stand out to you?"

Edna glanced out the window at a passing boat before answering. "Because I knew her," she finally said.

Tony had moved to the edge of the couch. "You knew the murder victim?"

Edna nodded. "Yes."

"Was she your doctor, or something?" he asked.

"Maybe I should just tell you about the murder scene first."

"Yes," Lucy said, glaring at Tony.

"There weren't many women detectives in the 60's in New Orleans. My partner Big Jim was an Irish Channel slob who I doubt ever brushed his teeth. He all but had his twenty years in and was scared he'd never see retirement. He hated having me as a partner and let me know it every chance he got. Mind if I turn on some music?"

Edna put a vinyl record on her turntable and adjusted the volume. The song was a blues guitar that sounded more like John Lee Hooker than Elvis.

"Hope you don't mind," she said. "Sometimes I need a little white noise in the background."

Lucy patted her hand when she returned to the couch. "Men can be pricks."

"Not all men," Edna said, looking at Tony.

Tony averted her gaze, glancing out the window as she closed her eyes.

"Not sure I agree with you on that one," Lucy said, flashing me a dirty look.

Edna took my empty glass, grabbed the pitcher of tea and started for the kitchen. "I'm a horrible hostess. Everyone's glass is empty. I'll bring more."

Lucy followed her, frowning at me as if Edna's hesitance to tell her story was all my fault. They returned with a full pitcher of tea.

"Please, Edna," Lucy said. "Tell us about the murder scene."

"Late July. Dog days of summer in New Orleans. Our squad car had no air conditioning, and I remember thinking how bad Big Jim smelled. It was Tuesday night, not much happening when we got a call to investigate a fire."

"Cops usually aren't called for fires, are they?" I asked.

"This wasn't a usual fire. Firefighters didn't find much of a blaze when they broke down the door of Dr. Mary's apartment. What they found was her body. The scene was quite bizarre when Big Jim and I arrived."

"Please continue," Lucy said when Edna drew silent.

"The body was lying on the floor beside her bed. The fire department put out the blaze."

"She died in a fire?" I asked.

Edna shook her head. "The flames were barely big enough to singe her hair. She was burned, but whatever did it wasn't that tiny pile of smoldering underwear."

"Sure about that?" Tony said.

"If you'd seen her body, you'd understand," Edna said. "Her right arm was missing, her organs exposed, her skin the color of boiled crawfish. I have a picture."

Edna went into another part of the house, returning with a box stuffed with photos, mostly black and white. Retrieving one from the top of the pile, she handed it to Lucy."

"Oh, my God!" Lucy said, quickly handing the photo to me.

What I glanced at was a faded, dog-eared crime scene photo of the deceased doctor. As Edna had said, something stronger than a small fire had charred the right side of the victim's body like a well-toasted marshmallow. Her right arm was missing, right side organs fully exposed. Her hair was undamaged. The skin on her left side, as Edna had said, mimicked the color of boiled crawfish. I handed the photo to Tony as a noisy flock of seagulls flew over the house on their way to Lake Pontchartrain.

"Holy hell!" Tony said as he viewed the photo. "Where did you get this?"

"Dug it out of the evidence room trash bin."

"What was it doing in there?" Lucy asked.

"The report we filed managed to disappear. Big Jim was retired early. I was given a desk job. A year had passed before they gave me my detective's job back."

The photo of Mary Taggert's damaged body had visibly shaken Lucy. "Was there anything unusual about the crime scene that caught your attention?"

"The apartment was small. Minimal. Almost no furniture. The painting on the living room mantle seemed out of place."

"Because?" Lucy said.

"It was Satan painted in reds and blacks. I remember thinking how weird it seemed in the apartment of a respected doctor. The beast was smiling, grasping a large pendant hanging from his neck."

"Any signs of forcible entry?" Tony asked.

Edna shook her head. "Nothing. Big Jim was a drunken lout but a good detective. He figured the burns had happened somewhere else. Someone who knew her and had access to her apartment transported her there, setting the fire and mutilating her genitals to cover the real cause of death."

"Is Big Jim still alive?" Lucy asked.

"Hit by a car a few days after retiring and dead before the ambulance got him to the hospital."

"Good God!" Lucy said.

The record had finished playing, and Edna flipped it to the other side before responding to Lucy's comment.

"Every time I asked about the murder my superiors acted as if it had never happened. I was either lucky or unlucky to find that crime scene picture. Depends on how you look at it."

"What happened to her arm?" Tony asked.

"Don't know," Edna said.

"So you don't believe it was a crime of passion?" Tony asked.

"Not no but hell no!"

"Was there a coroner's report?" I asked.

"An official one, yes."

"What do you mean?" Lucy asked.

"The story in the papers was nothing more than a pile of fabricated alligator crap."

"So an autopsy was never conducted."

"Didn't say that. I just don't believe the results."

"Please explain."

"The report concluded she died from a stab wound to the heart."

"Why don't you believe it?" Lucy asked.

Edna pointed to the picture on the coffee table. "Something killed her all right, but I'd say it was whatever burned her arm off and not a knife through the heart."

"You think the coroner falsified the autopsy to make the scene seem like a crime of passion?" I asked.

She nodded. "That's what Big Jim and I believed."

Edna refilled her glass from the pitcher on the coffee table.

"Who did the autopsy?" Tony asked.

"Someone I'd never heard of."

"This is starting to sound a little slimy," Tony said.

Lucy wasn't as convinced. "Then why are you still alive?"

The LP skipped across a scratch, abruptly ending the music. Edna didn't bother fixing it, crying again, shaking her head. Lucy began rocking her like a baby.

"Edna," she said. "Were you and Holly . . ."

Edna nodded again. "Four decades together. She passed three years ago, and I've been alone ever since."

By now, Tony's eyes were really rolling. I poured more tea for all of us, wishing I had some scotch for Tony.

"Something happened, didn't it?" Lucy said.

Edna gazed at the ceiling. "Holly and I didn't live together. Relationships such as ours were unacceptable in 60's New Orleans. Four men broke into her apartment on a night I was working late. They raped and terrorized her for hours."

"Oh my God!" Lucy said. "Did she recognize anyone?"

"Two Cubans and two Americans dressed in black, like cat burglars."

"How did she identify two of the men as Cubans?" I asked.

"There were lots of Cubans living in the city at the time. One managed the apartment complex where Dr. Mary lived. Holly had seen him there."

"What about the Americans?" Tony asked.

"Their names were Slink and Tex."

"They didn't bother concealing their identities?" Lucy asked.

Edna's head drooped as she recalled a particularly bad memory. "When I tell you what they did you'll understand why," she said.

"Sorry to put you through all of this," Tony said.

"It's okay. The man named Slink had a razor-sharp switchblade and made sure Holly knew it. He and Tex, the man with the southern drawl, did all the torturing. The Cubans didn't participate. They just watched."

By now, Edna was trembling. Lucy held the tea to her lips until she stopped shaking.

"I take it her assailants were never apprehended?"

"No one even cared. It was a message for me to keep my mouth shut or they would kill Holly. Before they left, they branded her."

"No way! You mean with a branding iron?"

Edna's head lowered, and she closed her eyes as if trying to make the mental image disappear.

"Exactly what I mean," she finally said.

You gotta be kidding me," Tony said.

"The same symbol hanging from Satan's neck in the painting on Dr. Taggert's mantle."

I pulled the doubloon from my pocket, showing her the engraving.

"Like this?"

"Yes."

"Here," Tony said, reaching for the doubloon.

With his cell phone camera, he took a picture of both sides of the coin before returning it to me. I was more interested in what Edna had to say.

"You knew Mary Taggert?" I asked.

"There were two kinds of gays in New Orleans during the 60s: flamers who didn't care who knew about their sexuality, and buttoned-down professionals that chose to remain closeted. The two groups had little contact or mutual venues. Mary had a companion.

Edna nodded when Lucy said, "A woman?"

"Angelica. She seemed half Dr. Mary's age. Her name fit her because she had the face of an angel and a body to match. She stood an inch or so taller than Dr. Mary. Both had dark hair and eyes, but Angelica's skin was the color of coffee and cream."

"Was she Hispanic?" Lucy asked.

Edna shook her head. "Around New Orleans, we'd say she was Creole. "

"I'm not from New Orleans," Lucy said.

"A mixture of French, Spanish, African and American Indian," I said.

"You and Holly met Angelica and Dr. Mary at the office? Which office?" Lucy asked.

"A landmark nightclub in the Quarter," I said. "It's named the Office."

Edna nodded. "Downstairs was a souvenir shop complete with cheesy tee shirts and stuffed animals made in China. Upstairs was a gathering spot for gay and lesbian judges, doctors, lawyers, and business people."

"What was Angelica's last name?" Tony asked.

"Closeted gays and lesbians keep their secrets. Angelica never told us her last name. We never asked."

"What else do you remember about her?" I said.

"She was about the same age as Holly and me and lots younger than Dr. Mary."

56

"Where did she work?" Tony asked. "Was she from around here?"

"Don't know. Like I said, they kept things to themselves."

"Is she still around?" I asked.

Edna glanced out the window, toward the river. "She disappeared after the murder."

"You've thought about all this, haven't you?" Tony asked.

"More times than I'd care to admit."

"You must hate the men who branded Holly."

"You can't imagine. Even years later, Holly would wake up screaming."

"Wonder if they're still alive?" Lucy said

Edna's frown told the story even before she spoke. "If they are, and I ever meet them face to face, I'll kill them with my bare hands."

Chapter 8

July heat blasted us when we stepped out the door. Lucy glared at me as if it were my fault. I didn't bother denying it.

"Dirty Edna, indeed!" Lucy said. "She's just a nostalgic old woman."

Tony smirked as he climbed into his car. "Yeah? Well, she wasn't kidding about killing those two bastards with her bare hands. What's your take, Wyatt?"

"That I need to visit Madeline's Magic Shop, and then the Office Bar."

"Who is Madeline?" Lucy asked.

"I thought you didn't need my help," I said.

"Fine."

"She's Rafael Romanov's mother. Dr. Mary and Jeribeth Briggs used to attend séances there."

"Rafael never mentioned his mother to me."

"Maybe because he didn't think you'd believe him. She's a former Catholic nun, and a witch, by all accounts."

Tony had lowered the top on his convertible and Lucy glanced at the fat gray clouds floating above us.

"Give me a break."

"You asked me; I told you. Now, what?"

"That pay phone you promised to take me to."

"Is there one around here, Cowboy?" Tony said.

"JL's Riverside Cafe. Around the corner on Magazine."

"Great," Lucy said. "I need a drink in the worst way, and I can get one while I'm waiting for my ride."

Tony pulled into JL's and parked. This part of Magazine Street, from the Audubon Zoo to Canal, is six miles of restaurants, art galleries, antiques and tourist shops. JL's fit right in, a trendy watering hole occupying the rustic brick shell of an old building. The new owners had added a modern deck with colorful umbrellas topping the tables.

Light jazz piped through hidden speakers resonated with the sound of boats on the nearby Mississippi. Though still early, many smiling patrons occupied the patio, drinking, listening to the music and watching scores of tourists ambling past. The pay phone, looking lonely and unused, was on the wall in front of our car.

"I'll wait for you," Tony said.

"No, you won't. When I finish my call, I'm going inside for a martini. I don't care if I ever see either one of you again."

We watched her stroll to the phone without looking back. In a moment, she returned to the car. Tony was waiting, a quarter in hand. She took it without saying thanks.

"Now what?" Tony asked.

"I'm leaving now."

"Sure about that?" he asked. "I can drop you somewhere else. It's obvious Miss Network T.V. don't want nothing more to do with you."

"I'll hang around until I see her safely disappear in her boss's car."

"You know something I don't?"

59

"Just that I got her into this mess, and I have an obligation to see she gets out of it," I said.

"Don't get yourself killed doing it. With that mouth on her, she ain't worth it. How will we stay in touch?"

"We won't. No need in you getting involved any more than you already are."

"Sure about that?" he asked as I got out of the car.

"If I need you, I'll find you."

"Stay safe, Cowboy," he said as I hurried through the throng of tourists milling in front of JL's patio.

Too busy with her phone call, Lucy didn't see me walk behind her and enter the crowded cafe through the front door. The dimly lit establishment hummed with activity, harried waiters and waitresses working the tables. The sound of zydeco accordion music was barely audible. I spotted an empty table partially hidden from the bar area by hanging ferns and a large potted plant.

"Can I sit here?" I asked a passing waitress dressed in khaki shorts and tee shirt emblazoned with JL's red logo on the front.

She smiled and took the twenty I handed her. "You got it, handsome. What can I get you to drink?"

"Ice tea."

"Sweet or unsweet?"

She smiled and winked when I said, "Sweet."

Sitting on the stool at the tall bar table, I pulled the brim of my cap down over my eyes. My shoulder had started aching again, and I took two more of Sonora's painkillers, hoping they would hurry up and start working as I washed them down with sweet tea.

Lucy didn't notice me when she entered the front door, heading straight for the bar. The first thing she did after ordering a drink was to remove her cap and sunglasses. The couple sitting next to her noticed, as did the bartender. Lucy was busy signing an autograph when the bartender returned with her drink.

Everyone in JL's soon knew they were in the midst of a celebrity. Many ventured to the bar for her autograph. Euphoric from her first double of the day, and the prospect of soon being safely back in the folds of her network, she smiled and ordered a second drink.

Not everyone was smiling. I watched as the bartender stepped into the shadows and made a frenzied call on his cell phone, looking at Lucy as he did. Heading for the bar, I grabbed her hand.

"We have to get out of here," I said.

"What the hell! Are you still stalking me? Leave me the hell alone," she said, causing the man sitting on the stool next to her to give me a dirty look.

"No can do," I said, pulling her off the seat and out the door to the raised deck.

The man beside Lucy at the bar started to say something, thought better of it and turned his back to us as we exited the restaurant. By now, she was kicking and flailing her arms as she called me every name in the book at the top of her lungs. When I saw a familiar black sedan screech to a stop at the front door, I quit trying to avoid her fist and feet. I lowered my head, banging into her midsection and throwing her over my shoulder.

The patio was a good six feet above the parking lot pavement. There was no exit from the cafe on the deck. Lifting her over the railing, I lowered her unceremoniously to the ground and then jumped over after her.

"Are you truly crazy?" she screamed at me.

"Shut up and run," I said as the same two men that had shot me rushed out the patio door with their pistols drawn.

Lucy's hand went to her mouth.

"Oh my God!" she said.

"Believe me now?" I said, turning her around and pushing her toward the alleyway.

When a bullet whistled over our heads, ricocheting off the ancient mortar, she heeded my instructions and ran. I wasn't far behind, tipping trash cans along the way in an attempt to slow down the two gunmen when they came after us.

When we reached a junction in the alleyway, we took a left, not knowing which direction our pursuers would take. Lucy soon drew to a halt, breathing hard as she leaned against old walls of the brick canyon.

"Who are those men?"

"The same two that shot me and killed my client. Hispanics; now it seems they're probably Cubans."

Lucy glanced behind us. "This is a maze. How do you know where to go?"

"I don't, but neither do they," I said.

"Doesn't matter because they'll be waiting for us if we ever reach the other end."

"You're right about that. We have to get out of this alley before they trap us."

I began running from backdoor to backdoor, trying to find one that someone had left unlocked. Not locating one, I broke out a pane in the glass part of a door with my elbow, stuck my hand through the break and unlocked the bolt.

"You're crazy!" Lucy said. "Someone's probably in there with a shotgun.

"Then choose your poison," I said, grabbing her wrist and pulling her through the door.

The moment we shut it behind us we knew the old apartment was unoccupied. Sweltering heat, smell of must, dust and mouse droppings almost overpowered us. Lucy grabbed my wrist and drew closer.

"Jesus, this place is creeping me out."

I tried the lights. No electricity. Except for beams of light shining through missing slats, blinds tightly cloaked the windows and darkened the room. Fishing for my keychain flashlight, I flashed the beam around the dusty room.

"There's no one here except us."

"Then why does it remind me of a tomb?" she said.

"Maybe a few ghosts in here."

My flashlight quickly answered her question. Sitting lifelike in a stuffed chair was the mummified body of an old black woman, cobwebs on her face and body attesting to the length of time she'd sat there.

"Oh my God!" Lucy said. "We have to do something."

"She's long dead. Let's get the hell out of here."

"You can't just leave her. What about her family?"

"If she had a family someone would have already found her."

"You're a monster."

"Just a realist," I said, opening a closet and rummaging through the dusty clothes hanging on the rack. I tossed Lucy a dress. "We have to get rid of the clothes we're wearing. Put this on."

She removed her blouse and shorts, wiggling into the dress. "This barely covers my ass," she said. "I can't believe that old lady ever wore this."

"Maybe her daughter or granddaughter. Doesn't matter because there's not much to choose from."

"Thirteen-year-old daughter, maybe," Lucy said.

"Here's a pair of sandals that'll probably fit you. Less conspicuous than your red tennis shoes."

Lucy tossed her shoes into a corner and slipped on the sandals. I found a pair of khakis, plaid shirt and slightly used Panama hat that I pulled down over my eyes.

"What about me?"

"Try putting your hair in a ponytail. that will alter your appearance."

"I've never worn a ponytail in my life," she said.

I pulled her blond tresses behind her head.

"Maybe not thirteen, but your ponytail and that miniskirt make you look about fifteen. Even your mother wouldn't recognize you."

"Does that turn you on, buster?"

"Let's worry about what turns me on some other time. Right now we need to find something to keep your pretty little ponytail in place and then get the hell out of here."

Rummaging through a drawer, I found a rubber band and handed it to her. Lucy shrieked when a mouse raced across her foot. Grabbing her wrist, I pulled her to the front door.

"You're just going to rob the old woman and then leave her body here to rot?"

"Trust me; the body isn't going anywhere. When we're safe, we'll send someone to retrieve it. Meantime, we need to think about our hides. I figure we've got about fifteen minutes before those two thugs notice the broken pane."

We were soon out front at a cross street leading to St. Charles Avenue.

"What now?" Lucy asked.

"I was on my way to the French Quarter to talk with Madeline. Don't know now. The Quarter will be swarming with people looking for us. What happened to your producer?"

"Sandy can't pick me up until ten tonight."

"You were going to wait for him that long?"

She didn't answer as a vehicle approached, slowing as it neared us. We both froze. It was a couple of teenage boys in a pickup truck, slowing when they spotted Lucy. Rolling down their windows, both boys howled, and wolf whistled before racing away in a wake of burning rubber.

"Don't say a word," she said when she saw me smiling.

Vehicles continued to slow, their passengers gawking as they drove past us. Lucy wasn't happy.

"I stick out like a sore thumb. This outfit is drawing too much attention."

"No one has a clue you're the world famous Lucy Diamond. You look more like a . . ."

"Hooker?"

"You said it, not me. People are staring because you look sexy as hell."

"I don't smell sexy as hell, and neither do you."

"We both could use a little deodorant," I said.

"Even last night's fleabag shower stall seems inviting right about now."

She wasn't exaggerating. Summer heat continued to swelter, and we were both sweating when we reached the streetcar stop on St. Charles. Live oaks draped the Avenue, providing a bit of a shelter when the sky darkened, and it began to rain. Lucy propped her sunglasses on top of her head, mopping water out of her eyes with the back of her arm.

"Hey, at least it's cooler than it was," I said when she crossed her arms and glared at me."

The rain was falling harder when an army green streetcar rattled to a halt. The old rumble buggy was empty, so we grabbed a seat by the rear exit. Lucy continued to frown.

"Does it rain every day in this town?"

"Just seems like it sometimes. And it's cooler now."

"At least until the sun comes back out."

The rest of the ride, we watched in silence as drops of rain trickled down glass panes on the streetcar. At least until I fell asleep. The rain had stopped when we reached Canal. Lucy nudged my arm to wake me. It took me a moment to remember where I was.

"Guess I didn't sleep very well last night," I said as we exited the streetcar.

"No, and you kept me awake with your moans and groans."

"You'll sleep well when you're safe again. Where are you meeting your producer?"

"The end of the 17th Street Canal."

"For what reason?"

"Because that's where he wants to pick me up."

"How were you planning to get there?"

"Cab, of course."

"Aren't you forgetting something? You lost your purse. You have no money."

Lucy didn't cry but turned so I wouldn't see her wipe away a tear.

"I would have thought of something," she said.

"I'll take you."

"Just lend me a twenty. I'll go by myself."

"Every cabbie in the city is probably looking for us by now. No matter. I don't own a car, but I do know every bus and streetcar route in the city."

"You're weird. What do you do when you go out of town?"

"Then I use planes, boats, cabs and public transportation."

"Like I said. Weird."

Chapter 9

When sunlight finally broke through the clouds, humidity began to sizzle. Beads of sweat started forming on Lucy's neck. She wasn't a happy camper and let me know it.

"My stomach's growling and this heat's starting to fry my brain. A martini and dark bar are calling me."

"You had lots of luck with that one earlier today, and I have another place to stop. Maybe we can find out something about this doubloon."

"At least get me some air conditioning. Please."

She followed me as I started up the sidewalk. With a wealth of one-owner shops, restaurants and art galleries, New Orleans defies corporate America. Not even half of these unique establishments are located in the French Quarter. Canal Street had long housed an abundance of camera, electronics, and Carnival-related shops. Most had suffered looting and vandalism during Hurricane Katrina, and many had never reopened.

One such shop was a place on Canal I hadn't visited since I was a boy. With Lucy glaring at me, I crossed my fingers it was still there.

"If this is a snipe hunt, you're a dead man," she said.

"We're almost there."

As we walked, she mumbled obscenities I tried to ignore. The day was busy, tourists hustling up the sidewalk, attempting to stay ahead of the rain. A red streetcar filled with tourists on their way to explore the city's cemeteries passed on the palm tree-lined median. When we reached the familiar shop, I had to stop. The sign on the door said Haney's Coins and Collectibles.

"What's up, buster? This it?"

I could only nod. The sight of the little shop had sent a wave of nostalgia cresting across my bow.

"Haven't been here in years, and it looks the same as when I was twelve."

Lucy shook her ponytail and entered the shop. "Wait outside if you want. I'm going in for some cooler air."

If refrigeration was what Lucy sought, the shop didn't provide much, a single ceiling fan stirring the air almost as warm as outside on the sidewalk. Tinkling bells signaled our presence causing the little man behind a display cabinet to glance up from his paperback. He barely managed a constipated smile.

"Help you?"

"I'm Wyatt Thomas, Mr. Haney. You probably don't remember me, but I used to come with my dad."

"Of course, I remember you," he said, his smile expanding. "So sorry about your father."

Though probably pushing ninety, Haney's hair, except for his sideburns, was still brown. From men's hair dye, I suspected. He still had the same toothbrush mustache and pince-nez glasses he'd probably bought when he was twenty.

The shop was small, lined with faded posters and Mardi Gras masks, the cabinets filled with rare coins and Carnival doubloons. Caught in an apparent time warp, it hadn't changed much since the last time I'd seen it.

"This is Lucy, and we have a few questions."

"Your little sister?" he asked.

"Something like that," I said, imagining Lucy's expression without bothering to look.

"Ask away."

"Ever seen one of these?" I said, handing him the doubloon.

Haney perched his glasses atop his head and drew the Carnival toss closer to his eyes.

"This is relatively rare," he finally said. "I don't remember ever seeing a doubloon like this, much less selling it to your father."

"I didn't get it from Dad."

"What kind of coin is it?" Lucy asked.

"Not a coin, young lady, a doubloon from the Krewe of Rex formed in 1872 to honor Alexis Romanoff, the Russian Grand Duke."

"What's so special about Rex?" Lucy asked.

Haney's little mustache twitched before he answered.

"The King of Rex is also King of Carnival. With the possible exception of Comus, it's the most influential krewe in all of Mardi Gras, the King often the richest and most powerful man in the city."

"Who was King of Rex in 1948?" I asked.

"Don't know, but I can look it up."

The old man disappeared into the back of his shop, returning with a thick book. Placing it on the counter, he began thumbing the pages.

"Well?" I said when he glanced up for a moment to watch a group of tourists walk by on the sidewalk.

"Dr. Louis Hollingsworth, founder of the Hollingsworth Clinic," he said.

Lucy's jaw dropped, and it took her a moment to recover before speaking.

"What about the engraving on back?"

Haney flipped the coin and looked. "No earthly idea," he finally said. "It was added later. Not part of the original doubloon."

"How do you know?" Lucy asked.

Haney turned the book around so she could see it. "Here's a picture of the original doubloon, front and back. No engraving."

"You said this particular doubloon is rare. Why is that?" she asked.

Haney hefted it in his hand before giving it to her. "Feel it? Solid gold. One of a kind, not a Carnival toss. Only one person owned this doubloon."

"Who?" Lucy asked.

"Dr. Louis Hollingsworth. The doubloon you're holding was personally made for the King of Rex. There's not another like it in the whole world."

Lucy had already started for the door without bothering to say thanks. She stopped when I pointed to an elaborate Mardi Gras mask in Haney's display case.

"How much?" I asked

He smiled for the second time. "Just like your old man," he said as he removed the mask and handed it to me. "Always able to recognize the very best. The Queen of Venus wore this mask in 1964. A hundred dollars and cheap at twice the price."

I pulled out five twenties and handed them to him. After placing the mask in a brown paper bag, he shook my hand.

"Glad to see you again, young man. You're all grown now and remind me so much of your dad. Don't make yourself scarce."

It was late afternoon when we left Haney's. Clouds had grown dark, the humidity through the roof. I was worried about Lucy because she had stopped complaining.

"You all right?" I asked.

70

"It was almost as hot in there as it is out here. The little man wasn't even sweating?"

"Probably like the woman in the apartment. Already mummified."

"Why did you buy the mask?"

"Because valuable information is never free."

"You're a weirdo," she said.

Not bothering to rebut her comment, I tossed the bag into a trashcan on the sidewalk. Lucy reached into the trash and retrieved the brown sack.

"It's much too beautiful to toss away. The old man knew your father. What's the deal?"

"Dad collected coins and doubloons. He used to take me with him when he visited Haney's shop. Probably the only thing we ever did together as father and son."

"What happened to him?"

"Long story."

"Give me the abbreviated version," she said.

"You're good."

"Then answer me."

"He killed himself."

Something in my voice caused her to discontinue her questions.

"Sorry," she said.

"No problem. It happened long ago."

"Give me your take on what the old man told us about the doubloon," she said, changing the subject.

"Dr. Mary's boss Louis Hollingsworth owned the doubloon. Its engraving has something to do with Dr. Mary, as well as the rape of Edna's significant other."

"Now what?"

"It's too early to take you to the West End."

"Then let's find a dark bar and get out of this heat. I needed a drink an hour ago."

"I have just the place," I said.

Lightning zigzagged across the darkening sky. Thunder that rattled slate roofs on nearby buildings quickly followed.

"Better hurry before we get drenched. Which way?"

When I pointed, she ran up the street without waiting for me, and I hurried after her. The rain had begun sprinkling our shoulders as we reached our destination a few blocks away.

Allemandes is an eclectic bar on the edge of the Quarter. Unknown by most tourists, the regulars eyed us with disdain as we entered. I knew our disguises were working because I'd known the bartender for years and he didn't recognize me. Otis Redding blared from the jukebox as we made our way to a dark booth in the back.

"Help you?" the man in the booth asked.

"Armand, it's me," I said, lifting my Panama so he could see my face.

"Cowboy. You the talk of the town right about now. Who'd you piss off this time?"

"Seems like everybody. Safe to join you?"

He grinned. "I can only speak for myself. Madam Toulouse Joubert has always had a thing for you."

"I'll take my chances," I said, sliding in beside her. "This is Lucy."

"Honey, you're too young for this bar, even if this is New Orleans," Madam Toulouse said.

"Don't let this short skirt and ponytail fool you," Lucy said. "I'm much older than twenty-one."

"Don't worry, honey. I won't let the bartender card you."

"Good, because I need a drink, and I don't have my I.D. on me."

"Honey, you can get most anything you want in this place, even if you ain't legal yet," Madam Toulouse said, raising a finger to get the bartender's attention.

Armand had thinning black hair, a tiny black mustache and was dressed totally in black, including his shoes. If he'd been wearing socks, they would also have been black.

Madam Toulouse's red miniskirt highlighted her long legs and muscular thighs that never moved far from Armand's. Her bouffant hair pointed toward the ceiling as she sucked a sugary drink through a long red straw, and eyed Lucy's bare legs.

"Love your ponytail, and your skirt."

"What there is of it," Lucy said, trying to hike it down an inch or two.

Madam Toulouse noticed the paper bag Lucy was holding.

"What's in the sack?" she asked.

Lucy removed the mask and showed her. "Something Mr. Culture bought on the way over," she said.

"Oh, it's beautiful," Madam Toulouse said.

A waiter interrupted the conversation, arriving with drinks. Lucy licked the edge of the frosty glass, and then took a sip, savoring the martini and the bar's nippy temperature. I'd popped two of Senora's pills after leaving Haney's. Now, I felt better than I had in a while as I sipped my first lemonade in two days.

"Armand and Madam Toulouse are dealers in art, antiques and old books, especially anything concerning New Orleans. They also know more about the inner circle of this city than probably anyone alive."

"Yeah, yeah," Armand said. "When you're through stroking us, you can tell us what you come for."

"We're in trouble. Sorry to involve you and Madam Toulouse."

"You family, Cowboy. That's what families are for. Besides, your mother wouldn't recognize you in that outfit."

"You're wrong about that. Whoever we're dealing with is tailing us so close, I almost feel as if I have a bug in my underwear."

"Could be," Armand said. "What do you need from the Madam and me? A place to hide out?"

"I wouldn't do that to you. The people looking for us aren't playing games."

"I hear that," Madam Toulouse said, touching my shoulder. "You okay?"

"I got some pain pills from Madam Aja's daughter Senora."

"How can we help?" Armand asked.

I handed him the doubloon. "A little problem, this my only clue."

Armand shook his head slowly and glanced at the ceiling after studying the doubloon. "You got more than a little problem, Cowboy. Who'd you kill to get this?"

"A client gave it to me. Someone told us it's very rare."

"Not another like it in the world. No telling what it would go for at auction."

"High six figures at least," Madam Toulouse said. "Where did you say you got it?"

"From my client."

"You know this is stolen property, don't you?" Armand said. "Missing from the estate of Louis Hollingsworth for several years now. There's a healthy reward for its return."

"I didn't steal it."

"Didn't say you did, but I wouldn't let the police find it in my possession if I was you."

"Don't intend to. Any idea what the symbol means?"

Madam Toulouse gazed over Armand's shoulder at the doubloon and was the first to answer.

"Something that could get us all killed."

"Can you elaborate?" I said.

"I need another drink first," Armand said, raising a finger to get the barkeep's attention.

When someone exited the bar, we heard thunder rumbling outside the door. I hoped the weather wouldn't get any worse. Lucy, working on her third martini, didn't seem to care.

"I can tell you're reluctant to talk about the symbol. Is there anything you can tell us?"

"We ain't just reluctant, Cowboy, we downright scared," Armand said. "Whatever we say can't go beyond this table. Comprendre?"

"Je comprends," I said.

Armand grinned. "Don't know why I'm even bothering worrying about it. You the most tight-lipped person I ever met. You wouldn't give it up to God."

"Yes I would," I said. "But not a mere mortal."

Thunder rumbled again, louder this time. Armand sipped his scotch and relaxed against the booth's cushion.

"Nawlins has secret and exclusive clubs, societies and organizations."

"Like the Boston Club." I said.

"That's one of them, but it ain't all by any stretch."

"What's the Boston Club?" Lucy asked.

"Formed before the Civil War by a group of the city's elite," Madam Toulouse said. "Associated with the Krewe of Rex."

Lucy was suddenly all ears. "What's so secret and exclusive about it?"

"No Jews, blacks, women or Texans can ever join; its members are sworn to total secrecy about what goes on inside the club walls."

"Do you know?" Lucy asked.

"I ain't white, honey. I've never been inside, but I know what goes on."

"Please tell me," Lucy said.

"Control. Everything from politics to garbage collection. You want something important done in this city you better be a member of the Boston Club."

"Is that their symbol on the back of the doubloon?"

"Another club even more sinister. You can see it's a bastardized pentagram."

"I'm not sure what you mean," Lucy said.

"A pentagram is a five-pointed star within a circle, one point always at the top. It was a Christian symbol for the five senses or the five wounds of Christ. All the points have meaning. The high point symbolizes spirit; the other four are fire, air, water and earth."

"But this symbol is opposite."

"Yes," Madam Toulouse said. "When the top point is inverted, it becomes the symbol of Satan. The goat's head is the goat of lust, its horns attacking the heavens. It's the symbol of dark magic."

"What does it supposed to mean?" Lucy asked.

"Honey, it symbolizes New Orleans and the Mississippi River, black magic, and all that's dark and ominous in this town."

"Can you put a name to these people?" I asked.

"The Forces of Darkness. The most secret cult our fair city has ever seen."

Thunder rumbled the walls of the bar, and Lucy finished the last of her martini. "Are you a member?"

"If I were," she said. "We wouldn't be sitting here right now."

Armand handed me the doubloon, and I rolled it in my hand.

"Louis Hollingsworth was the King of Rex in 1948. He owned this doubloon. What can you tell us about him?"

"Lots of public information out there. Being from Nawlins, I thought you'd already know all about him."

"I'd like to hear your take."

"By all accounts, Hollingsworth was one of the greatest surgeons that ever lived. He was charismatic. When he walked into a room, people stopped whatever they were doing and took notice."

"We know all that," Lucy said. "Tell us something we don't know."

Madam Toulouse rolled her big brown eyes.

"Don't mind Lucy," I said. "She means well."

Madam Toulouse was between us, and Lucy calmed down when her next martini arrived. Armand just shook his head, sipped his scotch and continued.

"He wasn't born in Nawlins, but someplace in the Midwest. He taught at Tulane and Charity, and soon had funding for Hollingsworth Clinic. Before long, he was treating every dignitary and prominent political figure from the Caribbean, Central, and South America, and had the respect of the city's inner circle. Something almost no outsider ever does."

"What's the significance of the foreign dignitaries?"

"People in the C.I.A. noticed and got involved," Madam Toulouse said.

Lucy's eyes widened. Placing her martini on the table, she touched knees with Madam Joubert.

"C.I.A.?"

"That's right, honey, and Hollingsworth ate the attention up. He had his rightwing organization called NOFF which stood for New Orleans for Freedom."

Armand nodded. "Because of his Caribbean and Central American connections, he hated the Kennedy's for what he perceived was betrayal at the Bay of Pigs in Cuba."

"What was the connection with the C.I.A.?" I asked.

"You'll have to ask someone besides me on that one, Cowboy," Armand said.

There was no clock in the bar. Used to checking my phone for the time, I reached for it, quickly remembering I no longer had it. Rain poured through the door when a patron hurried inside.

"Either of you have the time?"

"You taking medicine?" Armand asked.

"We need to be someplace at nine."

"Unless the storm lets up, none of us are going anyplace. Might as well drink up."

Lucy took his advice and hoisted her martini.

"Easy," I said. "We still have unfinished business and the West End's several miles from here."

Armand glanced at the Rolex on his wrist. "Then you better think about leaving or you won't make it by nine."

"What's happening at the West End?" Madam Toulouse asked.

"We're meeting Lucy's boss near there. He's taking her to safety."

"Maybe you better go with her," Armand said.

"I'll be okay. One more question before we go. Was Hollingsworth a member of the Forces of Darkness?"

Armand glanced at Madame Joubert before answering. "Sorry, Cowboy. Right now you know as much about Hollingsworth as I do."

Lucy and I slid out of the booth and started for the door, Lucy returning before she'd gone ten steps. She handed the Mardi Gras mask to Madam Toulouse.

"You keep it," she said. "It's too beautiful to let the rain ruin it."

Chapter 10

Lucy stumbled as a gust of wind blasted through the door. Other than that, I was amazed at how well she held her liquor. We found the sidewalks soaked, water pouring down the street, but at least it had stopped raining.

"How far to the West End?" she asked.

"Twenty miles, as the crow flies. Plenty of time to get there if we haven't missed our bus."

"You and your buses! Why don't you own a car?"

"I told you, I like public transportation."

"You're a dork. Why do Armand and Tony call you Cowboy?"

"My parents were socialites, jet-setting all over the world. They didn't have much time for a child, so I spent most of my summers and holidays on a cattle ranch in southwest Louisiana with my aunt and uncle."

"They raise cows in Louisiana?"

"Lots of them," I said. "I learned to rope and ride so well, my cousins nicknamed me. The name stuck and most of my friends still call me Cowboy."

We waited for fifteen minutes beneath a covered bus stop. Though the heavy rain had ceased, pools of water reflected in the flickering light of a lone streetlamp. Lucy had a sudden chill; her arms clasped tightly against her chest. She must have been cold because when I put my hands on her shoulders, she didn't move away.

"When I make it to a hotel I'm going to fill a tub to the brim with water hot as I can stand. I'm going to soak up to my nose until it turns cold. Then I'm going to crawl beneath a big down comforter and sleep until noon tomorrow."

"Sounds like a plan. Won't be long. Here's our ride."

We had our pick of seats on the nearly empty bus. Lightning flashed outside the hazy windows as we passed miles of streetlights on the way to the West End. Lucy sat in silence, not bothering to wipe the drops of water beading her thighs.

"You okay?" I finally said.

"Why don't you come with me? Sandy and the network will protect you until this mess blows over."

"You don't hate me anymore?"

"I don't hate anyone. Detest, maybe."

"That's the girl I know and love," I said with a smile. "I was starting to worry about you."

"What's that wall?" she asked, changing the subject.

"Floodwall," I said. "There's a canal on the other side that's designed to relieve flooding if the water gets too high. It empties north of here into Lake Pontchartrain."

"It must be eight feet tall. Does water ever get that high?"

"It's precautionary since some of the levees became breached during Katrina."

"I can only imagine what it would be like here during a hurricane. Doesn't it ever stop raining?"

"Every so often," I said.

"I wasn't kidding about you coming with me."

"Can't. I'm going no place until I find out who killed Dr. Mary."

"Or get killed first."

"That's not in the plan."

"How do you intend to prevent it?" she asked. "The people chasing us seem to know every time we burp."

"Maybe, but they don't know the city as I do."

"Even if you find out who killed Dr. Mary, it's not going to call off the killers. How do you plan to solve that little problem?"

"I'll think of something."

"You're just bull-headed," she said. "Sandy and I will find Dr. Mary's murderer. Step out of the picture until then."

"I'll think about it."

"You'd better think fast. Once Sandy and I drive away, you'll be on your own, and I won't be able to help you."

"My client must have stolen the Rex doubloon from the Hollingsworth estate," I said.

"That's what has me puzzled," Lucy said.

"Are you on to something?"

"Armand and Mr. Haney both said the doubloon is valuable. The people chasing us want it badly and have already killed to get it back. Why do they covet it so?"

"It's one of a kind. Maybe it's like the Holy Grail for the Forces of Darkness."

Lucy glanced at me. "Now and then you say something that almost makes sense."

The bus let us off a few blocks before we reached West End Park. It was drizzling again as we backed against the floodwall and huddled beneath a tree on the dark street. About ten minutes later, a white Mercedes pulled slowly to the side of the road and stopped.

"That's Sandy's car. You coming?"

"No, and I don't think you should either."

"It's just Sandy. What's the matter?"

"Don't know. I have a nagging feeling something's wrong here."

"That's just crazy," she said.

"Then why didn't he want to pick you up on Canal, or someplace with lots of people around."

"Don't know. Coming or not?"

When I shook my head, she stood on her toes, put her hands on my cheeks, stared into my eyes a moment, and then kissed me.

"You're a stubborn fool, Wyatt Thomas. Try not to get yourself killed."

She turned away and hurried toward the big Mercedes before I could reply. As she did, my warning whistles began blasting a clamorous siren in my brain. Feeling around on the ground for something to use as a weapon, I found a fallen branch. I hefted it to test its weight, hoping like hell I wouldn't need it.

Lucy had almost reached the car when I glanced up. She stopped when a man dressed in coat and tie burst out of the driver's side.

"Sandy," Lucy called. "It's me."

"It's a trap, Lucy. Run!" he yelled.

A man in a black sports coat came crashing out of the car behind him with pistol drawn. Lucy screamed when the weapon erupted, destroying the night's serenity. The impact knocked Sandy to the sidewalk where he lay struggling, trying to stand. The assailant put his foot on the small of Sandy's back, and then shot him again, this time in the back of the head. Lucy continued to scream.

"Lucy," I yelled. "Run!"

She turned and ran toward me as the lights of a black sedan came sliding in a squeal of rubber around the corner. After kicking the fallen Sandy for good measure, the man in black hurried after her. He wasn't expecting me when he reached the tree. I cold-cocked him in the head as hard as I could swing. Lucy had stopped running when I picked up the pistol, unloading it into the black sedan barreling toward us. At first, I thought I had missed. I hadn't.

The speeding car's tires screeched. It did a sudden three-sixty, almost turned over, then crashed in a burst of flame into the floodwall. I didn't wait to see if there were survivors as I grabbed Lucy's hand. She was in near hysterics when we reached Sandy's body.

"Oh my God!" she said, squatting beside his body.

"No time, he's dead," I said, looking to see if he'd left the key in the ignition.

I didn't bother opening the passenger door for Lucy, pulling her unceremoniously into the car. Cranking the engine, I wheeled the car around and headed west on the first major street, my foot crammed to the floorboard. After a few miles, I stood on the brakes and slid to the side of the road, leaving the car running. Lucy was in shock when I yanked her out and hurried away in the opposite direction. She was crying as she shook my hands away.

"Don't fight me, Lucy. We have to get away from here."

"That man killed Sandy," she said.

"Grieve later, unless you want to join him now."

"You're an asshole!"

"No time for feelings. The man that killed your boss could have killed you just as easily. He wanted you alive for some reason. We need to find out why."

"I'm sorry," she said. "It's just . . ."

"I'm the one who is sorry," I said, grabbing her shoulders. "I know you're in shock, but you have to fight through it, or we won't survive."

She pushed my hands away. "I'm okay. I've covered Afghanistan, Bhopal, and the earthquake in China. Believe me; I've seen my share of dead people. Stop treating me as if I'm a child."

"Good, then let's hurry before the clouds open and drown us."

"We won't get far on foot."

"There's a bus stop ahead."

"Then what?" she asked.

"Shut the hell up for a few minutes. I'm doing the best I can."

I managed a weak smile when she said, "Now who's acting like a baby?"

We must have looked a sight when the bus driver picked us up on Lake Side Drive. Likely used to seeing many strange things, he didn't comment as I paid our fare and directed Lucy toward the back of the empty bus.

"Sorry I yelled at you back there," I said. "You okay?"

"I feel so responsible for Sandy's death."

"You're not. He was just doing his job and you yours."

"How did you learn to shoot like that?"

"Like I told you, I practically grew up on a ranch. I started shooting by the age of ten, though I haven't used a pistol in more than twenty years until tonight."

"Like riding a bicycle, huh?"

"Something like that."

Any idea where we're going?" she asked.

"Bertram has a fishing camp near here. I know where he keeps the key."

"Who is Bertram?"

"Someone I trust with my life," I said.

Lake Pontchartrain was a shadow in the distance, dark clouds draping the water. We soon reached a long wooden walkway jutting far out into the lake. At the far end sat a rustic cabin. Rain began falling in sheets as I fumbled for the key and opened the door.

"What is this?" Lucy asked.

"Bertram's fishing camp. Used to be hundreds like this one on the lake. Katrina changed all that. Bertram's is one of the few remaining."

I expected the smell of must as I turned on a fluorescent lantern. There wasn't any. Bertram had recently visited and left an ice chest filled with lemonade, cold drinks, and a pot of gumbo. The lantern even had fresh batteries. I lit the propane stove and sat the pot on it.

"Good old Bertram," I said.

Bertram had also left the windows cracked, the storm flapping faded curtains. The floor was unpainted wood, as were the walls. There were no pictures; just some functional cabinets stocked with canned goods. My stomach churned when I smelled the fresh loaf of French bread on the counter.

Lucy popped the top on a soda, holding the cold can against her neck a moment before taking a sip.

"Your friend's an angel. I wish he'd left a bottle of gin."

She grinned when I opened a cabinet, showing her Bertram's larder.

"Bertram never goes anywhere without his liquor," I said.

Lucy flinched when thunder shook the cabin. "This isn't a hurricane, is it?"

"Just a normal summer storm for New Orleans. We'll be fine."

I lit the candle on the kitchen table and then turned off the lantern to conserve batteries. There were other candles in strategic locations and Lucy lit them as well. Shadows, flickering light, and flashes of lightning soon filled the little cabin.

86

"The wonderful aroma wafting from the pot is calling to me. Now, if I just had a shower and change of clothes I'd be in heaven."

"Don't know about clean clothes, but the cabin has a shower and chemical potty. Want to clean up before you eat?"

"Lead the way," she said.

There was no stall. The bare showerhead in a shallow basin drained into the lake.

"This place has running water?" she asked.

"A cistern on the roof that collects rainwater. You'll have to take a cold shower. It's all we have, so go easy on it."

"Great," she said, stripping off her clothes in front of me.

When I turned away to give her some privacy, she grabbed my arm.

"No, you don't. You stink as much as I do, and I'm not sleeping with a smelly man."

I didn't take much convincing.

Tepid water was soon pouring off our bodies producing smiles on both of our faces.

"Keep your hands to yourself," she said.

"Just trying to soap your back."

"That's not my back."

"Sorry, it's just that beautiful naked women have an effect on me."

"Stow it. It'll get you nowhere."

When lightning struck so close to us that resultant thunder rocked the walls, Lucy practically jumped into my arms."

"Change your mind?" I said.

"You wish."

At least she was laughing as she pushed me away.

Though the water was lukewarm, it felt like heaven. Despite our banter, neither of us wanted the shower to end. Moreover, we didn't want to put our dirty clothes back on. Bertram's little closet almost solved our problem.

The closet provided sleeveless tee shirts and cutoff blue jeans. We dined on gumbo and hot buttered French bread. Lucy's pants were about five sizes too large, and she had to hold them up with her free hand as she fished a cold beer out of the ice chest. Wind shook the little cabin on stilts, rain peppering its tin roof.

"You sure it's not a hurricane?" she asked.

I shook my head and said, "Not even close."

"Good. My body's clean and belly full. All I need is more gin to help me forget the sight of Sandy lying dead on the sidewalk with half his head blown off."

I sat my spoon on the table, hugging her. She didn't pull away.

"I don't care how many tours of the Middle East you've had. It's okay to feel sadness and grief. At least we're safe."

"What about tomorrow?"

"We'll lie low a few days. Bertram will return soon and bring us some clothes. He can also drive you out of town to someplace safe."

"Where would that be? Someone has even compromised my network."

"Looks like it," I said.

"I'm staying with you. We can't let this go."

"I never intended to."

"Then now what?"

"You heard what Armand and Madam Toulouse said. Nothing goes down in New Orleans unless the power hierarchy wants it that way. Whatever we're into apparently extends beyond the city limits of New Orleans."

"Conspiracy? But why?"

Lightning flashed outside the windows and nearby thunder rocked the cabin as I pondered Lucy's question.

"One of my close friends is the Assistant Federal District Attorney of New Orleans. We have to find a way to contact him without giving up our location."

"What's wrong with one of your vaunted pay phones?"

"Maybe. I'm having another bowl of gumbo. How about you?"

"I'll get it," she said, grabbing my bowl. "This was my first taste. Now I'm hooked. Your friend Bertram is a fabulous cook."

"You should try one of his fried oyster po'boys."

"If we ever get out of this mess alive."

Thunder shook Bertram's little fishing cottage on stilts before I could reply.

Chapter II

Tony had nursed a hunch ever since leaving Edna Callahan's earlier in the day. She knew more than she'd let on, and he intended to confront her about it. Shadows had grown dark in the street, and it was starting to rain as he rapped on her door.

"Tony? What the hell?" she asked when she peeked out to see who it was.

"Thought of another question," he said. "Got a minute?"

Edna opened the door without answering. An Elvis album was playing on the LP in the living room. The volume was a bit too loud, but she didn't bother lowering it as she motioned him to take a seat on the couch. Running lights of boats burned on the Mississippi but it was still early enough to see a flock of gulls circling a towboat headed upriver.

"Damn birds know when there's a free lunch," Edna said. "Cook must be throwing out the dinner leftovers."

"You watch the river a lot?"

"Not much else to do when you're my age."

"How old are you, if you don't mind me asking?"

Eric Wilder

"Seventy-something. I stopped counting years ago."

"I was just breaking out on the force when you retired. I don't remember you being that old. What have you done all these years?"

Holly and I traveled. Time just sort of slipped away," she said.

"Don't I know it," Tony said.

"You're still just a baby."

"Hardly. Investigating hundreds of murders can weigh on your mind."

"Tell me about it. I wasn't fifty when I retired, but I felt like a hundred."

A whistle blew on a passing tanker just as the Elvis LP ended. Edna didn't flip the record.

"Want something to drink, Lieutenant?"

"Just Tony," he said. "I haven't been a lieutenant for some time now."

"You're a legend at the precinct," she said. "I've kept in touch."

"A legend in my own mind," he said, grinning.

"Bullshit! No one in the Eighth District has solved as many murders as you. You're the best."

"Thanks, Edna, but now I'm just a burned out old private dick."

"Double bullshit! I knew you'd be back around."

"How so?"

"Cause I was a pretty good detective myself. When a bloodhound's on the scent, he don't quit till he tracks down his perp. You're on the scent, aren't you?"

"Got any scotch or whiskey in this place?" he asked.

Edna returned from the kitchen with a bottle of Wild Turkey. After taking a swig straight from the bottle, she handed it to him.

"Thought you'd never ask," she said.

A drop of whiskey dribbled down Tony's cheek, and he wiped it away with the back of his hand.

"About that question I got."

"Ask it in the car. I'm going with you," she said.

"Going where?"

"The Office in the Quarter," she said. "I've had questions now for twenty years and maybe someone there will have answers."

"I don't want to get you involved."

"I been involved for more than fifty years. Now that you're here to help me, we're going to get to the bottom of this murder."

The top was up on Tony's Mustang. Good thing as the rain began pouring in sheets as they headed for the French Quarter.

Edna couldn't take her eyes off the instruments on the lighted dashboard.

"When did you get this pussy wagon?" she asked. "You still married?"

"Barely," he said. "Had a little fling a while back. Lil's still not quite over it."

Edna snickered and said, "You men!"

"What, you never played around on Holly? I know you better that that."

"Nobody's perfect," she said.

"Then lay off of me and I'll do the same," he said.

"Partners, then?" she said.

"I haven't had a partner since Marlon Bando took a beating from a perp we were chasing."

"I thought Tommy Blackburn was your partner."

"Long story," he said.

Though tourist season was in full swing, the torrential downpour had prompted most of the city's visitors to remain in their hotel room, or retreat to the nearest French Quarter bar. Because of the lack of activity, Tony easily found a parking spot near the tee shirt shop below the Office. The rain had even slacked to a gentle sprinkle as they made their way through the lighted entrance.

Rows of cheesy tee shirts, alligators made from green foam, and pictures of St. Louis Cathedral mounted on slate filled the shop. A balding man dressed in black shorts and bright red Hawaiian shirt stood behind the counter reading a paperback.

"Help you?" he asked when he turned around.

"That you, Shinny?" she said.

"Do I know you?" he asked.

"Edna Callahan. Long time no see."

"Good God almighty!" he said, a smile appearing on his face. "Get over here and give me a big hug."

The man named Shinny reached across the counter, hugging Edna and slapping her shoulders.

"Good seeing you, Shinny."

"Where you been? I saw Holly's obit in the Picayune. You okay?"

"Hell, Shinny, I'll never be okay again, but I'm making it. You?"

"Same old, same old," he said.

Edna glanced around the shop. "Things haven't changed much. Thought you'd be retired by now."

"I'll retire the day I die," he said. "Who's your friend?"

"Shinny Black, this is Tony Nicosia."

"I know you?"

"Used to be a cop but I don't think I ever ran you in for anything."

"That's a relief," Shinny said.

"Was in homicide. I only busted murderers."

"Not guilty," he said, holding up his hands. "Though I thought about killing some of my crazy customers a time or two."

"Thoughts don't count," Tony said.

"Thank God! You ain't here just to shoot the shit with old Shinny. What's up, Edna?"

"I been grieving for Holly too long now. Thought I'd try out the scene again. See if I'm too old for another love affair. Things still hopping upstairs?"

They heard a buzz as Shinny punched a button. "Door's open. Welcome back, baby. Just don't tell anyone you're a pair of ex-cops."

Shinny returned to reading his paperback as they ascended the short flight of stairs.

"Why do they call him Shinny?" Tony asked.

"His bald head," Edna said. "Someone misspelled shiny, and everyone started calling him Shinny. The name stuck."

"You still haven't told me why we're here?"

"A gay couple. Holly and I used to double date with them. They knew Mary and Angelica. For years now, I've meant to ask them if they know where Angelica disappeared to."

"You think they'll be here?"

"Haven't kept up with them, but this is as good a place as any to start looking."

Tony expected a manic scene when they opened the door to the Office. He wasn't disappointed. Loud music, couples dancing, and bright flashing lights engulfed them, drawing them in. What he saw was anything but raucous. The room was vast and open, cozy tables fronting windows and old brick masonry looking down on the French Quarter. Lighting was dim, potted palms separating the tables and Boston ferns hanging from the rustic rafters. Soft music provided white noise, just enough for comfort but not enough to distract. A waiter, dressed much like Shinny, met them with a smile.

"Welcome to the Office. I'm Gus. Will you be dining, or visiting the bar?"

"The bar," Edna said. "Got a crowd tonight?"

"The usual suspects, though there're a few couples in from out of town."

Gus led them through the urban forest of potted palms to the center of the old building. The polished wooden bar formed a large octagon that sat on a stage elevated five feet above the club. A brass rail encircled the deck. Dozens of well-dressed people of both sexes sat on stools at the bar or congregated in bunches against the railing. Everyone held drinks and had smiles on their faces.

"Quite a crowd," Tony said. "See who you're looking for?"

"Not yet. Let's walk through the bar and see who's here."

"Right behind you," he said.

The bar was large, and it took them nearly ten minutes to circle it as they maneuvered through the crowd.

"Sorry, Tony," Edna said. "Don't see who I'm looking for."

"There are two empty stools. Let's take a load off and get a drink. Your friends may be running late because of the rain."

Tony was nursing his scotch, Edna her second shot of Wild Turkey when someone bellied up to the bar next to her. Tony recognized something about the man, maybe his shaved head, and salt and pepper mustache. When Edna spoke, he knew that he did.

"That you, Chad?"

"Edna?" the man said after giving her the once over. "How the hell you been?"

"You remember Chad, don't you Tony?"

"Sure I do," he said, shaking Chad's hand. "I was going crazy trying to put a name to your face."

"Oh my God! It's like old home week. Jeremy, look who I just bumped into."

It was then they noticed the much younger man standing directly behind Chad. They were both dressed alike in Bermuda shorts, sandals, and gaudy shirts. Jeremy was an inch or two taller than the height-challenged Chad.

"Glad to meet you, Jeremy. Chad, Tony and I all used to work together at the Eighth."

"Edna and Tony were the stars," Chad said. "Homicide dicks. They ran the place."

"You had an administration job, as I recall," Tony said. "You were always hanging around with the mayor, the chief, and all the city councilmen."

"Came in handy when I ran for office," Chad said. "I already knew who to schmooze to get to the top."

"I'm buying," Tony said. "What are you two drinking?"

"Thanks. Chardonnay, if you please. There's an empty table on the floor. Let's get our drinks, get out of this crowd, and catch up on things."

Ado from the noisy bar disappeared behind a potted palm as a waiter seated them by a large window overlooking the Quarter. The rain was falling in slow waves, occasional flashes of lightning racing across the darkened sky.

"You still drinking straight whiskey, Edna? It's a wonder you ain't pickled."

"Hell, Chad, I may be seventy, but I still feel twenty-five. When did you and Chad get together?"

"Been a while now."

"What are you doing since you left politics?" Tony asked.

"Just chilling. Thinking about making another run one of these days."

"Not if I have anything to say about it," Jeremy said.

"You two get lots of comments about your names?" Edna asked.

"Not so much. Most people we know are too young to remember the singing duo from Great Britain. Didn't know you were a fan, Edna."

"No one but Elvis for me," she said.

Thunder rattled the windows as a passing waiter checked on their drinks.

"Seems sort of strange a couple of retired homicide detectives out on a night together. You weren't here looking for me, were you?" Chad asked.

"Matter of fact we were," Edna said.

Chad's mustache wriggled as he glanced at the ceiling with a big grin on his face.

"I can't stand my ex-wife, even though I love our three kids. Don't matter cause I'd never kill her, or anyone else."

"Relax," Tony said. "We're only looking for information."

"Now you got my curiosity up. I heard you were a private eye now, Tony, but I didn't know you two were working together."

"Can't let good talent go to waste," Tony said. "Edna was the best homicide detective this town ever saw."

"I think he's angling for me to buy the drinks," she said."

"You're both pretty damn good," Chad said. "Now tell me how I can help you."

"You remember Holly?"

"Course I do. Sorry to hear about her passing, Edna."

"Thanks. I'll be over it one of these days. You remember the couple we used to hang with occasionally? Mary and Angelica?"

"Uh oh! I think I see where this is going. Dr. Mary was the victim of the most bizarre murders this town has ever seen," he said, turning to Jeremy.

"Angelica was much younger," Edna said.

97

"We know all about spring, winter relationships," Jeremy said, grabbing Chad's hand and squeezing.

"Hey now!" Chad said. "More like summer, fall."

"Didn't mean to scratch the scab off a wound," Edna said. "Angelica dropped off the face of the earth after the murder. I never knew her last name. She had no local accent."

"How did you know them?" Jeremy asked, directing his question to Chad.

"Me and James used to double date with them when I was still with the force, and before I came out."

Jeremy made a face. "I hate it when he talks about his exes."

"Didn't mean to cause a lovers spat," Tony said. "We're just wondering if you could give us a lead on Angelica to follow."

"Like you said, Edna, they were extra secretive. I never caught her last name either. One thing, though . . ."

"We're listening."

"They once let it slip that Angelica had recently graduated medical school from Tulane and was interning for Dr. Mary over at Charity. That's the only thing I know about Angelica that ain't public information."

Jeremy poked Chad in the side and glanced behind them at a man walking in their direction.

"It's that awful Judge Romberg," he said. "Let's get the hell out of here before he sees us."

"Too late," Chad said. "He's smiling and heading this way."

Chapter 12

Tony was fidgeting when the inebriated Judge Henry Romberg reached their table. So were Chad and Jeremy. The rotund man with a dimple in his chin rested his hand on Chad's squirming shoulder. He didn't look very judge-like, his Bermuda shorts and lime green shirt doing little to hide his beer belly and spindly legs.

"I was hoping I'd find you two here. With no one but those kids at the bar, I haven't had a decent conversation in a week"

"How you doing, Judge?" Chad said. "You know Tony and Edna here?"

"Don't believe I do," he said, bending to get a better look at Tony.

"Tony Nicosia," Tony said, shaking Judge Romberg's hand. "And this is Edna Callahan."

"I think I know you both, but I can't place your faces."

"Been awhile, Judge," Edna said. "We were both homicide cops. We testified in your court lots of times."

"Sure," he said. "Has been awhile."

Chad and Jeremy stood from the table, Chad slapping the much taller man's shoulder.

"Me and Jeremy got an appointment across town. Maybe you can join Tony and Edna here and catch up on old times. We gotta scoot."

They gave Judge Romberg no chance to respond, Chad saluting Tony as he turned and mouthed the words, "I owe you one."

Well into his cups, Romberg didn't seem to notice, plopping into the seat Chad had vacated.

"Been fishing in Florida since May. What's happening in the Big Easy?"

"Hot weather, crime and about a dozen murders," Tony said.

"What else is new? You're looking good, Edna. What's up with you and Tony?"

"Catching up with each other, Judge. How you been?"

"Retired a year now and it sucks. I'm so bored I could just puke." Using Tony's shoulder to help him to his feet, he started away from the table. "Gotta go to the little lawyer's room. Don't go nowhere. If my prostate cooperates, I'll be right back."

Tony waited until he'd disappeared behind the potted palms. "Jeez! I never expected to see him in a gay bar. I didn't know he was gay."

"Hell, Tony, he probably thinks you are, being here with me and all."

"What'll I do if he comes on to me?"

"Don't be so homophobic," Edna said. "Gays are no different than straights. We're all human."

"Yeah, well that's what's got me worried," Tony said.

"Suck it up. Romberg was around during the Doctor Mary murder. He likely knows lots more than we do."

"But will he tell us?" Tony said.

"Hell, he's drunker than Scooter Brown. Want to trade places? I'm not afraid of him."

"Neither am I."

"Just slap him if he tries to kiss you," Edna said with a grin.

"I get the picture. You can lay off of me now."

"Then get a grip."

Lightning rippled outside the picture window as Judge Romberg returned to the table. The waiter wasn't far behind.

"Make mine a double," Tony said. "You okay, Judge?"

"I thought you was married. Didn't know you played both sides of the fence," Romberg said, his words a mumbled slur.

Edna kicked Tony under the table before he had a chance to respond.

"You were around during the Doctor Mary murder," Tony said.

Mention of an apparently unsavory subject caused Romberg's slurred words to disappear.

"What about it?" he asked.

"Don't mind Tony, Judge. We've been drinking since noon. Now I feel like getting naughty," Edna said, motioning a passing waiter. "Bring us a round of tequila shots."

"You got it," the friendly waiter said.

"Hell, better make it three for each of us."

The waiter gave her a thumbs up before heading for the bar. When the shots arrived, Edna divided them.

"Here's to old times, Judge. Down the hatch."

After slugging their shots, Edna elbowed Tony.

"Screw the damn criminals," he said. "And let them rot in hell!"

Judge Romberg said, "Here, here," and drained his shot.

Edna slid one of her shots across the table as thunder rumbled the windows

"You look thirsty, your honor. Have one of mine."

Romberg killed the shot and then rested his head on Tony's shoulder.

"Someone may have to drive me home."

"We'll get you there," Edna said. "Am I wrong, or was there a cover-up going on in the Doctor Mary case?"

When Romberg hesitated, Tony touched his second shot to his lips.

"Have another and catch up with me, Judge. I'm just starting to have fun."

"You two trying to get me drunk?" he said, slamming the shot.

He laughed when Edna said, "Don't worry. We won't take advantage of you. Not much, anyway."

Romberg slid away from Tony's shoulder, mumbling something as he rested his head on the table.

"What?" Edna said.

Romberg lifted his head. "Cubans, mafia and C.I.A."

"I'm drunk, Judge. You got to spell it out for me," Tony said.

Romberg giggled as if remembering something humorous.

"Something funny?" Edna said.

"Lots of crazy shit going down in New Orleans during the sixties," he said.

"Like what?"

"Texas oilmen with more money than good sense. A doctor whose ego was bigger than the clinic he founded and the most powerful mafia don in the south."

"We've heard that old story before," Edna said. "Give us something we ain't heard."

"You know about the secret medical laboratory?"

"Maybe you better tell us," Tony said.

"The medical district. C.I.A. was funding primate research. Trying to mutate viruses to cure cancer and such."

"What did the C.I.A. care about cancer?" Edna asked.

"Maybe they wanted to infect Castro. Give him cancer and cause his pecker to fall off or something like that. Hell! I don't know."

When the judge's head returned to the table, Tony poked him with his elbow, and then shook his shoulders. The large man's eyes seemed to cross as he raised himself back into a sitting position.

"Why did they pick New Orleans?" Edna asked.

"Hotbed of rightwing crazies. Yellow fever, cholera, epidemic city . . ."

Romberg's eyes closed as his words trailed off. Tony shook him until he opened them again.

"You were telling us about the secret medical lab," Edna said. "Who controlled it?"

"ASH . . ."

"ASH who? Was that his last name?"

"ASH wasn't his name. It was. . ."

"Was what?" Tony said, shaking Romberg's shoulder.

Romberg tipped over his half-finished drink his elbow splattering melted ice and scotch.

"His name, Judge," Edna said. "Tell us his name."

"Admiral . . ."

"Admiral who?"

"Particle . . . accelerator . . ." Romberg said before snorting, laying his head on the table and starting to snore.

"Guess we gave him too many shots," Edna said.

"What now?"

"We're not getting anything else out of him. Let's pay up and get the hell out of here."

"And just leave him?"

"You stay and nursemaid him. I'm going to the library at Tulane."

"What's there?"

"Old yearbooks."

"Huh?" Tony said.

"Medical school. Remember what Chad told us about Angelica being a doctor. Find her graduation picture, and we'll learn her last name."

"Right," he said. "That last shot muddled my brain a bit."

"We'll get some coffee on the way. You coming?"

Damp air blowing in their faces revived Tony on their walk to the car. Handing Edna the keys, he reclined in the passenger seat, closing his eyes. They popped open when she slammed the door after returning from a quick detour to an all-night convenience store. He took the hot coffee she handed him without comment as rain misted the windshield.

"You okay?"

"Getting there," he said. "Where are we?"

"Almost to the parking lot. The rain has let up a bit. Maybe we can make it in without an umbrella."

"That last shot hit me like a ton of bricks."

"Surprises me. Always thought you macho detectives could hold your liquor."

"Not feeling very macho right about now. Romberg is gonna have a hell of a headache tomorrow. Hope he doesn't remember it was us that gave it to him."

"He'll be lucky if he remembers his name," she said.

The rain had slackened as she switched off the windshield wipers.

"What the hell do you think he was mumbling about?" Tony asked.

"Something about a secret medical project that has to do with Doctor Mary's murder. He wasn't making much sense."

"That's a fact." Tony began massaging his forehead. "You wouldn't have a couple of aspirins, would you?"

Edna handed him a tin from her pocket. "Just waiting for you to ask."

"I only worked with you on one case. I'd forgotten how intense you are."

"Try to keep up."

Humidity made it hard to breathe as they hurried to the front door of the library, refrigerated air blasting their faces when they entered. Summer session was in progress, only a few students studying or researching. Upstairs, they found the rows of yearbooks from the old university.

Torrential rains had abruptly returned, and Tony listened to it pounding the windows as Edna poured through yearbook after yearbook.

"Got her," she finally said.

"Let me see."

Edna pointed to a black and white of a young woman with dark hair.

"Last name's Moon," Edna said. "Graduated medical school in '62. Would have been a second-year resident at the time of Doctor Mary's murder."

"Strange last name. Wonder if she's from New Orleans."

"Call and see if there's a listing for her," Edna said.

She waited while he called information. "No listing," he said. "I'll call Tommy O'Rear."

"Who's that?"

Tony had his phone to his ear. "My old partner. He still works at the precinct and can run her name for us." After leaving a message, he said, "What now?"

"Start calling information to see if any of the doctors that graduated with Angelica still live here."

They divided the names, soon eliminating most of Angelica Moon's graduating class. Tony's phone rang as they worked.

"What you got?" Edna asked when Tony signed off.

"She's from N.O., all right. Daughter of a prominent Garden District doctor. No record of her after 1964."

"You mean she just dropped off the face of the earth?"

Tony's phone rang again before he could answer her question. She waited until he finished a rather long conversation.

"That was Mama Mulate. A friend of me and Wyatt. Called me because she's worried about him. She teaches here and knows most of the doctors at Tulane Medical Hospital. She invited us over to her house."

"You think she can help?"

Tony reached for his wallet. "Maybe. Something we need to do before heading to her house."

"Like what?"

He counted out five thousand dollars, pushing the bills across the table toward her.

"We're partners now. Here is your half of the retainer."

"I can't take this," she said.

"I ain't taking it back."

"Sure?"

She stashed the money in her pocket when he nodded. "Anybody looking?"

"No one on this floor except us. Why?"

"Cause we may need these," she said, ripping pages out of the yearbook.

Mama lived in an old blue-collar neighborhood not far from the river. Tony had recuperated enough to drive. Rain continued as they left the library.

"She has a Ph.D. in English lit and teaches at Tulane," he explained. "Something else about her I need to tell you."

"Oh?"

"She's a practicing voodoo mambo. It's her religion, and she takes it seriously. I wouldn't make fun if I was you."

"You're kidding, right?" Edna said.

"You're about to find out."

Chapter 13

Mama met them at the door and hugged Tony. She looked ready for bed in her tattered, terry-cloth robe. The handsome woman stood a couple of inches taller than Tony. She had dark eyes and hair, and skin the color of cafe au lait.

"Sorry to call you out on a night like this but I'm so worried about Wyatt, I had to talk to someone about it or explode."

"No problem. We were out anyway."

"Do you know what's going on?"

"We saw Wyatt this morning. He was all right. Meet Edna Callahan. She's a detective, and we're working a case with him."

She grabbed Edna's hand, shaking it in both of hers.

"Come in this house before we all get struck by lightning," she said.

Mama led them to the kitchen, the aroma of freshly brewed coffee wafting from a pot on the stove.

"Sit," she said. "I'll get coffee."

"Your gumbo smells awesome," he said.

"I'll get you a bowl."

They settled in at Mama's old chipped-enamel kitchen table. Before Edna could sip her coffee, a cat came running around the corner and jumped into her lap.

"I can tell by your body language you're not a cat person," Mama said, grabbing the cat and putting it on the floor.

"Never owned a pet," Edna said.

"Never?" Tony said.

"Not even as a little girl."

Mama's cat wound its way between Edna's legs, rubbing them.

"You never own a cat. It's the other way around," Mama Mulate said. "That's Bushy. He likes you."

Edna reached down and stroked him. "He's gorgeous. I never seen one quite like him."

"Tortoise-shell. I love his markings."

"Tony says you teach at Tulane."

"English lit, though sometimes I wonder if my students ever even listen to me."

"I have a hunch the girls do while all the boys are watching," Edna said.

Mama patted Edna's hand. Tony was eating, not talking. After licking the last succulent morsel of gumbo from his spoon, he sat back in the chair and sipped his coffee.

"The two of us worked together at the N.O.P.D. Wyatt set us on a case before he disappeared."

"With the news and all, I've been worried sick."

"He's in a heap of shit," Tony said. "Mind if I have some more gumbo?"

Mama grabbed his bowl and hurried to the stove. "I should have known one bowl of Mama's gumbo wouldn't be enough for you. Edna?"

"Just incredible, but no more for me," she said.

"We girls have to watch our figures," Mama said.

Before Edna could answer, Bushy jumped into her lap again. When Mama tried to grab him, Edna raised a palm.

"It's okay. I like this regal creature, and he's certainly not bothering me."

When nearby thunder shook the roof, the lights flickered and died, along with the air conditioning. Mama began lighting candles.

"Happens every time we have an electrical storm."

Mama's shadow played on the wall as she hurried around the room, returning to the table with a bottle of whiskey, three glasses and a bucket of ice.

"May as well relax and get comfy. Could be hours before the city restores power. A little alcohol makes the situation more tolerable," she said. "Now tell me about Wyatt."

"Bad trouble," Tony said. "He took a bullet in the shoulder."

"My God!" Mama said.

"Not fatal, but he's on the run."

"From who?"

Tony showed her the picture of the doubloon on his cell phone.

"Someone connected with the symbol on the back of the doubloon. I was hoping you'd know something about it," he said.

Lightning flashed outside the windows as Mama topped up her whiskey glass. Bushy curled closer to Edna.

"Did Tony tell you I'm a voodoo mambo?"

Edna nodded. "He did."

"I'm a mambo, but I practice the Vodoun religion and not voodoo."

"They aren't the same?" Edna asked.

"Related but not the same. Vodoun is an ancient West African religion. Voodoo and hoodoo are Vodoun's bastard children after illicit affairs with Catholicism, West Indian animism and who knows what else."

"I'm confused," Edna said.

"Vodoun came from West Africa, voodoo and hoodoo from Haiti, the West Indies, and right here in New Orleans. During the plague years when yellow fever, malaria, and cholera were killing thousands, many voodoo practitioners became very powerful."

"Because?" Tony said.

"They provided gris gris and amulets to protect the population from the epidemics. Some of these practitioners provided other things as well."

"Such as?"

"Spells, hexes, curses. The list goes on."

"You've never cast a spell on anyone, have you, Mama?" Tony asked.

"Many times," she said with a grin, "but never with evil intent."

Bushy had fallen asleep in Edna's lap. She scratched his ears as she listened to Mama amid the flickering candle light.

"But there are those that do?" she said.

"We're all ears," Tony said, catching Edna's drift.

"Voodoo practitioners are divided into Rado and Petro. White magic and black magic. The emblem on the back of the doubloon is the symbol of a particular group here in New Orleans."

"A voodoo group that practices black magic?" Edna asked.

Mama shook her head. "They practice neither white nor black magic. They are devil worshippers and the emblem a satanic symbol."

"What can you tell us about these devil worshippers?" Tony said.

"This cult is very secretive. I've heard they practice animal sacrifice, and use their powers for nefarious purposes."

111

"Does the cult have a name?" Edna asked.

"Forces of Darkness. They wield immense power stretching far beyond Louisiana's borders."

"Explain," Tony said.

"It's a power thing. Doctors, lawyers, judges, bankers, and politicians belong to the cult. What they gain from this unholy alliance is wealth, fame, influence, and power."

"How do you know so much about them?" Edna asked.

"I'm not a member if that's what you mean. I've heard things."

Tony's head had barely stopped hurting from the shot as he sipped his whiskey and listened to thunder rolling outside the house.

"What else do they do?" Edna asked.

"Bad things."

Tony's expression wasn't exactly one of disbelief, but close. "Then why hasn't someone put a stop to them?"

"Ain't gonna happen," Mama drawled. "Believe me, when I say these people are connected. Too many heads would have to roll if this group came to light."

Before Mama's words had died away, the lights flickered, and then came back on.

"Thank goodness for air conditioning," Mama said. "It was getting a bit stuffy in here."

Edna handed the pages she'd ripped from the Tulane yearbook to her.

"Tony said you know most of the medical staff at Tulane. Any of these faces look familiar?"

Mama nodded when she reached the last page. "Bruce Waters. He works at Tulane Medical Center."

"He must be in his seventies," Tony said.

"Doctors often work long past normal retirement age," Mama said. "Want me to call him?"

112

"Right now?" Edna asked.

"He has no family and works the all-night shift. He must like it because he has never worked anyplace else."

Mama punched a number on her cell phone. After a lengthy conversation to catch up on small talk and old times, she asked if he minded speaking to Edna. He didn't, and she handed her the phone.

Edna's conversation was brief, but she was smiling when she finished the call.

"Well," Tony said.

"You're not gonna believe what he just told me."

Chapter 14

A pattern of recurrent storms had stalled over New Orleans, damp clouds masking the sky when I awoke the following morning. A familiar voice was calling up to the loft where Lucy and I were lying on a mattress, beneath a sheet.

"You gonna sleep all day up there?"

It was then I realized it wasn't Bertram's deep drawl that had awakened me but the aroma of biscuits, eggs, and Cajun sausage wafting up the ladder.

"Who is that?" Lucy asked, pulling the sheet up around her neck.

"Just Bertram," I said.

"I heard that," Bertram said.

Lucy's eyes remained closed as she rubbed her forehead. "I'm so depressed. Sandy's dead, and it's my fault."

"No one's fault. You were both just doing your job."

"This wasn't supposed to happen."

I touched her shoulder, and she didn't draw away. "Things happen that aren't supposed to. Just karma. You can't blame yourself."

"You're a prick, you know, but sometimes you say the right things," she said.

"Try to forget about last night. There's nothing we can do about it now."

"Whatever he's cooking smells wonderful," Lucy said.

I slid off the frameless bed and pulled on my shorts and tee shirt. "Then let's get dressed and check it out."

Lucy was moving slowly, but at least she was moving. She even ventured a smile when Bertram greeted us.

"Well, look what the cat drug in," he said as we descended the ladder from the loft. And who is this pretty little gal you got with you?"

Too shell-shocked to let Bertram's sexist greeting offend her, Lucy just shrugged and shook her head.

"If you're Bertram, I want to thank you for the wonderful gumbo Wyatt, and I had last night."

"Yes ma'am," he said, ignoring her extended hand and giving her a big Cajun hug instead. "Can't cook good as my mama, but neither can nobody else."

When Lucy pulled away and sat at the kitchen table, Bertram poured her coffee from the pot on the burner.

"Your mama must be one fine cook."

"That she is, little lady. What's your name?"

"Lucy Diamond."

"No way," Bertram said, cocking his head to view her from a different angle. "Not the real Lucy Diamond?"

"No makeup and my hair is a mess," she said. "Sorry."

"Well, I'll be damn. The paper and news was right."

"About what?" I asked.

"That you two are on the lam together."

"What else did it say?"

115

"That you killed two people already, and are armed and dangerous."

"Up to two now? Who else did we kill?"

"Her boss. Last night near the West End."

"Sandy," Lucy said.

"Did the news also mention a car wreck involving several suspicious characters?"

"Nope," Bertram said.

"Why are we linked with the murder?" Lucy asked.

"They lifted Wyatt's fingerprints from the gun that killed him."

"I took the pistol from the killer, and used it to stop the car trying to run us down."

"Yours was the only prints they found, though you both left lots of them in his car you stole and escaped in," he said.

"Amazing," I said, joining Lucy at the table. "You don't believe that crap, do you?"

"Why hell no!" he said, pouring more coffee. "You won't even stomp a spider, much less kill someone."

"Thank you," I said. "And thanks for figuring out I'd come here."

"Cops are questioning everybody and keeping watch on your friend's goings and comings. Since you know where I keep the keys, I figured you'd wind up here sooner or later."

"Anyone follow you?"

"This old Cajun's dumb, but he ain't crazy. I drove halfway to Abbeville before turning around and taking side roads back here. Whatcha gonna do now?"

"Try to talk with Eddie. Seen him lately?"

"Tending bar for me while I'm gone."

"Who is Eddie?" Lucy asked.

"The Federal D.A. I told you about."

"Why is he bartending on the side?"

"He helps me out sometimes," Bertram said. "He has a few days of vacation and his main squeeze is out of town."

"Won't take long to rectify that little problem, if I know Eddie," I said.

Bertram nodded. "Got that right. That boy has a hard time keeping it in his pants."

"Eddie's a womanizer?" Lucy said.

Bertram and I both nodded.

"Next time you see him, ask him to find out what he can about Dr. Louis Hollingsworth and a secret cult called Forces of Darkness," I said.

"He's working the bar tonight. He was asking about you."

"He and everyone else in town," I said. "Guess this is my fifteen minutes of fame."

Bertram didn't bother commenting. Rolling thunder heralded the rain that had begun again, dimpling water outside the cabin and casting whitecaps against its stilt foundation. Bertram closed a window as the wind began spraying water across the floor. When he returned to the table, he removed a flask from his shirt pocket, lacing his coffee with Cuervo.

"You mind?" Lucy said, reaching for the flask.

"Give it hell, girl," Bertram said.

"Thanks," Lucy said. "Your cooking is fabulous but this coffee tastes like scorched shoe leather."

"Cajun coffee," he said. "That's how it's supposed to taste."

"Whatever!" Lucy said, lacing the dark brew. "Maybe I'll get drunk enough so as not to notice."

Bertram was glancing at our skimpy outfits. "You two won't go unnoticed five seconds dressed like that."

"It's all we could find," I said.

"Hell," Bertram said, pulling a footlocker down from a shelf. "I got clothes in here I don't remember wearing. Some I never wore."

117

Lucy grabbed a white blouse from the trunk and held it to the window for a better look.

"This is silk, and it's a designer label."

"Lilly Bliss," Bertram said. "She had expensive tastes. Maybe the reason she finally dumped me."

Lilly was one of Bertram's recent squeezes. A screenwriter who'd met him while working on a script in New Orleans. Their torrid affair had ended soon after the movie hit the can.

"Smart woman," I said.

Bertram was unfazed by my comment. "I'll be seeing her again," he said. "She's probably already missing me."

"Sounds like you're already missing her. Hope she doesn't want her clothes back," Lucy said, disappearing into the little bathroom with an armload.

She returned dressed in the silk blouse, knee-length black skirt, and red high heels. She'd taken her hair out of the ponytail and fluffed it with her fingertips.

"Nice legs!" Bertram said. "Now I know you're the real Lucy Diamond, the prettiest newscaster on prime time."

"Thanks, Bertram. The first compliment I've had in two days," she said, glaring at me.

"I said you are beautiful."

"Yeah, yeah! I was naked, and you were trying to get me to perform a random sex act on you."

Bertram glanced at Lucy, and then at me to see if she was joking. I simply grinned.

"Good thing I showed up when I did," he said.

Thunder shook the little cabin again. "You didn't get all these clothes from Lilly, did you?" I said, changing the subject.

"Exes," he said. "I've had a few."

"That's a fact. Too bad you don't have any men's clothes."

"Shut your mouth," he said, pulling down another footlocker from the shelf.

He opened it to reveal expensive shirts, pants, shoes, and accessories, many still in their original packaging.

"You've never worn a shirt like this in your life," I said, grabbing one still in the cellophane from the trunk.

"One thing all my exes tried to do," he said. "Change old Bertram."

"Maybe that's why they're all gone, and you're still wearing suspenders and checked shirts," I said.

Bertram nodded. "You ain't half as dumb as they say you are. Take what you want. I ain't ever gonna wear none of them. What now?"

"If you'll give us a ride to the Quarter, we need to see Madeline Romanov. Maybe you can return tomorrow and bring Eddie with you."

"I'll be here tomorrow but can't promise Eddie will be with me. He's going to the quarter horse races at the Fair Grounds when I relieve him. If I know the boy, and I do, he'll be pretty hung over by this time tomorrow."

"Probably right. Just do the best you can."

"I don't know what you're wearing to see Madeline, Cowboy, but if the little lady wears the outfit she has on, you'll be spotted pretty damn fast."

"What do you suggest?"

"Take a gander at what I got in here," he said, pulling yet another trunk from the shelf.

Chapter 15

Bertram dropped us off a few blocks from Madeline's shop on a deserted side street, Lucy and I clad in Mardi Gras costumes we'd found in the third trunk.

"In those outfits, you two will be all but invisible," Bertram said.

Lucy wasn't happy. "This is crazy. Everyone in the French Quarter will be looking at us."

"Bertram is right," I said. "Dressing in costume is normal for the Quarter. No one will think twice."

"There you go," Bertram said. "You two be careful."

We listened to the rattle of his old truck as he disappeared around the corner. Lucy wasn't in a good mood.

"Why do you get a cute pirate's costume and I have to wear this cat girl outfit? I feel half-naked."

Lucy's black leotard cat costume, complete with curling tail, was certainly sexy and highlighted her long legs.

"It's no more revealing than a bathing suit," I said. "Besides, you're wearing a mask and nobody knows who you are."

"Easy for you to say. You're not half-naked."

"Neither are you, so stop whining. No one's even looking at that gorgeous tail of yours."

"Shut up or I'm going to slap you."

I was laughing but backed away quickly when she raised her hand. The rain had stopped, at least for the moment, though clouds still covered the sky. We didn't need an umbrella for the first time in twenty-four hours. The sign on the antique door said Madeline's Magic Potions. The door was locked, and Lucy pounded on it, hoping to attract Madeline's attention.

"I think we missed her," I said.

"Why do you say that?"

I pointed at the black wreath on the front door. "Someone died, and she's at their funeral."

"Now what?"

I glanced down the sidewalk behind us.

"We aren't open," someone said from behind the door.

"Madeline, it's Wyatt Thomas. I need to talk to you."

The door opened a crack, and someone peered out. Remembering I was wearing a mask, I removed it so she could see my face. When she did, she opened the door and let us in.

"Wyatt," she said. "Everyone in town is looking for you. Are you okay?"

"People are chasing us, Madeline. Bad people. That's why we're in costume. I'd like you to meet Lucy Diamond."

Madeline shut the door behind us, locking it. She smiled when Lucy asked, "Why do you have the black wreath on your door?"

"Subterfuge, my dear. Sometimes I need a few hours to myself. The funeral wreath is the only way to achieve my needs."

"Sorry we're interrupting," I said.

"You aren't. I was preparing to remove it when I heard your knocks. Rafael has been worried sick."

"This is Rafael's mother," I said.

"I've heard so much about you," Lucy said.

Madeline smiled and patted Lucy's wrist. "Rafael told me you were beautiful. He didn't stretch the truth."

The rain had begun falling again dampening terra cotta pave stones in Madeline's courtyard. Fat drops dimpled the lily pads in her water garden as we followed her, beneath the overhang, to the open door of her little kitchen.

"Make yourself comfortable. I'll bring tea."

Lucy and I cozied together on a padded park bench situated beneath the second floor outside walkway.

"I've never been inside a French Quarter courtyard," Lucy said.

"Really?"

"It's enchanting. Like a hidden garden with all the ferns, flowers and tropical foliage."

Squawks and flapping of wings directed our attention to a big, black bird flying out of the rain to a roost beneath the overhang.

"Don't be frightened. It's just Calpurnia," Madeline said. "She comes and goes as she pleases and doesn't much like the rain."

"Is she a raven?"

"Yes, my dear." A black cat had followed Madeline out of the kitchen, winding between her legs. "And this is Jinx. He and Calpurnia dislike each other but somehow manage to coexist. Tea?"

"Yes, thank you," Lucy said.

"Now tell me what trouble you are into, and what I can do to help."

"It started at the wake of Jeribeth Briggs. A new client had requested I meet him there. He hired me to find the person who murdered his mother."

"Someone I know?"

"Very perceptive, Madeline. The murder victim was Dr. Mary Taggert."

"You saw Rafael at the wake. I assume it was he who told you I knew Mary and Jeribeth."

"He knew little about either except that you met with them occasionally for séances. He also said you never discuss business. Not even with him."

"Rafael is still a priest, and I am still a nun. We take our vows seriously."

"I respect that," I said. "Dr. Mary and Jeribeth Briggs are both deceased. Your input could help solve Dr. Mary's murder."

Calpurnia began flapping her wings again. "Hello, I'm Wyatt," she said.

Madeline grinned and started back for the kitchen. "She remembers you. She's also reminding me she hasn't eaten all day."

She returned with an ear of corn that she affixed to the spike on Calpurnia's perch. The large bird began plucking kernels from the cob.

"Now, what exactly do you need?" Madeline asked.

"Your take on Dr. Mary and Jeribeth Briggs," I said.

With a nod, Madeline said, "My silence would serve neither woman. Unfortunately, there is little I can tell you except why Rafael saw them occasionally."

"Which is?"

"Jeribeth had heard I perform séances. She wanted to contact her dead husband. She was so pleased with the results she continued to return every year or so for another conversation. She usually brought a friend along, and Dr. Mary was one of her friends."

"Did they always come alone?" Lucy asked.

"Dr. Mary had a companion. A much younger woman named Angelica. They never divulged her last name."

Madeline closed her eyes, cupping her hand as if shielding them from the sun. There was no sun; all the plants damp with rain.

"Were Mary and Angelica . . . ?"

"A couple? Yes. But there was also a man."

"You're losing me," I said. "Please explain."

"They would often arrive in a black chauffeur-driven limousine. A man usually dressed in a dark suit would wait on the street for them."

"Do you know who he was?" I asked.

A frog jumped into Madeline's koi pond from its perch on a lily pad, the splash disrupting her response.

"I never got a close look at him. He was older than both Angelica and Dr. Mary. He did seem strangely familiar."

"A relative, maybe," Lucy said.

Madeline shook her head. "I saw the three of them embrace and kiss. It wasn't platonic."

"And his name was never mentioned?" Lucy said.

"Never, and I didn't ask."

"Are you suggesting Dr. Mary was involved in a ménage à trois?" Lucy asked.

Madeline refilled her teacup from the old China teapot. Calpurnia squawked and ruffled her feathers as lightning crackled across the sky. When rain began again in a torrential deluge, Jinx jumped into Madeline's lap.

"This is the Big Easy. Anything is possible." Madeline must have noticed the concern on my face. "I don't know much more."

"You've raised more questions than we previously had. I'm stumped on where to go from here."

Madeline touched my hand. "Maybe it's something the crystal ball can tell us."

Lucy frowned at me as we left the rainy courtyard and followed Madeline through her shop. The room was dark, only flickering candles and refracted light through antique glass providing faint illumination. A Gregorian chant from a scratchy LP filled the room with guttural voices. Madeline stroked the head of a brass gargoyle before entering a room in the back.

Must and burning incense engulfed my senses as we followed her to a cluttered table. Everything, posters, crucifixes, brass figurines, projected the feel of age.

Lucy stared around the room. "I remember now that Rafael told me you are a witch. I thought he was talking figuratively," she said.

Madeline touched Lucy's hand. "I am a real witch, like my mother before me, and her mother before her. If Rafael ever has a daughter, she too will be a witch."

"What does being a witch involve?" Lucy asked.

"Great responsibility. I can view the past and foretell the future. It's a burden almost unbearable at times."

"Pardon me if I'm skeptical," Lucy said.

"Disbelief is another burden I bear," Madeline said. "You both have great pain. I can feel it. If I am to help you, you must suspend your disbelief."

"Then make something levitate," Lucy said with a smirk. "Maybe that would convince me."

"If I did, would you believe your own eyes?"

"Try me."

Madeline lit the massive candle in the center of the table. Red wax had dripped down its sides, congealing on the table's distressed wood.

"Look into the flame," Madeline said. "Not the surface, but into its burning heart. Fix your gaze. The candle will begin to move and then float up from the table. Be prepared."

The door to the room was ajar, Jinx opening it further when he padded toward us. Lucy didn't notice, her gaze locked on the flickering flame. Suddenly, her chin lifted, her unfocused eyes following a slow arc to the ceiling. She jumped and stretched her neck when the candle tipped over with a waxy thud.

Obviously confused, she glanced first at the candle and then at Madeline.

"You hypnotized me," she said.

The candle lay on its side, its flame sputtering in dripping wax.

"Did you not see it levitate?"

"I'm not sure what I saw."

Did you see me touch it?"

"You must have," Lucy said.

"There are spirits behind every shadow. All you see is the shadow. Your eyes are open, now open your mind."

Madeline grasped Lucy's hand.

"I . . .," Lucy stammered.

"Take a leap of faith," Madeline said. "I'll guide you."

The sound of monks chanting Dies Irae grew louder as Madeline retrieved an ornate case from the shelf behind her. From it, she removed a sphere that flashed in the light of the upended candle.

"This crystal is as old as time, cut from a seam of quartz in a Romanian coal mine. Light refracts from fractures and veils. At least that's what some say. The real reason is that the rock is alive, and a fount of knowledge only a few can even begin to understand. Mother and Grandmother had the gift. They did not possess the crystal; it possessed them. Now it possesses me. Do I have your trust?"

"I'm trying," Lucy said.

"You have something I need," Madeline said, looking at me.

She nodded when I handed her the Mardi Gras doubloon and said, "This?"

Madeline righted the candle its sputtering flame melding with fire bleeding from the crystal. Her eyes closed as she clasped the doubloon. Thunder rattled the windows as a low moan began issuing from her pursed lips. I shook my head when Lucy cast me a worried glance.

Madeline didn't notice, her own eyes opened wide, staring at the ceiling, drool suspended from her parted lips. The room went deadly quiet, no thunder shaking the windows or monks chanting from the other room. There was only the rasp of a voice trying to escape. Madeline's mouth had opened wide as her head tilted backward, and her lifeless eyes stared at nothing.

> A devil lives on winding road
> in a house beside the river
> round Satan's Bend bad water flows
> waiting for his dead to deliver

Lucy's eyes were as wide as Madeline's as the last word droned from the seer's mouth. I filled their water glasses, then lifted Madeline's head and held the goblet to her lips. It revived her, but not quickly. After several slow sips, she shook her head as if trying to clear the cobwebs.

"Thank you," she said when she saw me smiling.

"Please," Lucy said. "You must interpret your message for us."

127

"Sorry," Madeline said, rubbing her brow as she slowly rotated her head. "It wasn't I that spoke."

"You quoted a poem. You don't remember?"

"The Oracle often speaks in verse, her answers always a riddle for the listener to solve. Or not," she added.

Lucy cast me another anxious glance.

"Are you okay, Madeline?" I asked.

"This migraine will stay with me the remainder of the day, and much of the night."

I stowed the crystal ball in its case and returned it to the shelf. After pouring her more water, I left five twenties on the table and motioned Lucy it was time to go. Madeline stopped us before we got out the door

"Wait," she said. "There's more."

The rain had ceased as we followed her back to the table in her courtyard. This time, she offered us no tea.

"I'm confused," Lucy said.

Madeline closed her eyes and rotated her head around her neck. "What I said about the verse is correct. I don't remember it nor do I know its meaning."

"What, then?"

"Sometimes when I'm deep in trance, I have visions that I remember. I had one just now, and it disturbs me greatly."

"Can I get you some tea?" I asked.

"Let me," Lucy said.

Madeline's head was still hanging when Lucy returned to the garden table with a pot of freshly brewed tea.

"Thank you," she said after sipping the hot liquid.

"Are you sure you're up to telling us about your vision?" I asked.

Madeline placed the cup on the table and began massaging her forehead.

"I'll lie down for a bit and take a nap. What I have to tell you may be crucial."

"We're listening," I said.

"I call my visions spirit walks because I'm like a ghost visiting a place that exists only in my mind. All the experiences are eerily coincidental."

"How so?"

"I float through the scenes engulfed by a mist that no one else seems to notice. The people I see move in slow motion and are unaware of my presence."

"Like a ghost?" Lucy said.

"Yes, and the sensation is ominously frightful."

Lucy squeezed her hand. "You aren't dead. You are very much alive."

Madeline nodded. "The spirit walk from which I just returned frightened me."

"I can tell," Lucy said. "You're trembling like a leaf."

When thunder rumbled in the distance, Calpurnia ruffled her feathers and Jinx jumped into Madeline's lap.

"I was in the front yard of a Garden District mansion. A streetcar rumbled behind me so it must have been closc to St. Charles Avenue. A man and a little girl were playing with a ball."

When Madeline grew silent, Lucy held the cup of tea to her lips. Nodding her thanks, she began again.

"The man was old, his hair snowy white. He was a white man, and I say this because the little girl was probably Creole. She called the man Grandpa. He smiled as he knelt before her and pinned a gold pendant to the neck of her blouse. The inscription said Rex, 1948."

Madeline winced and made a face as if recalling something particularly repulsive. Lucy squeezed her hand again. Jinx also seemed to sense her distress, rubbing his head against her breast.

"Can I get you anything?" Lucy asked.

Madeline shook her head and continued.

"The sky was cloudy and gray as bird noises, and beating of wings caused us to look upward. It was a flock of white doves. As we watched, a dark falcon shot from the sky, ripping through the doves. It descended in front of us with a dead dove in its talons.

"The little girl broke away from her grandfather and ran toward the bird. The falcon waited for her, unafraid when she approached it. She bent down to touch the dove as the grandfather hurried toward her. He recoiled when she turned to face him."

"It's okay, Madeline," Lucy said. "We're here."

Madeline stroked her cat with a trembling hand. "The little girl turned around when her grandfather touched her shoulder. She was smiling, her face and mouth bloody from contact with the dove."

Nearby thunder rocked the windows behind us as the rain began falling in bucket loads. Madeline's story concluded, Jinx jumped to the ground. Lucy gave her a consoling hug and then refreshed her tea.

"Thanks for drawing the courage to tell us," Lucy said.

"One more thing," Madeline said. "I have an address on Carondelet I need to tell you about."

Chapter 16

"We can't go out there," Lucy said as I pulled her to the door. "We'll drown."

"Bertram's waiting for us. We won't melt."

Bertram's old pickup was parked against the sidewalk and barely visible. When he saw us standing in the doorway, he drove up on the sidewalk and held the door for us to jump in. The maneuver took less than ten seconds but left Lucy and me drenched. Bertram threw us a towel.

"Thought you might need one of these," he said. "Learn anything."

Lucy and I began speaking at the same time. She said "no," and I said "yes."

Bertram scratched the stubble on his chin. "Well, which one is it?"

"Ask him," Lucy said. "I need a drink."

Bertram passed her his bottle of Cuervo. "Never go anyplace without my vitamins," he said.

Lucy tippled straight from the bottle and said, "Thanks, I needed that."

Bertram stared at me as I took the Cuervo from Lucy and took a hearty swig.

"You okay, Cowboy?" he asked.

"My shoulder's throbbing like a bass drum and I took the last of Senora's pills a while ago."

"Must be," he said. "That was a mighty healthy slug of my tequila you just drank. You falling off the wagon?"

"Drugs aren't addictive when you need them, and I may need more."

I took another swig before handing Lucy the bottle. She wiped her mouth with the back of her hand and belched after drinking another slug.

"Excuse you," I said.

Lucy ignored my comment. "What now?" she asked.

"Maybe we better stop by Madam Aja's. I'm having trouble thinking, and Bertram's Cuervo isn't doing the trick."

When Bertram pulled in front of Madam Aja's cottage in Faubourg Marigny, Lucy jumped out and ran through the driving rain to the porch. Bertram parked in front, and we waited until she came running out, the black cat's tail of her costume whipping behind her. She thanked Bertram when he tossed her a towel.

"Madam Aja wanted us to come inside, but I told her it was too dangerous. Here are your pills."

I quickly swallowed one, washing it down with another healthy slug of Bertram's Cuervo.

"Sure you ain't reverting to your old ways?" he asked.

"If you need pain medication, it won't addict you," I said. "My arm hurts like hell, and I wouldn't be functioning right now without your tequila. Besides, I hate tequila."

Senora's pain medication soon began washing over me in a gentle wave, relieving my persistent shoulder pain that had felt like someone was stabbing me with a knife.

Rain continued pouring so hard, Bertram's old wipers couldn't work fast enough to remove water from the windshield. He managed to pull over at a little walking park.

132

"Well?" Lucy finally asked.

"Think I'm going to make it," I said.

"I have to tell you," she said. "I made absolutely nothing out of Madeline's gibberish. We're no closer to an answer than we were last night."

"Wrong," I said.

"Then maybe you should enlighten me."

"The riddle."

"What about it?" she said.

"I think I've solved it. Head up River Road when the rain slacks, Bertram."

My shoulder was comfortably numb when the rain eased enough for Bertram to leave the parking lot. River Road follows the path of the Mississippi River. Many of the plantations not destroyed during the Civil War remain as restored remnants of a bygone era. We hadn't gone far before Lucy quizzed me again about the riddle.

"Okay, I'll bite. What does it mean?"

"I grew up in an old plantation house on River Road. The question jogged my memory about something I'd heard when I was a boy. I can't quite put my finger on it."

"This riddle," Bertram said. "What the hell you talking about?"

"Madeline summoned a spirit with her crystal ball. It quoted a riddle in the form of verse."

"Uh huh," Bertram said. "And what did this spirit say?"

"Some gibberish about the devil, the river and a place called Satan's Bend," Lucy said.

"What the hell's that supposed to mean?"

"Something hidden deep in my memory bank. Like I said, I can't quite put my finger on it. I sense the riddle explains something about Dr. Mary's murder. We can turn around if you think this is a wild goose chase."

"Mind if I have another pop of your Cuervo?" Lucy asked.

Bertram didn't look happy about doing it but handed her the bottle.

"It's getting short, but why the hell not?" he said. "You?"

"No thanks," I said. "Senora's painkillers are starting to work."

For an hour or more, the pain in my shoulder had encompassed my every thought. All was forgotten as Senora's drug numbed the pain. I fell asleep, finally opening my eyes to Lucy's prods.

"You were talking gibberish. When you started shouting, I decided to wake you."

"How long was I asleep?"

"Long enough that we need directions," Bertram said.

My eyes were still cloudy as I glanced around, looking for a landmark. Torrential rains had ceased, though slow drops of water continued to speckle the scenic blacktop road. The old engine of Bertram's truck sounded throaty as he slowed, waiting for me to give him directions.

"Can't quite remember," I said.

"Maybe this is a wild goose chase," he said.

"Hope not."

"You said some things while you were asleep," Lucy said.

"Like what?"

"Crazy things. I need more tequila to even talk about it," she said.

Bertram didn't look happy but handed her the bottle. "It's almost empty," he said. "Want the last swig?"

"No thanks," I said. "Senora's pain killers are working just fine."

"Good, cause Lucy here drinks as much as I do, and I don't have another bottle in the truck.

Maybe we oughta think about turning around," he said.

"A few more miles can't hurt anything," Lucy said.

Bertram was no longer smiling. "Fine, but we're out of Cuervo."

"You didn't tell me what I said that sounded crazy."

Lucy glanced at Bertram. "You were ranting about murder and tortured slaves. Remember?"

I had no memory of my dream. "You can turn around if you like. I'm lost."

"Not so fast," Bertram said. "Looks like a roadside bar up ahead and I need a drink."

Bertram's bar looked more like a shack thrown together with scrap lumber and galvanized tin, and decorated with faded Coca-Cola and other colorful signs. Gravel and shell crunched beneath the tires as he pulled into the parking lot.

"You can't be serious," Lucy said. "This place looks dangerous."

Bertram's big Cajun grin had returned. "No worries, little lady. If you ain't got a knife, they'll issue you one at the door."

"Not funny," she said.

"Come on," Bertram said. "Your boyfriend and me'll take care of you."

"He's not my boyfriend," she said, following us out of the truck.

Only one other vehicle a beat up pickup older than Bertram's was in the parking lot. It had started to drizzle again, so Lucy hurriedly entered the dark bar, the ingrained odor of stale smoke and spilled beer accosting her as she did. The only customer was throwing money on the bar and rising to leave. Bertram took his place atop the barstool.

"Need some service," he said, slapping his palm on wood stained by years of spilled drinks.

A wiry little man in an armless tee shirt was facing away from the bar as he polished glasses. Faded tattoos on his arms and bare shoulders pegged him as a former Marine, though he didn't look very menacing. He had no hair on top of his head, only Clarabell tufts of red around his neck and ears.

"Don't usually serve coonasses," he said without turning around.

"Then you don't sell much whiskey, do you?"

The skinny little man polishing a glass with a bar rag turned with a grin. "Hell, I make even more. I charge them double."

Bertram whipped out his wallet and tossed it on the bar. "Then take what you need, cause me and my friends here are powerful thirsty."

"Put it back in your pocket," the bartender said, sliding it back to Bertram. "I'm Red. First one's on me. Whatcha drinking?"

"Glad to meet you, Red. I'm Bertram, and I'll have a Dixie and a shot of Cuervo.

Lucy and I had joined Bertram at the bar. "I'm Lucy. I don't suppose you serve martinis."

"Baby, I was the bartender at an officer's club in Korea for nine years. Believe me when I tell you I mix the best martini on this side of the old Mississippi. Hey, and I like your tail."

"Wonderful. Make me one and don't call me baby."

"You got it, baby. You, bro?"

"Whatever you got that's not alcoholic," I said.

"You one of them teetotalers?"

"Ex-drunk," I said.

"Gotcha, bro," he said. "Drinks coming right up."

Bertram and Lucy were soon happily nursing their drinks. I was also happy as Red brought me an icy glass of pink lemonade. Good thing, as the lone ceiling fan in the old dive was barely enough to ease the heat and humidity.

"You two going to a costume party?" he asked.

"We're hiding from the cops, and this is our cover outfits," Lucy said.

"Fine by me," Red said. "Not many cops out this way."

"I Like your place, Red," Bertram said. "I got my bar up in the city."

"Shoulda known," Red said with a snicker. "Your martini okay, baby?"

"Best I've ever tasted, but I'm going to dump it on your head if you don't stop calling me baby."

Red grinned. "What brings you folks to my neck of the woods?"

"Wild goose chase. My friend Wyatt thought he remembered something out this way. Seems he's losing it."

"Like what?" Red asked.

"An old plantation home, not easy to see from the road. When I was a boy, we thought it was haunted. Any ideas?"

"No, but there's someone in back that will. Trey, can you come out here a minute?"

A young black man dressed in a blue work shirt and starched jeans appeared from a door in the back. Red introduced us, and Trey flashed a movie star smile as he shook our hands. Lucy was instantly smitten and suddenly conscious of the cat costume she still wore, and the long black tail extended over the barstool.

"Do I know you?" he asked, ignoring her skimpy costume.

"Don't think so," she said. "I have an ordinary face."

Trey smiled. "Anything but. I'll figure it out."

"These folks are looking for an old plantation home. Trey here was a tour guide at the Myrtles while he was going to Tulane. Ain't much he don't know about that era. Just ask him."

"I'm impressed," Lucy said.

I suddenly felt foolish dressed in the pirate's outfit and placed my hat on the bar.

"I grew up nearby. There was a plantation home my friends and I thought was haunted."

"Dessalines Plantation," he said. "Not far from here."

"Never heard of it," Lucy said.

"Because it's not open to the public. It's haunted I assure you."

Trey topped up Lucy's martini from the chilled shaker on the bar, then poured himself a shot of whiskey. Red popped the top on three beers, handing one to Bertram, one to Trey and keeping one. He also poured a shot of whiskey for himself.

"Trey's been working here off and on since he was tall enough to see over the bar. He's my son," he said.

"Stepson," Trey said when Lucy looked confused.

"Tell him the riddle," Bertram said.

It was Trey's turn for confusion. "Riddle?"

"Lucy and I consulted a seer this morning. She had a vision and told us a riddle. It jogged something in my memory, and it's what caused us to drive down River Road."

Red refilled my glass with lemonade, and then leaned on the bar.

"Let's hear it," he said.

"A devil lives on winding road
in a house beside the river,
round Satan's Bend bad water flows
waiting for his dead to deliver."

"Why hell!" Red said. "We didn't need Trey for that. You didn't see the name of the bar on the roof?"

He nodded when I said, "Satan's Bend?"

"This old bar sits right in the crook of Satan's Bend," he said.

"He glanced at Trey when Bertram asked, "What's the damn riddle mean?"

"The rich alluvium deposited for centuries by the river makes the land adjacent to it perfect for agriculture," he said. "Sugar and cotton farms began popping up, their crops making the owners wealthy beyond their imaginations. Slavery provided the bodies to work the fields. Massive plantation homes were built and furnished with shipments from France, Italy and Spain. Before long, no expense was too great. They mostly treated the slaves with benevolence."

"You say that with a tone of cynicism," Lucy said.

"For good reason," he said. "They were chattel, like prized horses or cattle. Plantation owners bred them like animals and families were routinely torn apart if the price was right. It always was."

"Most owners took good care of their slaves. Not out of brotherly love but because they were valuable. It was the only way they could maintain their wealth and position," I said.

"Most owners," Trey said. "Some treated their slaves horribly, torturing and mutilating them. The owners of the Dessalines Plantation fell into that category."

Trey grew silent and poured himself another shot of whiskey, sighing deeply after taking a sip. Lucy reached across the bar and patted his hand.

"We are sorry," she said.

"No need to apologize for something you didn't do. The story affects me every time I tell it."

"What's the deal about Satan's Bend?" Bertram asked.

"It's okay," Trey said when Lucy gave Bertram her best frown. "Satan's Bend is where the river takes a healthy jog. Currents become lots stronger after rounding the bend. It's where the Dessalines discarded the bodies of dead slaves. The current would pull them under the water, and they wouldn't surface until they reached the Gulf of Mexico."

"So the bend is haunted by spirits of dead slaves?" I said.

"So they say. Dessalines Plantation is where the real evil occurred. If ghosts and spirits indeed exist, it is surely the place you'll find them."

"I remember the house," I said. "It's away from the river, masked by giant oaks. It was foreboding during the day and downright scary at night. We kids thought that spirits haunted it."

"The evil continues. The present owner descended from the people that built and ran it. They often have ceremonies there."

"Tell us about them," Lucy said.

"They supposedly perform satanic rituals. I've heard they practice human sacrifice, among other things."

Lucy sipped her martini. "Oh my," she said.

"You wouldn't happen to know the present owner's name, would you?" I asked.

Trey nodded. "Guy Marc Gagnon."

Chapter 17

After Bertram had dropped us off, deserted streets prevailed. Rain covered Chartres in a mild deluge. We huddled against the door of an antique shop, water spraying up from the curb. Lucy wasn't happy.

"What now?" she asked.

"Find a cab and check the address Madeline gave us."

"Trey sounded convincing, though I'm still not sure Madeline wasn't faking the séance."

"If she was faking her fright, then she's one hell of an actress. And what about the riddle? How did she know about Satan's Bend and the Dessalines Plantation?"

Lightning lit the sky as Lucy crossed her arms. "Sorry, but I have a hard time believing in ghosts and spirits," she said.

"It's obvious to me she saw something on her spirit walk that scared the crap out of her."

"You sound as if you believe her."

"I've lived here all my life. Trust me when I tell you this old city is alive with spirits."

"Maybe so. That cutie Trey seemed way too sincere to be a liar. Still, I've never seen a ghost or no anyone that has."

"You think they'd tell you?"

Thunder rattled the window behind us before she could reply. When I spotted a cab tooling down the street, I braved the rain to flag him down. The old vehicle wheeled to a stop, splashing water on my pants. Mingo's Cab Service was hand painted on the door.

"Get in," he said. "And hurry before we drown."

Lucy came rushing from the sidewalk, and we piled into the backseat of the cab, an 80's vintage Ford that had seen better days.

"Thanks for stopping," I said.

The Hispanic cabbie flashed us a grin. "Kind of early for a costume party," he said.

He nodded and gave us a thumbs up when I said, "Never too early for a party in the Big Easy."

"Got that right. Where to?"

"Somewhere on Carondelet Street."

"Big street, amigo. Know the address?"

"Not exactly," I said.

"What's the name of the business?"

"Don't know that either. Only that it has something to do with a flock of doves."

"Hell, amigo, why didn't you say so?"

"You know where it is?"

"Me and everyone else in the CBD. Now I know why you two dressed as you did."

"Oh yeah?"

"Hell yeah! There's a ceremony getting ready to start."

The young man had a swath of white in his otherwise dark hair. His Saints tee shirt and black tennis shoes didn't quite go with his freshly pressed khakis. He also had a gold earring and sported a shiny Rolex on his wrist.

"Guess we grabbed the right cab."

He gave me another thumbs up. "Mingo knows where all the bones are buried. I'm Domingo, but my friends call me Mingo. And you are?"

"Lucy and Wyatt," I said.

Lucy glared at me and banged an elbow into my ribs. "We're from out of town," she said.

"You, maybe," he said. "Mister Wyatt sounds like a local to me."

"You're good, Mingo," I said.

Mingo saw me looking. Without turning around, he grinned and saluted the rearview mirror.

"Thanks, Mr. Wyatt. I always try harder."

CBD was what the locals called the Central Business District. The rain had abated as Mingo took us into the heart of the area. Storefront cafes occupied old stone buildings beside law offices, Scottish Rite Temples, and other nondescript businesses. Construction was going on everywhere, chain link fencing and makeshift scaffolds jutting far into the street, all to the backdrop of forklifts, cranes, plywood, and porta-potties.

"Lot of work going on," I said.

"Torn to hell ever since Katrina. Worked on some of the buildings myself."

"You from N.O.?" I asked.

"Mexico, but I been here a while."

Katrina and plentiful FEMA money had brought a throng of people to Louisiana to help in the cleanup. Many had never left. From the faint odor of mold in the backseat of the taxi, I wondered if Mingo had rescued it from the hurricane. He pulled up to the sidewalk before I had a chance to ask.

We're here," he said.

"Where is it?"

"That building," he said, pointing.

"Sure about that?" Lucy asked.

"I'm very sure, pretty señorita. If you aren't, then maybe you better stay in the cab with me."

"Kiss my ass," she said.

143

He was still grinning as he tooled away down the street.

"Are you just trying to get us caught?" Lucy asked.

"What are you talking about?"

"You didn't have to tell him our names. He could be working with the Cubans."

"He's Mexican, not Cuban. I sensed he meant us no harm."

Lucy didn't seem convinced. "What makes you say that?"

"His positive vibes. I had the feeling he knows something about this place he wanted to tell us."

"Then why didn't you just ask him?"

"Because that's not the way you get the answers you want in New Orleans."

Lucy let my remark pass. "He did make the place sound a bit ominous. But why?" she said.

"We're about to find out."

The two-story building was yellow contrasting with the one beside it that was white, and the orange one beside it. Army-green shutters shrouded the two front windows. Filigree ironwork adorned the second-story balcony. A locked iron gate protected the only entrance. As Lucy stood with her arms clasped, I rang the antique doorbell. The woman that appeared did a double take when she saw our costumes.

"I'm Jubah. Are you here for the ceremony?"

"Yes," I said.

Jubah was dressed in a floor-length white dress and matching tignon—a turban-like hat slaves and free women of color were required to wear before the Civil War. Despite her name and antebellum costume, I could see she was a descendant of neither slave nor Creole. Her light skin, blond hair, and blue eyes belied that particular heritage.

"We take donations, but not credit cards," she said, holding her hand through the gate.

I gave her five twenties. "That enough?"

"Most generous," she said as she opened the gate, and motioned us to follow her. "The ceremony hasn't started yet because of the rain," she said.

Lucy responded with one of her patented wise-ass comments. "December, maybe?"

"Today, I assure you," Jubah said.

Unmindful of Lucy's remark, she led us down a dark corridor that opened into a large courtyard. The rain had ceased, at least for the moment. Like Madeline's courtyard, this one was charming and damp. Six women, all white and all dressed like Jubah, were gathered against a wall.

A small bleacher complete with canvas roof for protection against impending rain sat against the opposite wall. Several observers, probably all tourists braving the stormy weather, occupied the bleacher. Jubah motioned for us to take a seat and then joined us.

"We are the Order of the White Doves. What you are about to witness is a lave tet. In French, this means a cleansing of the head. While this is not an initiation into our order, it is a requirement."

Boots, jeans, western shirts and cowboy hats adorned the couple behind us. The man looked old enough to be his companion's father.

"We're Dennis and Jill from Omaha," he said. "Mind if we ask questions during the ceremony?"

"Only in undertones, please. Do you mind telling me how you heard about us?"

"From someone at a bar, we visited last night. You remember which one, Jill baby?" he asked.

"Don't remember much of anything about last night, big daddy," she said with a grin.

Dennis and Jill grew quiet when someone began drumming a rhythmic cadence. The women standing opposite us swayed to the beat of the drum as two more similarly dressed women appeared from the corridor. Their arms encircled another young woman. Unlike the Doves, her dress was brown, old and frazzled, and she wore no tignon. They escorted her to the center of the courtyard and assisted her as she lay prone on her back.

Though the damp flagstone looked less than comfortable, the young woman didn't seem to mind as the other women supported her head in their hands.

"The acolyte is about to receive the lave tet," Jubah said.

Three Doves approached the woman, kneeling around her in a semi-circle. They began bathing her forehead with sponges dipped in a ceremonial ceramic pan.

Jubah turned to face the small group witnessing the ceremony.

"We believe everything from wisdom to emotion begins with the head," she said. "Every person is different. The bath water is a mixture of herbs, flower petals, and perfume that uniquely matches the personality of each receiving the lave tet."

She smiled when Big Daddy Dennis asked, "Is this a voodoo ceremony?"

"New Orleans voodoo is a mixture of hoodoo conjured up by the local Indian tribes and Caribbean voodoo. Our order is much more than that; a blend of elements from many beliefs and religions."

"How so?" I asked.

"A full description would take me too much time to explain," she said.

"I love the costumes," a woman behind us said.

"They aren't costumes," Jubah said. "It is what we wear every day."

When the cadence of the drums changed, another woman appeared from the corridor.

"Please be reverent," Jubah said. "It is Madam Moon."

The woman appearing for the first time was striking; neither white nor black, but more the color of strong Creole coffee liberally laced with fresh milk. Her black silk dress looked Chinese. The most striking thing about her costume was the gold pendant on the neck of the dress. The man beside me had a pair of opera glasses.

"Mind if I borrow your binoculars a moment?"

He handed them to me with a nod, and I had a start when I focused on the gold pendant on her blouse. It said Rex, 1948. I had to remove my gaze from the object to hand the opera glasses to Lucy. When I looked at her, I could see she was having the same problem.

"Thanks," I said, returning the opera glasses to the man seated beside me.

Madam Moon was strikingly beautiful, with expressive eyes and delicate features. Taking a position behind the acolyte's head, she chanted as she bathed her forehead. The Doves closed their eyes, raised their arms and began singing an African melody. A distant clap of thunder didn't disturb the ceremony.

"What's the story on the pendant?" I asked.

"A priceless gift from Madam Moon's grandfather," Jubah said.

"You mean the King of Rex?"

Jubah nodded. "Yes," she said.

I drew a deep breath trying not to look astonished when something unexplainable interrupted the ceremony. Madam Moon rose to her feet, a solemn expression of anger on her face. As rain began to drizzle, she stalked through the confused Doves, stopping in front of the bleachers.

For a long moment, she stared directly at the black mask covering my eyes.

"Someone is here that should not be. You," she said.

When I glanced around, I could see everyone was looking at me, waiting for an explanation.

"You must have me mistaken for someone else," I said.

"I know who you are. Call for assistance, Jubah. These two must not leave."

Madam Moon and the Doves jumped when lightning flashed across the sky, followed by an ear-splitting clap of thunder, and then a heavy downpour.

Seeing the ceremony was at an end, everyone opened their umbrellas and hurried to their cars through the gate opening on Carondelet. I grabbed Lucy's hand, and we followed them.

"Stop!" Madam Moon shouted through the din.

Lucy skidded to a halt, wheeled around and shot her the finger.

"You two are walking dead," Madam Moon shouted as Lucy and I raced through the gate.

We ran down the sidewalk, drenched from the downpour when a familiar car slid to a stop beside us. It was Mingo. I opened the back door, pushed Lucy in ahead of me and then joined her.

Mingo barely heard the door slam before floor boarding the old heap and then fishtailing down the wet street at a dangerous clip. He made several evasive detours before slowing the car.

"Been driving around the block," he said. "Thought you might need me."

Chapter 18

Tony glanced at his watch when they left Mama's, realizing he wasn't going to make it home anytime soon. Mama, trying to get comfortable in the cramped rear seat, had insisted on going with them. She and Edna listened as he called his wife Lil to explain. He was frowning when he put the phone back in his pocket.

"Trouble in paradise?" Edna asked.

"More like the dog house when I get home."

"Want us to drop you off? Mama and I can interview Dr. Waters. We'll fill you in tomorrow."

"Don't think so."

"Why not?"

"My car, remember?"

"Just offering," she said.

Mama gave his shoulder a comforting pat. "Take Lil some roses."

"I've been keeping a flower shop in business, lately, so it might not work this time."

Edna gave Mama a glance, frowned and shook her head, both deciding to drop the subject. For the first time in hours, the car's wipers weren't moving. Gone was the rain. Only ground fog remained, wafting across the street in supple waves. Tony slowed, hoping not to crash into a stalled car, or someone walking on the sidewalk.

The New Orleans hospital district spans many city blocks, encompassing doctor's offices, medical buildings, and several hospitals. That included Charity the massive old monstrosity still abandoned a decade after Hurricane Katrina. They found the doctor in a Tulane Medical Center break room.

Coins rattled as a nurse bought candy from one of the vending machines. She didn't glance at them as she hurried out of the dimly-lit room, the candy bar in her mouth already half-eaten. Except for a single slump-shouldered man sitting with his back to the door, the place was empty. Mama recoiled when she touched his bony arm.

"Bruce, is that you?"

She gasped when he turned to face her and said, "How you been, Mama?"

Sallow skin was wrapped tightly around his sunken cheeks and bald skull. His blue eyes were bloodshot. Mama grabbed his shoulders, rocking him like a baby.

"Oh my God, Bruce! What's happened to you?"

"Bad case of leukemia's got me by the throat," he said with a grin.

"Why didn't you call me?"

"Didn't want to worry you."

"You've lost so much weight."

"Nothing like the cancer diet to slim you down," he said.

"Not funny," Mama said, staring into his eyes that were still very much alive. "How long have you been like this?"

Dr. Waters answered with a drug-induced catch in his throat.

"About a year," he said in his cornpone, North Louisiana drawl. "Went into remission for a while, and then relapsed."

150

"Why are you still working?"

"Don't golf. Got no hobbies, and I never was much for daytime T.V."

"You could travel; see the world," she said.

"Too puny for that. Damn sure don't want to die in Timbuktu on the side of the road."

Mama hugged him again. "Same old Bruce. You'll never change, will you?"

"Good to see you, Mama. Who you brung with you?"

"Edna Callahan and Tony Nicosia. They have questions about Dr. Mary Taggert."

"You the police?"

"Private investigators," Tony said.

"Kind of a day late and a dollar short, I'd say."

"Hope not," Tony said.

When he shook Doc Bruce's hand a bit too hard, he realized the man's arms were little more than skin and bones.

"Edna says you may know something about the case."

"That I do."

"Something we haven't already heard?" Tony said.

"You ain't never heard what I'm going to tell you."

"Then why haven't you come forward before now?" Edna asked.

"Well, ma'am, guess I didn't want to wind up with a bullet between my eyes. Right now, it don't matter so much."

Edna pulled up a chair at the table. "That's why we're here. Tell us what you got."

Mama joined them as Tony browsed the flickering candy machines.

"Didn't you get enough gumbo?" Mama asked.

"Long night," he said. "I could use another cup of coffee."

151

"Two doors down," Doc Bruce said, pointing. "I'll take a cup if you don't mind."

Tony returned with coffee, sugar and creamer packets that nobody used.

Doc Bruce grinned when Mama took a sip and made a face.

"You get used to it after a few years."

"Hope I never find out," she said.

"Don't mean to rush you, but please tell us what you know," Edna said.

"I was there the night Mary died," he said, his drawl suddenly disappearing.

"At her apartment?" Tony said.

Doc Bruce glanced at Mama and winked. "You think she died in her apartment?"

"You tell us. That's what we're here for."

The vent above them began to rattle when the air conditioning kicked on. Clasping his arms tightly to his chest, Doc Bruce began to shiver. He smiled when he noticed Mama's worried look.

"Sorry about that. Don't take much to get a chill when you got no meat on the old bones."

Tony went into the hall, returning with a hospital blanket.

"Someone left a linen closet open. Bet they'll never miss this one."

When Mama wrapped it around Doc Bruce's shoulders, he nodded as color began returning to his face.

"You familiar with the U.S. Public Health Service?"

Tony and Edna shook their heads. "What about it?" Mama said.

"Mary's murder has U.S.P.H.S. fingerprints all over it."

"Maybe you better explain," Edna said.

"The U.S.P.H.S. is possibly the most powerful agency in the government. Center for Disease Control, Food and Drug Administration, National

Institute of Health, Substance Abuse and Mental Health Services, etcetera, etcetera, all report to the presiding officer of the U.S. Public Health Service."

"And?"

"You'd be correct in saying he wields as much power as anyone in the F.B.I. and the C.I.A. Hell! Maybe even more than the President."

"Who is this person?" Mama asked.

"ASH."

"His name is ASH?" Edna said.

"His title. An acronym for Assistant Secretary of Health. The first ASH wasn't yet appointed when Mary's murder occurred. Don't matter because Guy Marc Gagnon was the titular head of the U.S.P.H.S. and became the ASH when they created the title. Though he's retired from the agency, he still dresses in uniform."

"He wears a uniform?" Tony said, downing the rest of his coffee.

"The military isn't the only government group that wears uniforms. Members of the U.S.P.H.S. are recruited, just like soldiers. They all have specific skills and dress in uniforms similar to those worn in the Navy. They even have naval ranks. The ASH is a four-star Admiral. The only four-star Admiral outside of the military."

"Why haven't I heard of this before now?" Tony asked.

"Don't know what to tell you. Lyndon Johnson appointed the first ASH. The agency existed years before. Ever hear of the Tuskegee Experiments?"

"Hold that thought," Tony said, pushing away from the table. "Gotta have another shot of java."

Two nurses entered the break room while they waited for Tony. Their coins rang as they dropped through the slot of the candy machine. They exited as quickly as they'd entered, candy wrappers rustling as they ignored Edna, Mama and Doc

Bruce. They brushed past Tony as he returned with fresh coffee.

"Okay, I'll bite," he said. "Tell us about the Tuskegee Experiments?"

"One of the darkest periods in American medical history. Some have even likened it to experiments Nazis performed on the Jews. Doctors, under the auspices of the U.S.P.H.S., injected healthy individuals with syphilis bacteria."

"Come on," Tony said.

"Surely you're exaggerating," Edna said. "Was this covered up?"

Doc Bruce sipped his coffee and shook his head. "Nope. It's been out there for everyone to see, and Gagnon was a primary player."

"Jesus!" Tony said.

"I know. Hard to believe, but true. The U.S.P.H.S. initiated and controlled the experiments. That's not all. They did further syphilis experiments on men, women and orphan children in Guatemala."

"Is this man Gagnon still alive?"

"Very much so. Been awhile, but I saw him last time I ate at Brennan's."

"Dr. Mary was murdered more than fifty years ago. How old is this guy?" Edna asked.

"A hundred, at least, though he doesn't look or act a day over sixty," Doc Bruce said.

"Into plastic surgery?" Mama asked.

"More than that."

"What, then?"

"I can't tell you right now."

"Why wouldn't we believe you?" Edna said.

"You wouldn't. Just trust me on this. It'll all come clear, I promise."

"Okay, then what does the U.S. Public Health Service have to do with the murder of Dr. Taggert?" Edna asked.

Eric Wilder

"The U.S.P.H.S. has a gated compound not far from here. It's abandoned. It wasn't in 1964. Researchers there were performing experiments on mice and primates. Mary Taggert worked at the compound as a primary researcher. So did I."

When the air conditioning came on again, Doc Bruce quit talking as he pulled the blanket tightly around his shoulders. Seeing his discomfort, Mama embraced him. Edna and Tony didn't seem to notice.

"Did you ever meet Angelica Moon?"

The grimace on Doc Bruce's face drew into a smile. "You kidding? Mary never went anywhere without her."

"That close, huh?"

"Mary was jealous and didn't like her out of sight."

"Did she have a reason to be jealous?"

Doc Bruce nodded. "That woman was a looker. Everyone had the hots for her."

"And?" Mama said.

"She was also a certifiable nympho, and everyone including me had her."

"She liked men?" Edna asked.

"Postmen, firemen, he men, she-men; you name it," he said. "She wasn't picky."

Not liking where the conversation was heading, Mama stopped hugging Doc Bruce and pushed her chair away.

"I can see how that would have made Dr. Taggert angry," she said.

"Dr. Mary wasn't exactly chaste. She liked to play around a bit herself."

"With other women?" Edna asked.

"Mary was married once and had a son. She liked women but would bed a man if she thought she needed to make one of her girlfriends jealous. She tried it with Angelica and it backfired on her."

155

Edna had drawn closer, her elbows resting on the table. When a nurse came in for a bag of potato chips, she waited until she'd left before asking her next question.

"Please. Tell us what happened."

"Ménage à trois. Lasted until Mary died."

"Who was the third person?"

"Dr. Louis Hollingsworth."

"You gotta be kidding," Edna said.

"I kid you not! Mary and Lou had an off-and-on thing going before Angelica ever showed up. They'd cooled things when Lou and Angie hooked up for a little tete-a-tete. When Mary found out about it, she jumped back in bed with Lou to make Angie jealous."

"But it didn't work out that way?" Tony said.

"Hardly. Angie loved it. Before long, the three of them were going at it like cats and dogs."

Talk of the sexual fireworks had heated up Doc Bruce. Removing the blanket from his shoulders, he tossed it to a chair behind him.

"Did Guy Marc Gagnon know Dr. Mary, Angelica, and Dr. Hollingsworth?" Tony asked.

"Lou was Guy Marc's right-hand-man."

"Hollingsworth was a powerful man in his own right. Seems like it should have been the other way around."

"Like I said, Marc was the ASH. I can't begin to tell you how much power he wields."

"Did he and Angelica ever . . . ?"

Doc Bruce nodded. "Guy Marc had anybody he wanted, and I mean that quite literally."

"Even . . . ?

Doc Bruce nodded again. "With Mary, Angie, Lou and Guy Marc, the kink factor was off the charts."

"Are you telling me that Guy Marc Gagnon and Dr. Louis Hollingsworth were homosexuals?" Edna said.

156

"Didn't say that. Guy Marc was into power and control and used any means to achieve his goals. Sex was his way of controlling Lou."

"I'm not following you," Tony said.

"If you were a former King of Rex, the highest social position in the Big Easy, would you want people knowing you were having a homosexual affair?

"Got it," Tony said. "Was Gagnon present the night Dr. Mary was murdered?"

"Yes, along with three of his goons."

"Name them," Edna said.

"A Cuban named Jesus Molina, a C.I.A. operative everyone called Slink, and a mafia hit man named Tex."

"Slink?" Mama said.

"A real alley cat," Doc Bruce said.

"This Cuban didn't happen to live in Dr. Mary's apartment complex, did he?" Edna asked.

"One in the same."

"Makes sense now," she said. "No one at the time knew exactly what he did, but he was always close by."

"And, as I remember," Tony said. "The person reporting the fire the night Dr. Mary was murdered."

"That's right," Edna said.

"But he was never mentioned as a possible suspect," Tony said.

"Very strange," Mama said.

"Lots of strange things going on back then," Doc Bruce said.

"What about Tex?" Tony asked.

"He had such an accent, everyone around here thought he was from Texas. He was really from Mississippi."

"And he killed people?"

"Lots of them," Doc Bruce said.

"What does Gagnon look like?" Edna asked.

157

"A little man with a shaved head and deep voice. And believe me he likes the sound of it."

Tony gave the tabletop a nervous tap. "Where is this compound? I'd like to pay it a little visit."

"Sure about that? The place is kind of creepy at night."

"Cemetery creepy?" Edna said.

"More like haunted house creepy," Doc Bruce said.

"I don't believe in haunted houses," Tony said.

"Then buckle up, gang. I'll take you there and you can see for yourself."

Chapter 19

Moonlight filtered through low-lying clouds as Mama, Edna, Tony, and Doc Bruce made their way on foot, to the U.S. Public Health Service compound. Doc Bruce wobbled along, his Irish shillelagh tapping a percussive melody on the sidewalk.

"You okay, Doc?" Tony asked. "I can get the car."

"I'm not fast, but I can walk as far as you can."

"Don't get your blood pressure up," Mama said. "You are a little shaky on your feet."

"I'm not as good as I once was, but like the country song says, I'm as good once as I ever was."

"No comment," Mama said with a straight face.

Doc Bruce didn't skip a beat. "Maybe I can demonstrate for you a little later on."

"You'll never change," she said.

They left the well-lighted sidewalk, heading into darkness as a slow-moving ambulance passed on the street. Almost hidden by a grove of large oaks, they approached a group of buildings surrounded by a ten-foot iron fence.

"This is it," Doc Bruce said. "Eight or ten buildings, the largest of which is the U.S. Public

Health Service Hospital. That's where we did all our experiments."

"Looks vacant," Tony said.

"We can get in through the entrance gate," Doc Bruce said.

He fumbled with his keys until Tony shined the light on them. He held the gate until everyone had entered, and then shut it behind them with a metallic clank.

"Still have keys?" Tony said.

"Nothing much has changed since I worked here. Not even the locks," Doc Bruce said.

"Is this going to be safe?" Mama asked.

"No Dobermans, if that's what you mean, but I can't guarantee we won't all come down with some dread disease."

Edna pointed her flashlight at one of the deserted buildings. "This place is contaminated?"

"Let's just say it's not City Park," Doc Bruce said.

The large building looming near the center of the compound looked like a government building built in the thirties or forties. The smell of freshly mown grass hung in the damp air. Shrubbery surrounding the building was neat and uniform as if a gardener still tended the grounds.

"Someone's taking care of the place. Must not have been deserted long," Tony said.

"Decades, actually," Doc Bruce said.

"Katrina flooded this area," Edna said. "I see no damage."

"She's right. What's the story on that?" Tony asked.

"Someone has their reasons for keeping the place from falling apart," Doc Bruce answered.

"And who would that someone be?" Edna asked.

"The people that still own this place."

"Who is?" Edna prompted.

"Our government," Doc Bruce said.

Thinking he'd heard something, Tony glanced over his shoulder. A feral cat, looking for something to eat, ran away when Mama called to him.

"You say this compound has been unused for decades, yet the government still provides constant upkeep. For what reason?"

"You're about to find out. You are looking at the hospital, the Infectious Disease Laboratory located inside."

The front door opened without a squeak. When a mouse ran between his legs, Tony jumped. An almost imperceptible noise emanated from behind a closed door.

"What was that?" Mama asked.

"Mice and monkeys," Doc Bruce said, opening the door. "We kept their cages in this room."

"No cages or animals in here," Tony said. "What's making that noise?"

"Spirits of the dead," Mama said.

"Animals don't have souls," Edna said. "Do they?"

No one answered, and the clamor grew louder as they moved through the windowless room.

The forlorn wails had brought Mama to tears. "They sound so tortured and helpless," she said.

Doc Bruce leaned against the wall. "They were. Hundreds of animals that endured countless gruesome medical experiments."

"Like what?" Tony asked.

"Amputations, induced paralysis, surgeries with no anesthesia, infecting with all manner of diseases. Auschwitz-type experiments routinely performed on our primate cousins. Shall I go on?"

"Oh my God!" Mama said.

"Some survived. A natural habitat primate rescue facility near Shreveport has saved a bunch. The animals sent there were so traumatized the facility must permanently separate them from almost all human contact."

"This is creeping me out," Tony said.

"Thought you didn't believe in haunted houses, Tony," Edna said.

"I don't, and neither do you. We probably activated a sound system in place to scare away derelicts."

"There's a possible rational explanation for almost everything," Mama said. "It still doesn't prove or disprove the presence of a spirit world."

"Forget the spirits for a bit. We have lots more to see," Doc Bruce said. "Follow me."

Tony nudged an empty wastebasket with his toe. "Freshly polished floors," he said.

In a large, open room, Edna aimed her flashlight at an opening that extended upward to the support struts in the top floor tower.

"That's where they had the particle accelerator," Doc Bruce said.

"Must have been a doozy," Edna said.

"A cylinder-shaped behemoth at least two stories tall capable of producing focused beams of electrons traveling near the speed of light."

"For what purpose?" Mama asked.

"To change things: metal, plastic, flesh, you name it."

"This is just an open room," Edna said. "Surely they didn't perform medical experiments here."

"Concrete walls surrounded the linac when I worked here."

"Linac?" Tony said.

Sarcasm colored Doc Bruce's words. "Short for a linear particle accelerator. A maze leading into the laboratory shielded the rest of the hospital from radiation. There was even asbestos in the walls to help avert exposure."

"Oh my," Mama said.

"It's hard taking a bath without getting your toes wet."

Mama grasped Doc Bruce's frail arm. "Your leukemia?" she asked.

"I'm probably lucky that's all I have," he said.

"What kind of experiments did they perform with this linac?" Edna asked.

Doc Bruce's voice was almost imperceptible when he said, "Doctor Frankenstein shit."

"We're not scientists," Tony said. "I don't know about Mama and Edna, but you need to spell it out for me."

"A linac is capable of changing things in a molecular sense. Converting things into something they're not."

He nodded when Mama said, "Living things?"

"Monkeys and mice?" Edna said.

Doc Bruce nodded again.

"Humans?" Tony asked.

"Yes," was Doc Bruce's terse reply. "The linac was Guy Marc's baby. He liked being around when it was in operation."

"You knew all this and continued working here?" Mama said.

"I was young and naive. Some doctors at the time thought viruses caused cancer. If cells were malignant, perhaps you could cause them to mutate into a benign form. We were searching for the Holy Grail. A cure for cancer. I bought into the pitch, like my daddy used to say, hook, line, and sinker."

"But you continued working here," Mama said.

"And paid the price," he said. "You know what's ironic?"

"Tell us," Edna said.

"I thought I was saving the world, but all I ever did was wind up polluting it even more."

Wails from the primate room continued, unnerving everyone. Tony pointed his flashlight into the rafters.

"Sorry about your illness, but this place gives me the creeps and I want to get out of here. Can you please tell us what happened the night Dr. Mary died?"

"I was here that night. I wasn't supposed to be, but I was working on notes in my office on the second floor. I'd flipped off the lights and had fallen asleep at my desk."

"Go on," Edna said when Doc Bruce paused.

"A commotion awakened me, a familiar voice shouting and raising cane. I peeked out to see who was screaming loud enough to wake the dead."

"Dr. Mary?" Edna said.

Doc Bruce nodded. "Slink and Tex were dragging her by the hair, kicking her as they did. They pulled her into the linac room. I should have run, but my curiosity got the best of me."

"You followed them into the linac room?" Tony said.

"I'm not that stupid. There was a protected room with a slit where you could view what was going on without exposing yourself to possible contamination. No one knew I was there."

"Tell us," Edna said.

"Guy Marc was waiting for them. Slink and Tex stripped her naked and strapped her to the bench beneath the linac. They didn't bother gagging her. She was fighting her restraints and screaming bloody murder."

"Could you hear what she was saying?" Tony asked.

Doc Bruce closed his eyes and rubbed his forehead. "The room was soundproof. I heard nothing, except in my mind."

"Tell us what happened," Edna said.

"Linacs have immense power and can disintegrate flesh and bone in a millisecond. I wanted to turn away but couldn't."

"Gagnon turned the linac on Dr. Mary?" Tony said.

"First, he burned the fingers off her hand, and then her wrist. She was screaming. I couldn't hear her words, but I know she was begging him to stop."

"But he didn't," Edna said.

"He just continued torturing her."

Doc Bruce grew silent, remembering Dr. Mary's agony, and apparently the fact that he could do nothing about it. Tony tapped his shoulder.

"I know this is painful for you, but Edna and I need to know what happened. Can you please finish your story?"

Doc Bruce's voice was barely audible when he continued. "He burned off her arm and part of her ribcage. Her organs were exposed, and she looked like charred meat."

"But she was still alive?" Edna asked.

Doc Bruce nodded. "Slink and Tex unstrapped her and carted her away. I didn't know what happened until I read the news the next day in the Picayune."

"Did Slink and Tex take her back to her apartment?" Tony asked.

"Apparently," Doc Bruce said.

"And started a fire to try and cover up what occurred?" Edna said.

Doc Bruce was looking at the floor. "Yes."

Tony gave Edna a glance. "Then it was Gagnon that killed Dr. Mary?"

A bullet echoed through the open room before Doc Bruce could answer.

Chapter 20

Floodlights, shining down from the second story balcony popped on, illuminating every nook of the vast building. Edna, Tony, Mama, and Doc Bruce all dived to the polished floor. When Tony glanced up, he saw at least six automatic weapons pointing down at them. A man laughed, and then spoke.

"Shoulda known to leave well enough alone, Dr. B. Maybe you'da lived a few more years before the big C took you."

"Screw you, whoever you are!" Doc Bruce shouted, his weak voice echoing against bare walls.

"Stay on the floor and we won't shoot you. I'm coming down."

The man's boot heels reverberated through the open room as he tromped down the stairs. When he reached them, he kicked Doc Bruce in the ribs.

"Don't remember me, Dr. B? I'm your old buddy Slink."

Doc Bruce's eyes closed as he twisted on the floor, holding his ribs. When he opened them, he looked up at the man who had kicked him.

"His son, maybe. Slink would be pushing eighty," he said.

"Eighty-two, to be exact. You had your chance, but you never got the message. Now, your rotting carcass is gonna wind up in the middle of the river, along with your buds here."

The wiry little man had a shaved head and was dressed in a black jumpsuit. The prominent tattoo on his right hand was that of a bloody dagger piercing a deadly looking spider.

"We've done nothing to you," Mama said.

"Shut up, bitch, and stay on the floor," Slink said, administering a vicious kick with the toe of his boot to make sure she complied.

When Tony rose to assist Mama, Slink nailed him across the mouth with his pistol. Then, like a cat playing with a group of trapped mice, he began circling them.

"Couldn't leave well enough alone, now could you?" he said, kicking Doc Bruce's legs out from under him when he attempted to stand.

"You leave us alone," Mama said. "We've done nothing to you."

"Well, your business partner Mr. Wyatt Thomas and his blond slut girlfriend did. Now, we're gonna make you pay for it, and believe me I'm gonna enjoy every minute of it."

By now, all the spotlights focused on a tight circle where Tony, Edna, Mama and Doc Bruce knelt. Slink continued his rant as he circled them, using his boots as he did. Doc Bruce grimaced and held his ribs, Mama's busted lip bleeding profusely.

He moved just a bit too close and Tony was quick to react. Getting his leg between Slink's, he tripped him, rolling him on the floor. Diving on top of him, he began pummeling him with both hands.

Edna got into the act, chasing down Slink's pistol as it bounced across the floor. Tony quit punching when Edna grabbed Slink's collar and stuffed the barrel deeply into his mouth. The men with their guns trained on them held their fire, afraid they might accidentally hit their boss.

"Drop your weapons," she shouted, "or I'm blowing this little prick's head right off his spindly neck."

"Do as she says," Tony said, standing and administering a knee to Slink's groin.

After helping Mama and Doc Bruce to their feet, he gave Edna a hand with Slink. She had him on the back of the collar, his pistol trained on the nape of his neck.

"You want to see eighty-three I suggest you have your goons stand down."

"And she don't mean next week," Tony said.

Slink didn't answer. He had a switchblade up his sleeve. With one precise motion, he stabbed Edna in the thigh, and then slammed her to the ground with a twirling karate kick to the chin. He and Tony dived for the sliding pistol at the same moment. It was then that the lights went out.

Automatic weapons illuminated the building with barrel flashes as all hell erupted, the goons on the second-floor balcony shot dead. Tony and Slink didn't notice, locked in a life or death battle. Neither had control of the pistol, but Slink still had the knife. He was doing his best to carve Tony's face with it. One of the gunmen ended the fight, knocking Slink out with a makeshift billy club.

"Who the hell . . . !"

"No time to explain, boss," the man said. "Come with us. Now!"

Body armor covered the two men dressed in black. Bordered by their black face paint, the whites of their eyes glinted in the dim illumination of their flashlights. They had bloused their pant legs into their combat boots and their metal helmets didn't look American.

Their stubby, tricked-out automatic weapons were still smoking. Though the two looked ominous, something in their foreign accents caused Tony to trust them, not to mention that they had just saved their lives. One of the men began wrapping Edna's thigh with a tourniquet.

"The doctor is comatose, and you must carry him," the man told Tony. "And hurry, please. We have no time to spare."

A black stretch limousine waited on the street by an open gate. It sped away in a screech of burning rubber after the tired and wounded group had piled in the back.

Tony hadn't ridden in a limousine since his youngest daughter had married some two years before. The interior was roomy and dimly lit. Tony got his first good look at the two men that had saved them.

"I am Sasha. The bald one is Borya. Our driver is Vladimir."

Sasha was young, probably no older than mid-twenties, his hair and eyes dark and his accent Russian. He had removed his armor and black shirt and spattered blood from Edna's wound stained his pink Izod shirt.

Borya was busily working on Edna's stab wound, having already applied a bag of ice to Mama's busted lip. Doc Bruce's head nestled in Mama's lap. Borya was also young and prematurely bald, as his thick-haired partner had said.

"Are we in trouble here?" Tony asked.

"You are safe with us," Sasha said. "That is all I can now say. Drink?"

"What you got?" Tony asked.

"Your favorite; Dalmore scotch, straight up."

"How'd you know that?" Tony asked as he took a sip from the expensive crystal tumbler.

"We are following you for two days. Good thing, as Slink almost had you."

"You know Slink?" Mama asked.

169

Sasha nodded. "Drink, pretty lady?"

"Bless you, child. I'll take anything you have short of turpentine," she said.

"I do not know turpentine, but I have vodka."

"Perfect," she said.

Ice clinked as he filled her tumbler. "Then you must have Russian in you."

"Baby," she said. "Mama's got a little bit of everything in her."

"You okay, Edna?" Tony asked.

Edna was wincing as Borya finished dressing her wound.

"Not worth a crap right about now," she said.

Borya patted her shoulder. "Please breathe deeply for me. You're not going to pass out, are you?"

Edna drew a deep breath. "Burns like hell."

Borya opened a vial of pills and gave her a couple. "I will get you water."

"Only if you mix it with a little whiskey."

"Alcohol is not to mix with medication for pain."

"I'm old enough to be your grandmother, young man. Let me worry about what your pills will do to me if I wash them down with something alcoholic."

"You will heal nicely," he said with a grin. "It is a clean wound; hit no bone. Barely missed your femoral artery. You are most lucky."

"I should have patted the little bastard down first," she said.

Tony handed her a drink, and she took the pills along with a healthy swallow of whiskey.

"I owe you a big one," Tony said. "You saved my neck back there."

"Another?" Edna said to Sasha. "A triple would work for me."

He grinned as he refilled her glass. Mama saw the blood dripping down Sasha's face and wiped it with a tissue.

"Your partner needs medical attention," she said to Borya.

"I am fine," Sasha said.

"You could have been killed back there. Half your eyebrow is missing," Mama said, holding the tissue to the wound.

"It is nothing. Please do not worry about me."

"You saved our lives. I have a right to worry."

"We were just doing our jobs."

"Then you need this," she said, removing a necklace from her neck and putting it around Sasha's.

"What is it?" he asked.

"Gris gris," she said. "It will keep you safe, but you must never take it off."

"I am not a superstitious man," he said.

"If you do what I think you do for a living, then never take it off. And I mean never."

Sasha touched the necklace and nodded.

By now, Borya had moved from Edna to Doc Bruce.

"How is he?" Sasha asked.

"Not good."

A passing semi's horn blasted as Vladimir powered up an entry ramp to a cross-town. Sasha turned to Tony.

"We are sending the doctor, Miss Edna, and Mama to a hospital in Baton Rouge. You and I must take a detour."

"Edna, you okay with that? Tony asked.

"Hell no!"

"You have lost much blood," Borya said. "I field-clamped your wound, but you need stitches."

"You and Sasha are just babies to me. Don't matter your age because I just saw you kill half a dozen men without batting an eye. You two are pros. So am I. I'm going with Tony."

"You heard her," Tony said. "You okay going with Doc Bruce to Baton Rouge, Mama?"

"I have to stop by the house. Can't leave my kitties."

"We have already cared for that, Miss Mama," Borya said. "You will need to stay somewhere else for a while. Your cats will join you."

"In Baton Rouge?" she said.

"A safe house on the river."

"And Tony and Edna?"

"With Borya, me, and Vladimir, they are very safe," Sasha said. "I promise."

A cloudy moon shined over Pontchartrain as the black limousine disappeared around the corner, leaving Tony, Edna and Sasha alone in the darkness. Tony nudged a broken shell with his shoe.

"What now?" he asked.

Sasha glanced at his watch. "You have many questions, and I have no answers."

"Why the secrecy?"

Sasha just shook his head and turned away. The whomp, whomp, whomp of an approaching helicopter interrupted the silence. Lights appeared through the cloudy darkness over the lake as an offshore supply chopper landed with a lot of noise, flying sand and debris. Two men in helmets pulled them into the open cargo door. They lifted off without shutting it.

"Our journey is long," Sasha said. "Please relax and enjoy the view."

As Tony and Edna settled into their seats, the big chopper turned south, toward the Gulf of Mexico. The light show coming from the city below was spectacular. Tony had flown in planes, but never in a helicopter. The sensation was a cross between a riding lawn mower and a hot air balloon.

When he glanced at Edna, she was grimacing and holding her stab wound.

"You okay?" he asked.

"Nothing another drink wouldn't fix," she said.

Sasha handed her two more pain pills and a flask of vodka from a pocket inside his coat.

She smiled and nodded when he said, "This will help."

"Thanks," she said, returning her attention to the vista below them. "It's beautiful."

"Wait until you see the Gulf. It is quite spectacular."

The chopper soon moved south of the lights of New Orleans, into the swamps and bayous leading to the Gulf of Mexico.

"Where are we headed?" Tony asked.

"Out of state," Sasha said.

"What are all those lights down there?" Edna asked.

"Offshore platforms. Some are jack-up drilling rigs, others permanent production facilities. Choppers like this one and crew boats supply them."

"They look like a thousand flickering fireflies," Edna said. "I had no idea how much activity goes on out here."

"Me either," Tony said. "I've lived in Louisiana all my life and never imagined there were so many wells in the Gulf."

"Then you are about to see something you have only visited in your wildest dreams," Sasha said.

Chapter 21

Tony and Edna had fallen asleep, both awakening when the chopper began a steep descent. Still dark, a dense fog covered the water below them. Feeling as if they were in a falling elevator, they braced for a crash that never came. Seeing their discomfort, Sasha grinned.

"You both can relax. We are simply descending for a landing," he said.

When the chopper emerged from the clouds, Tony saw a giant, offshore complex. It looked like a drilling platform except there were no draw works or drill pipe. The chopper touched down on a bull's eye near the top of the complex. When the door opened a man in a helmet appeared. Lights in hand, he motioned them out of the chopper. The rain had ceased, but angry clouds masked the moon.

"You coming?" Tony shouted to Sasha.

Sasha shook his head, waving slowly as the chopper lifted off the platform, rising through the clouds.

The noise of the chopper's engines diminished as they followed the man to a steel door. It slammed shut behind them with a metallic clank.

"I'm Louis," he said. "Welcome to the far end of the earth."

Tony awoke to a clanging in his ears, disoriented, and in a strange bed. When a voice outside the door called to him, he didn't immediately remember where he was.

"Good morning. I'm leaving a carafe of coffee at the door, and I'll be back to get you in half an hour."

When he retrieved the coffee, he found the person with a pleasant female voice was gone.

The little room where he'd caught up on a few hours of sleep was apparently crew quarters, complete with bed, head, shower, functional desk and chair, and little else.

A Picayune, the New Orleans' newspaper, was on the tray with the carafe of coffee. There was also a note informing him someone had laundered and pressed his clothes. He was reading the paper when the woman with the pleasant voice knocked on his door again.

"I'm Tamela," the young black woman said.

She looked sharp in her khaki shorts and Tulane tee shirt, a red bandanna tying her dark hair into a ponytail. After following her up a flight of metal stairs, Tony realized why she seemed so happy.

The sky was still cloudy but a shade of blue he'd never seen. So was the water around them. They were on a deck high above the Gulf of Mexico, a warm but persistent breeze blowing in their faces. Tamela couldn't stop smiling.

"I've never seen the water this clear, or this blue," he said.

"That's the same reaction I get from every person that visits."

"What's up?"

"The depth. We're way beyond the shallow waters near shore affected by silt dumping in from the rivers."

"Where's Edna?"

"Spent the night in the infirmary."

"She okay?"

"I checked on her earlier. We have around-the-clock medical staff and world-class facilities capable of handling any situation."

Edna was the center of attention when they reached the infirmary, a frown on her face and arms tightly crossed as a doctor and two nurses tried to convince her to use the wheelchair they had brought for her.

"I walked in and now I'm walking out," she said.

The young doctor dressed in a white smock and expensive shoes finally just shook his head.

"Your wound will never heal unless you stay off your feet," he said. "At least take these crutches."

"Not gonna happen," Edna said.

A frizzy-haired nurse ended the standoff as she hurried behind the doctor carrying a cane.

"Don't need it, but I'll take it, just to make you feel better."

Edna smiled as they walked out the door when Tony said, "Troublemaker."

Edna twirled the cane to show she didn't need it.

"Not as sexy as Doc Bruce's shillelagh, but it'll make a pretty good club next time we meet some bad guys."

"You're a hoot, Miss Callahan," Tamela said.

"Just Edna," she said. "Who are you?"

"I'm Tamela."

"And you are?"

"Your tour guide. Please relax and enjoy yourselves."

"Where are we going?" Tony asked.

"We have time for breakfast and a small tour," Tamela said, hurrying along a gangplank overlooking the Gulf. "Sorry," she said, slowing when she remembered Edna's injured leg.

Another storm was blowing in from the south, angry clouds bearing the threat of thunder, lightning, and lots of rain. Busy staring out over the broad expanse of seemingly endless water, Edna had forgotten her wound for the moment.

"Oh my," she said. "I don't see land in any direction."

Tamela pointed into the distance. "We're about a hundred miles south of the Louisiana coast," she said.

Properly impressed, Edna asked, "Is this a drilling platform?"

"More accurately, a production platform. This complex of raised structures overlies a part of the Gulf where a giant oilfield once was."

From where they stood, Tony could see another platform equally as large. The size of a football field, it rose high above the water on massive metal stilts. Futuristic buildings constructed of metal and glass topped the structures. A complex system of ramps, runways, and catwalks connected the structures. A flock of gulls circled above.

"Those buildings don't look like any offshore platform I ever seen," Tony said.

"When the old company abandoned the field, the entire facility was stripped. Boston architects designed the buildings that replaced them. There are three more ramps you can't see from here."

"Beautiful," Edna said. "Like something out of a sci-fi movie."

"We get that a lot," Tamela said. "They are designed specifically to accentuate the stark beauty surrounding us, and robust enough to withstand a hurricane's direct hit."

"It's a long way down to the water," Tony said. "How high up are we?"

"A hundred feet," Tamela said. "It can get rough fast out here in a storm."

"I bet," Edna said. "I have no sensation of motion. How is this thing anchored?"

"We're in a part of the Gulf known as the Flower Garden Banks. This field overlies a seamount."

"A what?" Tony asked.

"A high spot caused by a salt dome pushing things up. The water is only about sixty-five feet deep here. There's a coral reef beneath this complex."

"How deep is the rest of the Gulf?" Edna asked.

"Very," Tamela said.

"Two hundred feet?" Tony said.

"Some parts as deep as fourteen-thousand feet."

"No way."

Tamela nodded. "The Gulf of Mexico is the ninth largest geographic body on earth. Some people call the Sigsbee Deep the Grand Canyon under the Sea. It's almost three miles straight down."

"I had no idea," Edna said.

"Most people don't. Here is where the Gulfstream, one of the most powerful currents on earth, originates."

Edna glanced up at a flock of migratory birds flying overhead. "You're quite the tour guide. How do you know so much?"

"My degree in marine biology from Texas A&M. I've trained for this job all my life."

A large boat emerged from the fog beginning to cover the water.

"Damn!" Tony said. "That thing looks like a little destroyer."

"Our security boat," Tamela said. "It circles the resort continuously."

Tony did a double take. "With a cannon and machine guns?" he said. Looks ready for a major naval battle."

"Never know what might happen out here in the middle of the Gulf. We're in open water, far beyond continental waters of the U.S. We are responsible for our security."

"But . . ."

She stopped Tony with a wave of her arm. "Pirates and ne'er-do-wells reign out here. Our responsibility is to our guests. Our security must be locked down and iron tight."

"Pirates?" Edna said.

"Don't let it worry you. We're safe. You must be hungry. I'll answer your questions over bacon and eggs."

The complex of raised platforms was more extensive than either Tony or Edna had imagined. They followed Tamela through a long series of gangplanks, escalators, and elevators, finally reaching a commissary complete with wonderful aromas emanating from the kitchen.

Dozens of people occupied the area, eating, drinking, and conversing, and dressed in identical sea blue jumpsuits.

"All these people work here?" Edna asked.

"And many more," Tamela said.

"What the hell do they all do out here in the middle of the Gulf of Mexico?" Tony said.

"This is a resort. Flower Garden Banks Resort. It takes lots of people to run a world-class facility such as ours."

"I never knew there were reefs in the Gulf," Tony said. "Hundreds, actually," Tamela said.

"Some are man-made. A few, like this one, resulted naturally."

"If this is a resort, where are all the tourists?" Edna asked.

"We're on the platform reserved for employees," Tamela said. "The guests stay on the main structure."

"How the hell do they get here?" Tony said.

"Yachts, service boats, and helicopters."

"It's beautiful and eerie," Edna said. "But what else is the attraction?"

"Diving, deep sea fishing, gambling and world-class entertainment. For our guests that don't dive, there's the Aqua Room."

"What's that?" Tony said.

"Glad you asked. I'll show you after breakfast."

The commissary was more than functional, offering a breathtaking view through a wall-sized window overlooking the Gulf. Once seated, Edna spent a moment wincing as she rubbed her thigh.

"You gonna make it?" Tony asked.

"Sorry to be such a whine bag," she said.

Tony grinned. "I'd still be in the hospital bed if it was me."

They were soon feasting on eggs, bacon, biscuits and gravy. The smiling wait staff kept bringing food and drink until Tony could eat no more.

Other than Tony and Edna, Tamela was the only person not dressed in a blue jumpsuit. The kitchen workers stopped bringing food when she finally moved her index finger past her throat.

"This is just one of many commissaries at this facility," she said. "They're open around the clock."

"Quite a perk for the employees," Edna said.

"It's an excellent place to work. Food is good, pay high and you only have to work two weeks a month. It seems like no one ever quits," Tamela said.

"What about movies, or trips across town to eat at a new restaurant?" Edna asked.

"We have a theater that screens all the latest movies and a performing arts center for bands and other live entertainment. That's just for the workforce. Other than probably Vegas, tourists would have a hard time matching the dining experiences and entertainment available to them."

"You've sold me," Edna said. "Where's Elvis."

"Impersonators are the best I can do, but there are some good ones. We get a few from time to time."

"I'll pass," Edna said. "What else you got?"

"Finished eating?"

"Another bite and I'll need bigger pants," Tony said.

"Then let me show you something our guests pay thousands to see."

Tamela led them through yet another winding pathway of corridors, stairs, and hidden passages. Tony's ears popped as they descended in an elevator. When he exited, he realized why.

"Geez!" he said. "Are we at the bottom of the ocean?"

Tamela's smile was the only answer he needed. The four walls of the room were glass, the only thing separating them from the sea life swimming on the other side.

"Oh my God!" Edna said.

"We're surrounded by the reef's abundant plants and fishes. It's like a bathysphere at the bottom of the Gulf."

"Is that a whale?" Edna asked.

"A big one," Tamela said.

"Oh, my!" Edna said. "It can't get through the glass, can it?"

Tamela laughed. "I won't go into detail, but the walls are strong enough to prevent almost anything, even a very large hurricane."

A big shark swam toward Edna, bumping the glass with its nose. The beast stared at her with steely eyes before swimming away.

"That's comforting," she said. "That shark looked big enough to swallow me whole."

"The reef is a virtual paradise for creatures of the Gulf. Turtles, whales, sharks, manta rays, and exotic fish you can only imagine. You'll see them all if you stay here long enough," Tamela said.

"So colorful," Edna said.

"Sponges, star, boulder and brain coral. Commercial fishermen noticed the bright colors years ago. That's how the banks got its name. There's more."

They followed her through a steel-encased corridor, complete with observation portholes, to another viewing room at a different part of the reef. Finally, Tamela glanced at her watch.

"Almost time for your meeting," she said.

"We still don't have a clue why we're here. You gonna keep us in suspense?" Tony asked.

"You're about to find out."

A small train connected the platforms. Their car seconded as an observation vehicle. The walls, roof, and floor, were glass and afforded spectacular views in all directions. They began seeing tourists for the first time as they passed stops along the way. As the car went outside the steel and glass structure, Tony had the sensation of flying.

"What do you think?" Tamela asked with a smile.

"Beautiful but creepy," Edna said.

"This thing has never fallen, has it?" Tony asked.

"Though it feels like we're floating, I assure you we are safely connected to the primary structure. That's the marina," Tamela said, pointing below them.

"Wow!" Tony said. "Are those all private boats?"

"Sea-going yachts from all over the world. Saudi sheiks, Chinese and Russian billionaires, dignitaries from every country on earth. You name it, and they are here."

Not far from the yachts, a whale broke the Gulf's blue water, gulls disappearing into the fog as they chased after it. When Tamela manipulated an app on her cell phone, the single car halted and its glass door slid open. She led them around a granite wall to an elevator door.

"This is where I leave you."

Chapter 22

Torrential rains continued to fall as Mingo turned the old Ford toward the river. Lucy was still in panic mode from our visit to the Order of the White Doves.

"Where are you taking us?" she said.

"Someplace safe. You two in a whole lotta trouble."

"I've heard that before," I said. "Can we trust you, or should we be trying to jump out of the car about now?"

Mingo glanced in the rearview mirror, and I could see his grin.

"Don't do that," he said. "I'm on your side, amigo. When we get to where we're going, you'll understand why."

We began passing cranes, docks, and warehouses—all part of the Port of New Orleans. Confused by the persistent rain, I didn't know if we were headed upriver or down. It didn't matter because Mingo apparently did.

The rutted dirt road we raced over led us to a highway underpass. The vision that began unfolding before us looked surreal and like something from a Fellini fantasy.

Dozens of junker cars lay strewn in the valley below the underpass: destroyed victims of Katrina, mud caking the mangled vehicles indicating they'd spent time underwater. Mingo parked the car by a building sheltered beneath the underpass.

"You hungry?" he asked.

"My stomach's touching my backbone," I said.

"Good. Mina will get you dry clothes to wear and then feed you the best Mexican food you ever ate."

Lucy wasn't budging, frowning as she sat with her arms and legs tightly crossed.

"Wyatt, let's get out of here."

Mingo stuck his head in the door and placed his hand over his heart.

"I am sorry you do not trust me, pretty señorita. I promise I mean you no harm. Come eat and get dry clothes with me. You are safe here and nowhere else right now. There was a carload of angry Cubans chasing us back there. I do not think they will give up so easily."

"Someone was following us?" I said.

"Don't worry Mr. Wyatt. I lost them awhile back. As I said, you're safe here. I promise."

We finally managed to coax Lucy out of the car. The building was a café filled with hungry diners. It smelled as if we'd died and gone to culinary heaven, the aroma of tamales, enchiladas and fresh-cooked tortillas filling the room. All talk subsided when Mingo walked in with us. When he smiled, put his arms around our shoulders and then gave two thumbs up, the diners returned to their meals. A woman in the kitchen heard Mingo's voice and hurried out to meet us.

"This is mi amor, Mina," he said.

Mina was all smiles. Instead of shaking hands, she demanded a hug from each of us. Lucy seemed comforted by her appearance.

Mina was a beauty but not a Mexican as I had expected. She was black; not just chocolate brown but the color of burnished gunmetal. Bushy hair draped her bare shoulders. Gold rings dangled from her earlobes and framed her expressive face. She spoke clipped English, her accent not Spanish.

"Mingo called. Said he was bringing somebody. You two a mess," she said, grabbing Lucy's arm. "Come with me, honey. I get you some dry clothes."

"Mina will take care of her," Mingo said. "Don't worry, Mr. Wyatt. You're about my size and I got something dry for you to wear too."

He laughed when I said, "Mina's not Mexican, is she?"

"Let's get those clothes and some hot food in your bellies. Then we'll tell you all about me and Mina."

Mingo and Mina lived in rooms behind the café. When we returned, we found the lunch crowd had departed. An older Hispanic woman was bussing tables, and Mingo called her over.

"Mama, this is Wyatt and Lucy. Mama and Mina run the place while I'm off in the taxi."

Mingo's mama was short, no taller than five feet, and her gray hair rolled in a bun behind her head. She seemed to have a perpetual smile.

"I am Abril," she said. "I do my best to keep these two out of trouble."

"You're doing a fantastic job," I said.

"Yes, but I am getting old, and they refuse to have niñas and niños."

"They'll come around," I said.

Abril smiled and then returned to bussing the tables. It felt good to have dry clothes for a change. Mine looked like Mingo's, Lucy's a white blouse and peasant's skirt like Mina. Mingo sat with us at a table in the corner while Mina hurried away to the kitchen. She soon returned with a mango and plantain salad; tasty but decidedly not Mexican.

"Mina is from Haiti," Mingo said after she'd heaped a feast on the table in front of us.

"Didn't think you had a Mexican accent," I said. "How did you get here from Haiti?"

"Long story," she said.

"Mina got a job at the Order of the White Doves. That's how I met her."

Mina rolled her eyes. "Who is telling this story? You or me?" she said.

"What can I say?" Mingo asked. "She is the boss."

Mina ignored Mingo's comment. "I grew up speaking French, but Mingo still talks to me in Spanish," she said. "I stowed away on a banana boat. Ended up here in New Orleans. I could speak only a little English at the time. I cannot remember how I met Madam Moon but she hired me as the cook at the Order of the White Doves. Before too long, I realized I was little more than a prisoner."

"Someone would even accompany her when she shopped at the market," Mingo said.

"I'm telling this story," Mina said.

"Sorry," he said.

"At first, I didn't think much about it," Mina said, continuing. "I am, after all, an illegal alien. Then Madam Moon began telling me I couldn't leave, or else she'd have me arrested."

"Madam Moon and the Doves mistreated her," Mingo said.

Lucy glanced up from her salad. "They abused you?"

Mina nodded. "Both verbally and physically. I was frightened they would turn me over to the police if I made trouble."

"Please tell us more," I said.

"Except for Madam Moon and Jubah, the other women spoke only English. Because of that, they'd

187

say things in front of me they didn't think I'd understand."

"Such as?" I said.

"I first thought the sisters practiced Vodoun. Being from Haiti, I was comfortable with that. It is not what they practice or believe."

"What do they practice?" I asked.

"Something much direr. They are devil worshippers."

We had time to let Mina's pronouncement sink in as Mama appeared from the kitchen with platters of tamales, enchiladas, guacamole and lots of hot sauce.

"You wanna beer, Mr. Wyatt?" Mingo asked.

"This water's fine, Mingo. Thanks, though."

"You, Lucy?" Mina asked.

"Love one," she said.

Lucy's demeanor changed noticeably after clean clothes, a hot lunch and two chilled mugs of Tecate with salt and lime.

"You overheard the Doves talking about devil worship?" she asked.

"Yes, and I had a small room upstairs that overlooked the courtyard. One night, the sound of drums woke me. I got out of bed and looked out the window. Torches were burning, the Doves sitting in a circle. Madam Moon stood inside the circle in front of an altar made of stone. I'd seen it before but did not know its use until then."

Mina paused as if she were about to describe something distasteful. Her voice had grown softer when she began again.

"The Doves had captured an alley cat. It was lying on the altar. I thought it was dead because it was on its back and not moving. It was not. As I watched, Madam Moon cut out its heart with a ceremonial knife."

"How did you know the cat was still alive?" I asked.

"Because blood spurted when she stabbed the animal. I wanted to turn away and close the curtains but I could not."

Profoundly affected by the story she was telling us, Mina began to cry. Lucy grasped her shoulders, giving them a comforting squeeze.

"I know this is painful for you. Please don't continue just for our sakes," she said.

"You need to know," Mina said. "Blood was everywhere. The Doves began circling the dead cat, each dipping their fingers into the wound where the heart had been and then tasting the blood. Madam Moon cut the heart into small pieces on the altar. One by one, the Doves knelt before her, opening their mouths and receiving pieces of the heart."

"Oh my God!" Lucy said.

"Madam Moon glanced up at my window and saw me looking. I dropped the curtain I was peeking through and hurried back to bed. Next morning, she slapped me so hard it rattled my teeth."

"Tell them what she said," Mingo said.

"Forget what I saw or else become the next to have their heart cut out and eaten."

"Crap!" Lucy finally said.

"She was kidding, don't you think?" I said.

Mina left the table, returning with a bottle of tequila. Abril had joined us, and Mina poured five shots.

"Not for me," I said. "I can't drink. I'm an alcoholic."

"I'll take his," Lucy said. "I need two after the story you just told."

"Then you'll need more," Mina said. "I've only just begun to tell you about the White Doves."

The rain had started up again in earnest, the lights in the café flickering briefly. When Mina excused herself for a moment to show Lucy the bathroom, I asked Mingo about the electricity.

"We live off the grid. A city power line runs overhead. I hooked into it."

"You don't pay for electricity?"

He laughed. "We got phone service, running water, and indoor plumbing with sewage disposal. Hard to beat Mexican engineering."

"What about the police?" I asked.

"They don't come here. Far as the city is concerned, we don't exist. Our customers are all illegals. We deal only in cash and trade."

"How did you meet Mina?"

Mingo leaned back in his chair and grinned as if remembering a pleasant memory.

"I work the CBD a lot and often pass the White Dove place. I began to see Mina staring out at the street through the gate. When I waved, she waved back. I soon began stopping and talking to her. We used to hold hands through the gate."

Mina and Lucy returned before Mingo could finish his story. After Mina had poured more tequila, they all had another shot. The buzz left Lucy in the best mood I'd seen her in for a while.

"You want to hear the rest of the story?" Mina asked.

"Please," I said.

Thunder rumbled down the gully, shaking the shutters and causing the lights to flutter again. Mina found some candles behind the counter, placed them around the room and lit them.

"Just in case," she said.

"Love it," Lucy said. "Feels like you're about to tell us something very creepy."

"I am," she said. "Madam Moon had some close friends. Three men: Marc, Slink, and Tex. Marc was a little man with a shaved head and dark gray eyes. I shivered whenever he looked at me. Tex and

Slink were just as creepy. They often arrived with several Cubans."

"How did you know they were Cuban?" I asked.

"I'm from Haiti. I know Cubans."

"What did they do at the compound?" Lucy asked.

"Sordid, sadistic, sexual things," Mina said. "There were orgies."

Lucy glanced at me. "You mean with the Doves?" she asked.

"Yes. Lots of drugs and alcohol were involved. I could hear their antics through the walls. Madam Moon had sex with all of them, including the Doves."

"Other than the ceremony with the cat, did you see anything else as macabre?"

"No, but I heard the Doves talking. One of the acolytes had agreed to sacrifice herself on the altar so she could join Father Satan in Hades. There were ceremonies for a week culminating with a lave tet ritual. She disappeared from the compound following the night of a full moon. She never returned."

"You think they killed her in the courtyard like the cat?"

Mina's demeanor darkened as she spoke. "There is another place. They call it their cathedral. I never learned where it was. I'm sure it is where they sacrificed the Dove."

"The lave tet ceremony isn't performed regularly?" I asked.

"I only saw it that one time," Mina said.

Lucy's eyes opened wide, and her hand went to her mouth.

Chapter 23

Lights continued to flicker in the building beneath the underpass. Mingo's cow dog was howling at the door, so he let him come in. The big dog's tail wagged as he crawled under the table beneath Mingo's legs. Mingo rubbed his neck and fed him half of the tamale he hadn't eaten. Mama and Mina shook their heads.

"We tell him a thousand times. Don't feed Pancho off your plate. He don't listen to nobody."

"Pancho's brave, but he don't like thunder and lightning," Mingo said.

"Welcome to the club," Lucy said, scratching behind Pancho's ears.

"You say you're off the grid, yet you have a cell phone. Someone must know where you are," I said.

"Pay-as-you-go," he said. "No contract and I buy extra minutes at the convenience store. No hassle. No one even knows we are alive, or cares."

I wasn't convinced. "Sure about that?" I asked.

"Trust me. No one bothers with pay-as-you-go people."

"Then can you make a call for me?"

"I can, Mr. Wyatt but I cannot guarantee the phone of the person you are calling will be secure."

"Hmm," I said.

Lucy had other things on her mind. "My tequila's wearing off. Mind if I have another shot?"

Mina poured everyone another round. Abril waved hers off.

"Too much excitement for an old woman. I am going to bed."

"She goes to sleep with the chickens," Mingo said.

"You have chickens?" Lucy asked.

"Yes, along with Pancho, several cats and a couple of goats."

"Mingo don't like paying for milk and eggs," Mina said.

Mingo nodded. "We got lots of room here," he said. "You are welcome to stay for as long as you like."

We appreciate your hospitality but there are things we need to do or we'll never be able to leave."

"I understand," Mingo said. "Want me to make that call for you?"

"There's someone I need to speak with, but calling probably wouldn't be wise. Can you take us to see him?"

"Why not?" he said. "Mingo's Taxi Service is always ready."

Rain was falling in a steady drizzle as we exited the dirt road onto a paved street. This time, Lucy and I were sitting in the front seat with Mingo. Even in the rain, a few tourists still roamed the sidewalks as we entered the French Quarter. Mingo stopped in front of Bertram's Bar. Leaving the motor running, he hurried inside. Lucy was nervous, practically ducking whenever car lights approached.

"I'll get in the backseat," I said.

"How do you know your friend is here?" Lucy asked.

"Bertram told us. Remember?"

"If you say so. Who is this guy again?"

"Eddie Toledo. Assistant Federal D.A."

"The womanizer?"

"That's Eddie," I said.

"What makes you think he won't turn us in?"

"Not gonna happen. Eddie's one of my best friends."

Lucy wasn't convinced. "Sure he doesn't have a conflict of interest when it comes to his bread and butter?" she said.

Mingo and Eddie came hurrying out of Bertram's before I could answer. Eddie climbed into the backseat with me.

"Where you been, Cowboy?" he said, pumping my hand.

"Hiding out, but you already knew that."

Eddie was from New Jersey. Even though his hair was a bit too long, he held the second highest government position in New Orleans. Eddie liked women, booze and gambling. A smooth operator, he had the ability to talk his way out of almost any situation. I had little doubt it was the only way he managed to retain his lofty, politically sensitive position.

Mingo pulled away from the curb. "Where to, Mr. Wyatt?"

"Circle around without being conspicuous. You know the drill."

Mingo was already heading toward Canal but gave me a thumbs up and a wink in the rearview mirror. Lucy turned to get a look at Eddie.

"I'm Eddie," he said, taking her hand. "You're even prettier than you are on T.V."

He didn't let go of her hand, and she didn't protest. Eddie had a way with women and Lucy took the bait.

"I don't feel very pretty right now," she said.

"Well I'm an expert on the subject, and I think you're gorgeous."

Eric Wilder

Lucy was probably blushing. The kaleidoscope of color caused by flashing neon and prismatic drops of water on the windows made it impossible to tell.

"Stop it," I said. "We have important things to discuss. Let go of her hand, Eddie."

Eddie and Lucy glared at me but both complied. "Sorry, Cowboy," Eddie said. "I get carried away when I'm around beautiful women."

"Stop working it. We need your help, or we wouldn't have risked coming downtown."

"Bertram said you wanted me to check out Dr. Louis Hollingsworth and a cult called Forces of Darkness."

"Find anything?"

"You kidding me? There are volumes written about Hollingsworth in this town. He's an icon."

"One with skeletons in his closet," I said. "Tell us something we don't already know."

"Maybe I better start with a few things you do know. Southern politics is corrupt. Louisiana takes it to a whole new level. You can get anything you want here in New Orleans with power and money."

"And?"

"Louis Hollingsworth had both. Dignitaries from Central and South America and every island in the Caribbean came to his clinic for treatment. They all knew him on a first-name basis. It made him a target for those seeking power and influence in the southern hemisphere."

"Such as the C.I.A.?" Lucy said.

"Yes. The Agency has been entrenched in New Orleans for decades, partially for that very reason," Eddie said.

"Who else?"

"Russia, Cuba, you name it," he said. "New Orleans is the door to the southern hemisphere, and everyone is looking for the key."

195

"What about Hollingsworth's connection with the Forces of Darkness?"

Eddie glanced out the window at a passing streetcar heading toward the river. Rain beaded off the windows, the lone passenger in the old rumble buggy nothing but a damp blur.

"A new one on me. I could find nothing on it, or anyone that knew anything," he said. "People in New Orleans have lots of crazy notions. Where did you come up with this one?"

I handed him the gold doubloon. "Check it out," I said.

Eddie hefted it in his hand and used the tiny flashlight on his keychain to get a better look at it.

"Gold," he said. "What's the significance of the engraving on the back?"

"Good eyes," I said. "Mark of the Beast, according to Madam Aja. Armand says it's the satanic symbol for Forces of Darkness. That's a 1948 Rex doubloon. Hollingsworth was King of Rex in 1948."

Eddie tossed the doubloon back to me. "How did you get involved in this mess?"

"A client hired me to find his mother's killer. None other than Dr. Mary Taggert. She worked with Hollingsworth and taught at Tulane.

"Heard about it," he said. "Probably the most macabre murder ever committed in a town where no murder is run-of-the-mill."

"The man never gave me his name, even though the police are tagging me as his murderer."

"Tim Taggert," Eddie said.

I glanced at Lucy to check her reaction. "So Dr. Mary did have a son?" she said.

"Yes she did. A loner raised mostly by his father although he spent summers here in the city with Dr. Mary and her female lover."

"How do you know?" I asked.

"Trust me, I know," he said.

Eric Wilder

Lucy peered over the bench seat, her chin resting on her forearms. "You know her lover's name?"

Eddie fidgeted. "I'm a Fed. I have access to dossiers on practically everyone of importance."

"Then do you know who killed Dr. Mary?"

"I know the name of her lesbian lover."

Mingo drove through a deep puddle and it splashed water on the windshield, impairing his vision until the wipers had time to catch up with the deluge.

"Don't keep us in suspense," I said.

"One of Dr. Mary's former students. A graduate of Tulane Medical School. Her name was Angelica Moon."

"Was?" I said.

"She disappeared the night Dr. Mary was murdered."

This time, Lucy gave me a glance. "Angelica is the name of the woman who accompanied Dr. Mary to the séances at Madeline's," Lucy said.

"The older man in the limo was probably Hollingsworth," I said.

"What older man?" Eddie asked.

"Madeline told us an older man would often wait for Angelica and Dr. Mary. She said it appeared the three might be romantically linked."

"Did she have a daughter named Tiana?" Lucy asked.

"Haven't heard that name," Eddie said. "Who is she?"

"Headmistress of the Order of the White Doves, a cult here in New Orleans possibly connected with the Forces of Darkness."

"What's her claim to fame?" he asked.

"She's possibly the granddaughter of Louis Hollingsworth."

"Did Madeline tell you Angelica was Creole?"

"I'm not following you," Lucy said.

"In Old New Orleans Creoles were people that had both black and white heritage," I said.

"Then Tiana Moon fits the description," Lucy said. "What's the significance?"

"Angelica Moon was the daughter of a very wealthy Creole businessman. She grew up in the Garden District. Her parents passed when she was in medical school."

"Then it's likely that Hollingsworth knew Angelica Moon," I said.

"And Dr. Mary," Lucy added.

"You think Hollingsworth killed Dr. Mary?" Eddie asked.

"Don't know," I said.

"At least you've established a connection."

"Wyatt's known it since Tim Taggert gave him the doubloon," Lucy said. "There's more to the story. I'd bet big on it."

"Why do you say that?" Eddie asked.

"Because when it comes to murder, the obvious suspect isn't always guilty," she said.

Eddie looked at me for confirmation. "Lucy's probably covered more murders than both of us," I said. "I trust her judgment."

Eddie was less than convinced. "Then what's the connection?"

"Forces of Darkness, Tiana Moon and her mother Angelica," Lucy said.

Mingo had circled through the cemeteries and was driving slowly toward Lake Pontchartrain. Rain continued to fall, the streets deserted. Eddie scratched his chin.

"Tell me again how you heard about Tiana Moon?" he said.

"Long story," I said. "Madeline had a vision during a spirit walk. She saw Tiana as a child, along with a much older man we now believe to be Hollingsworth. She gave us enough information, along with Mingo's help, to find the White Dove compound on Carondelet."

"The order is sinister," Lucy said. "They are into many bizarre practices, possibly even human sacrifice."

"You have to be kidding," Eddie said.

"Mingo's wife Mina worked at the compound," I said. "She witnessed some pretty unusual things."

"Such as?"

"Orgies involving the Doves, a bunch of expatriate Cubans and three men that frequented the compound."

"Cubans? You remember the three men's names?"

"Slink, Tex and . . ."

"Guy Marc," Lucy said.

Mention of the names must have piqued Eddie's interest. "Really?" he said.

"You know who we're talking about?" I asked.

"Maybe."

"Then don't keep us in suspense."

"This picture is becoming suddenly clearer. You've both probably heard of the secret monkey lab here in the city," he said.

"Lots of rumors; nothing concrete," Lucy said. "What do you know about it?"

"I managed to find this classified report," he said, showing it to us. "It's thick, and I didn't have time to read everything in it."

"Let me see," I said, taking the government publication. "Can I borrow your light?"

Eddie handed it to me and I used it to flip through the pages. A large, telescope-like instrument caught my attention. Lucy was hanging over the seat.

"What the hell is that?" she asked.

"Linear particle accelerator," Eddie said.

"Looks like a giant ray gun," I said.

"Pretty good analogy," Eddie said. "It's so powerful it can completely destroy matter."

"What was it used for?" Lucy asked.

"Mutating viruses, among other things."

"Like burning off an arm?" I asked.

"Huh?"

"Mary Taggert was a doctor. Maybe she worked at the monkey lab. Just a thought."

Eddie looked stumped. "Don't know," he said.

"Who headed this secret lab? The C.I.A.?" I asked.

"They funded it. No doubt about that. Don't know who ran it," he said.

Lucy flinched when a clap of thunder rocked Mingo's cab. Eddie reached across the seat and tapped his shoulder.

"Mingo," he said. "Can you turn this old doll around and head back to Canal?"

Chapter 24

Mingo was happy to comply, turning the car around and starting back toward Canal Street. Lucy could let Eddie's silence pass no longer.

"You know something else, don't you? Tell us," she said.

"The three men you mentioned. Slink is an ex-C.I.A. operative, Tex a mob hit man possibly linked to Kennedy's assassination."

"And the third man?" I said.

"Guy Marc Gagnon."

Lucy was growing impatient with Eddie's coyness. "Who is he?" she asked.

"The first Assistant Secretary of Health for the U.S. Public Health Service."

"Doesn't sound menacing to me," Lucy said.

"Maybe not, but every government health organization falls under the auspices of the U.S.P.H.S. It's civilian, not military and all the employees wear uniforms. The ASH has a rank equivalent to an Admiral in the Navy. Gagnon still wears his uniform."

I was still thinking about the secret lab described in Eddie's report. "Did his position as ASH make him the head man at the monkey lab?" I asked.

"Wouldn't be surprised," Eddie said.

Lucy had her mind on other things. "He must be pretty old. Sounds unlikely he'd be participating in orgies," she said.

"You'd think," Eddie said. "He has to be pushing a hundred."

"No way," Lucy said. "Surely Mina was talking about someone else."

"Don't think so," Eddie said. "I saw him a few months back at a government function, and he didn't look a day over sixty."

"Clean living?" I asked.

"I doubt anyone's ever accused him of that," Eddie said.

Lucy glanced out the window at the passing streetlamps. "I can understand the connection between the ASH and the C.I.A. How is the mob connected?"

"Maybe because Hollingsworth was a rightwing loony," Eddie said. "He founded an organization called New Orleans for Freedom. Lee Harvey Oswald distributed pamphlets for NOFF. Hollingsworth hated the Kennedys and everything about them."

"Organized crime didn't hate Kennedy," I said. "JFK had a mob girlfriend: Judith Campbell Exner. She supposedly carried on a relationship with Sam Giancana and Kennedy. Many of his friends had mafia ties."

"And organized crime didn't lose their casinos and resorts in Cuba because of him," Lucy said. "He did everything short of starting a nuclear war with Russia trying to oust Castro."

"Then why do lots of influential people suggest the mafia was complicit in the assassination?" Eddie asked.

"Good question," I said.

"Sounds like something we should look into," Lucy said.

"Good, because I uncovered a juicy bit of information while I was researching Hollingsworth for you," Eddie said.

"Tell us."

"NOFF dissolved after Hollingsworth's death. While he was alive, they maintained a small office here in town. I believe it's still at its original location."

"Where is that?" Lucy asked.

"On Canal, not far from here. It might be interesting to take a look."

"I'm game," Lucy said.

Eddie clutched her hand again. "You know anything I've told you is strictly off the record. My head would roll if anyone knew I'd met with you."

"My contacts are protected," she said. "I would never disclose this conversation."

"Believe me when I tell you that my nuts would roll if you did."

"Wouldn't want to put your family jewels in jeopardy," she said with a grin.

Eddie tapped Mingo's shoulder. "There's an office building up ahead on the left. Can you circle the block?"

Mingo glanced in the rearview mirror and saluted. For the first time in an hour, the rain had subsided to a slow trickle. Eddie pointed at an upper floor of the old building.

"No one has occupied this building for more than a decade. Interesting, because it's in a high-traffic area, right here on Canal Street."

"Who owns the building?" I asked.

"Someone with lots of stroke. There's no record of ownership; no deed, no tax records, no nothing."

"How can anyone get away with that?" Lucy said.

"We see such things all the time in the Justice Department. Limited liability corporations with

203

untraceable owners often buy buildings and significant properties."

"To hide assets and launder money," I said in answer to Lucy's puzzled look.

"Is this building owned by an LLC?" she asked.

"I found no record of ownership, not even by an LLC," he said.

"But you learned the NOFF office is located there," I said.

"Only because I'm a nosy bastard."

I had to laugh. "Better watch your back or someone will find you out and then have your family jewels on a platter."

"Thanks for your concern. Does this mean you're going to let me case the building alone?"

"You know better than that," I said.

Mingo drove into the shadows and let us out in the alley behind the building. Eddie was fired up and ready to go. For the first time since I'd met her, Lucy was speechless. She finally found her voice.

"Surely you can't be serious. You're a Federal D.A. Breaking and entering can't be part of your job description."

"Why not?" he said.

"How do you plan to get into the building? Bust a window and climb through?"

"No need for that," Eddie said. "If our man Wyatt hadn't been a lawyer and a P.I., he'd have made a hell of a cat burglar. There's not a lock around he can't pick or a door he can't open."

Lucy gave me a dubious look. "Is that right?"

"I worked for HUD during college. They paid me to break into houses they were trying to repossess. Once in, I'd cause a small ruckus. Just enough to get the police called. When the former owners were out of the house, we'd take possession and not let them return."

Lucy glared at me. "If we ever get out of this mess remind me never to speak to you again."

"Hey, I was a student, and that was a long time ago."

Lucy waved off my explanation. "Forget it. I'd already figured out you aren't exactly the Dalai Lama."

Ignoring our diatribe, Eddie was wandering around the back of the building looking for a place to enter.

"Over here," he called.

He'd found a loading dock with a sliding metal door big enough to drive a truck through. Lucy wasn't impressed.

"You can't be serious," she said.

"What do you think, Cowboy?"

"There's a keypad. The door opens with a code. Let me take a look."

Eddie and Lucy watched as I raised the plastic cover and studied the illuminated buttons.

"Think you can hack it?" Eddie asked.

I punched four buttons, and the door screeched as it began to open slowly.

"How'd you do that so fast?" Lucy asked.

"Some genius wrote the code on the back of the keypad cover with a magic marker. What now?"

Eddie was already heading down a dark corridor, the tiny keychain light his only illumination."

"My notes say the NOFF office is on the sixth floor. Here's a service elevator. Should we take it?"

"From the dust we're stirring up, I'd say we're the first visitors for a long time. Why not?"

"The electricity still works," Eddie said, punching the up button.

"I didn't think it could get any hotter or damper in this God-forsaken town. I was wrong and may have to come out of this blouse," Lucy said.

"Please do," Eddie said.

"Forget it, Eddie, and get your mind back on business. No one's taking their shirt off. At least not until we get out of this hell hole."

The old building was hot, the service elevator almost unbearable. Cables screeched as the cab rose slowly toward the sixth floor. When the doors opened, we saw a single entrance. The sign on the glass said, NOFF.

"Can you open it?" Eddie asked.

"If you have a credit card."

There was no deadbolt, and I easily opened the door with Eddie's American Express. The room we entered was even moldier and dustier than the hallway. When Lucy started sneezing, I thought we might have to abort our mission. Eddie came to the rescue, handing her a clean tissue, an allergy pill and a flask from the pocket of his linen jacket.

"I learned shortly after moving to N.O. that you should never be without certain necessities," he said.

Lucy blew her nose, took an allergy pill and swallowed it with a slug of Eddie's scotch.

"I could grow to like you," she said.

She blew her nose again and then used the crumpled tissue to wipe her eyes.

"That's my plan. Keep the tissue."

"And the flask?"

"I'll take care of the flask. You good now?"

"I'm okay. Where do we start?"

Eddie's flashlight cut a narrow swath through the swirling dust we'd stirred up. Lucy sneezed again.

"Great," she said. "I won't be able to breathe for a week."

Eddie ignored her discomfort. "Think we dare turn on the lights?"

"Don't do it," I said. "You have your light, and there's neon flashing through the window."

"I thought you said no one has been here for years."

"Something doesn't feel right," I said. "Let's just check these file cabinets and then get the hell out of here."

One desk and a dozen file cabinets filled the room. All were metal, Army green, and vintage 1950's. Two old electric fans hanging from the ceiling sat idle, frozen in time. A painting of Dwight Eisenhower hung from the wall along with a dusty old American flag. Linoleum covering the floors had started peeling away because of the heat and humidity rampant in the room.

"I'm going to open a window and let in some fresh air," I said.

"Start here," Eddie said, opening the file cabinet nearest to Lucy.

She grabbed the flashlight from his hand. "Let me. Everyone knows women are more efficient than men."

A gust of damp air filled the room as I opened two of the windows facing Canal.

"Don't argue with her, Eddie. She's always right."

Lucy ignored my wry comment, too busy rifling through the dusty files.

"Oh my God! Here's a dossier on Lee Harvey Oswald."

Eddie grabbed the file out of her hand. "Let me see it. Damn it! Let's turn on the lights."

"Don't do it," I said.

Lucy began stacking manila folders on top of the dusty old file cabinet. The stack was soon three feet thick. Eddie opened the file cabinet beside the one she was working and began sharing the light with her as he scanned the dusty files.

"Don't know if NOFF was complicit in the Kennedy assassination, but they were damn sure interested in the players," he said.

While Eddie and Lucy worked the file cabinets, I began opening desk drawers to see what I could find. The light filtering in from Canal was dim but just enough for me to see a mouse scurrying beneath my feet. It disappeared beneath a large rubber mat on the floor beside me. I lifted the edge of the mat to see where it had gone.

"Hey. Stop what you're doing a minute and bring the light."

"What is it?" Eddie asked.

I was on my knees, rolling up the mat and pushing it aside. "Shine your light down here."

"Lucy, see what Wyatt found," he said.

"This better be good," she said.

"It's a floor safe. Wyatt found a floor safe."

Eddie pointed the light at a rectangle incised in the floor, a recessed combination lock at its edge. I was already playing with the dial.

"Too large for that," I said. "I think it's a door."

"Can you open it?" Lucy said.

The cantilevered door popped open before I could reply. Eddie shined his light into the chasm.

"What is it?" he asked.

"A hidden room and there's a ladder."

"You're not going down there, are you?"

"Someone needs to."

"Then more power to you, big boy," he said.

Eddie shined the light for me while I climbed down the ladder. The eight by ten room was even mustier than the one above me. I felt around on the wall until I found a light switch. It didn't work.

"Toss me your keychain. There's an old fluorescent fixture, but it must be burned out."

Eddie threw me his keys. I missed his toss, and the keychain bounced across the cement floor, the impact extinguishing the tiny swath of light. I crawled around on hands and knees, trying to find it and hoping it still worked. I recoiled when I grabbed a beetle, and it squirmed in my hand.

Eddie's voice echoed off bare cement walls when he spoke.

"You okay?"

"Fine," I said as I found the flashlight and pressed the on button.

It came to life and I shined it at the table beside me. An old encryption device used during the Post-World War II era rested on it. A Big Chief pad of writing paper like the one I'd used in grade school sat beside it.

"What's down there?" Eddie asked.

"Don't know yet. Give me a minute."

There were no file cabinets. No furniture except for a single chair and the table where the encryption device sat. Not quite. There was a natural gas incinerator, vented to the outside. For destroying documents, I thought. As I continued surveilling the room, another sound began reverberating off the walls. Someone on the street below was laying on a car horn, the sound blaring through the open windows.

I knew I had to get out of the little room in a hurry, but a protruding sheet of paper in the encryption device caught my eye. A faded line below the perforations said page 2. I fumbled until I found a start button. When I pushed it, the device began to hum, and paper began slowly moving out of its feeder. Eddie was getting nervous.

"What's taking you so long?"

"Hang on," I said.

It seemed like an eternity for the device to stop printing. When it did, I grabbed the sheet and climbed back up the ladder, almost dropping the flashlight when Eddie grabbed my hand.

"Something's going on downstairs, and that has to be Mingo sitting on the horn trying to warn us. We need to get out of here, and fast."

By the errant light of damp neon floating up from Canal, I could see the anxious looks on their faces. They'd left a stack of manila folders atop one of the file cabinets. Lucy stopped to retrieve them. Instead, she managed only to drop the stack onto the floor. Outside, the horn continued to blare.

"Too late," I said. "I heard a metal door slam. Someone's coming up the stairs."

"Shit, shit, shit!" she said as she followed Eddie and me out into the hall.

"The service elevator," I said. "They probably don't know it still works."

We heard footsteps running up the stairs as we waited for what seemed an eternity for the elevator door to open. I didn't have to push Eddie and Lucy inside. Just in time. Spanish voices were shouting as they exited the stairwell.

"Hope no one's waiting on the bottom floor," Eddie said.

"If they are," I said, "Get out the door and run like hell."

A man waiting in the darkness reacted when the elevator door opened. Eddie punched him and he sank to his knees. Lucy kicked him for good measure and then hurried after us.

"Come on!" I yelled.

Once out the door, we ran into a southern squall, winds blowing at gale force. The headlights of a vehicle on the street shined through the storm. I had to shout for Lucy and Eddie to hear me.

"It's Mingo."

"What if it's not?" Lucy shouted back.

Mingo answered our questions, jumping the curb and sliding to a stop beside us.

"Hurry!" he said, holding open the front door.

He raced away from the curb, even before the door closed. Eddie grabbed Lucy's hand, pulling her inside as we slid around the corner onto Canal and headed for the river.

Lucy was distraught. "Dammit! So much valuable information we almost got killed looking at, and we came out with nothing."

"Not quite," I said.

Chapter 25

Tamela waved as the elevator door closed on Tony and Edna. Bent at the waist, eyes closed and holding her thigh, Edna was clearly in pain.

"You don't look so good," Tony said.

"I don't feel so good, either," she said.

"Gonna make it?"

She gave the floor a nervous tap with her cane. "Do I have a choice?"

Someone Tony recognized was waiting for them when the elevator door opened. Styling mousse slicked back his thinning hair, darkening it more than it already was. Lifts in his expensive Italian shoes rendered him a hair taller than Tony remembered. His silk ascot went well with his expensive maroon lounge jacket, and his Roman nose would have honored Caesar himself. At least ten years older than Tony, the man's teeth were anomalously straight and white.

Frankie Castalano was the infamous crime lord of New Orleans. Involved in everything from gambling to trash hauling, he'd recently hired Tony to find a missing cornet.

"Frankie!" Tony said. "You the last person I expected to see."

"You right. The real Frankie Castalano," he said when Edna cast him a frowning glance. "We got things to talk about."

They followed him into his penthouse suite, floor to ceiling windows highlighting the decor.

"Quite a spread," Tony said. "Never knew you owned a resort in the middle of the Gulf."

"My little secret. Adele asked me to say hello. My wife," he said to Edna.

Edna cast Tony another quizzical glance.

"Adele and her dad own the Via Veneto Italian Restaurant in Metairie. I introduced her to Frankie during a case I was working on," Tony explained.

Frankie wasn't smiling when he asked, "How's my old man's cat?"

"Didn't know you knew about that?" Tony said.

"I heard."

"Silky's fine. Lil fell in love with her, and now she's queen of the house. Gets more attention than me. Your pop would be proud."

"And your dog?"

"Patch has the run of the backyard. Lil's finally getting used to him, but he has hell to pay if he even looks at Silky sideways."

"Never knew you liked cats and dogs," Edna said.

"Late bloomer."

"Enough about pets and my old man," Frankie said. "We got a big problem."

He led them to the wet bar. From their vantage, they could see miles of rolling blue water. Frankie handed Tony a tumbler filled with scotch over ice.

"Thanks," he said.

"Edna? You ain't a teetotaler, are you?"

"Been called lots of names. Teetotaler isn't one of them."

"Glad to hear it," Frankie said. "I hate holier-than-thou types. What you drinking?"

213

"Whiskey, straight up. Wild Turkey, if you got it."

"Not much around here I ain't got," he said, pouring her whiskey.

The voice of Etta James singing Little Red Rooster gushed from hidden speakers as Tony and Edna sipped their drinks.

Frankie took a drink and then said, "Guess you're wondering what's going on."

"You didn't bring us all the way out here just to say hello."

"Adele made me promise I wouldn't let you get hurt. You owe her one, Tony. I like you, but if it wasn't for her, I woulda saved myself a shit-pot load of trouble and let Slink and his gang of Cuban crazies kill you."

"How'd you know about that?"

"Not much around here I don't know," Frankie said.

"Then maybe you can tell me what the C.I.A. and Cuba have to do with Mary Taggert's murder?"

"I ain't here to give history lessons. Figure it out for yourself."

"Mama Mulate's friend Doc Bruce thinks it has to do with the U.S. Public Health Service and a man named Gagnon."

Frankie smiled for the first time. "Not bad. The Admiral's in this up to his neck."

"Who are those men that rescued us? You hiring Russians to do your dirty work now?"

Frankie smiled again. "Spetsnaz."

"Pardon me?" Edna said.

"Russian special forces. The most elite military group in the world."

Tony scratched his chin. "Borya and Sasha don't work for you?"

"Just doing me a favor, though they seem to have an agenda I didn't know about."

"Spetsnaz?" Edna said.

214

"Baddest of the bad. Putin uses them when everything else goes to hell in a hand basket. Even ISIS and al-Qaeda are afraid of them."

"Why is that?" Edna asked.

"When Iraqi terrorists kidnapped a bunch of Russian dignitaries, Russian intelligence learned their identities. Spetsnaz corralled their relatives and began cutting off body parts until the militant group released the Russians. Believe me, when I tell you they kill without constraint."

"We found out as much last night," Tony said. "The little creep named Slink would have killed me, Mama, and Doc Bruce if Edna and your Russians hadn't stepped in."

Frankie became suddenly interested. "There was other people with you?"

"Mama Mulate knows Dr. Waters and arranged for him to take us to the medical compound. She went with us."

"What happened to them?"

"Borya took Mama and Doc Bruce to a hospital in Baton Rouge. What's the problem?"

"Nothing, except for a new layer of complications I don't need."

"Sasha was going to take them to a safe house after the hospital checked them out."

"Well, Sasha didn't make it," Frankie said.

"What happened?"

"Cuban mercenaries shot my chopper down with a ground-to-air missile."

"You shitting me?" Tony asked.

"Sasha's dead?" Edna said.

"I ain't shitting you and no, he ain't dead."

"How?"

My security boat patrols the platforms. When they saw the flash and heard the explosion, they high-tailed it out and reached the chopper before it sank."

"Good heavens!" Edna said.

Sasha was hanging onto the wreckage. My boys were pulling him out of the water when things got a little sticky."

"How so?" Tony asked.

"The Cuban gunboat that shot down the chopper came blasting through the fog, strafing everything with machine guns. My boys put a cannon round through their bow. Their gunboat sank like a sack of cement."

"What about Sasha?" Edna said.

"Shrapnel wounds, but no organ damage or broken bones. He's one lucky Russian."

"Those Cubans wouldn't attack your resort, would they?" Edna asked.

"Not unless they want to start a war with the U.S. and half the countries in Central and South America. The convention center downstairs is swarming with foreign dignitaries here for a conference. Hell, even Raoul Castro's in the building. Nobody's attacking nobody."

"Then what are you worried about?" Tony asked.

"The place is crawling with spies and secret agents looking for you and Sasha. I gotta get you out of here, or you'll be shark bait at the bottom of the Gulf before dark."

"What does any of this have to do with Tony and me trying to find out who killed Dr. Mary? Who the hell even cares anymore?"

"You'd be surprised," Frankie said. "Your leg okay?"

"A doctor shot me up with some good drugs, but it's starting to throb again."

"We'll get you some more. Meantime, I got plenty of whiskey."

"You know how to please a lady, Mr. Castalano," Edna said.

"Just Frankie," he said, topping up her glass with straight Wild Turkey.

216

"Russians, C.I.A., Cubans, U.S. Public Health Service, and now the mob. What else?" Tony asked.

"F.B.I., Krewe of Rex and an exclusive little satanic sect called Forces of Darkness."

"Can't you tell us anything else about what's going on?" Edna asked.

"If you're on a case, then you're getting paid. You figure it out. I'm not into charity cases."

Frankie slugged his drink and stood with his back to them, glancing out the window at a dark cloud moving up from the south. He didn't speak again until his cell phone rang.

"Bring him up," he said.

When the elevator bell sounded, Tamela appeared, pushing a man in a wheelchair. It was Sasha dressed in a blue jumpsuit. Tamela returned to the elevator, coming back with a rolling clothes rack. She handed Edna two pills.

"These might make you a little woozy," she said.

Edna put them in her pocket. "Right now, Frankie's whiskey is doing the trick. I'll save these for later." She knelt beside the wheelchair and touched Sasha's shoulder. "Sounds like you're lucky to be here."

He nodded. "Mama's gris gris. I was at the bottom of the Gulf when a hand grabbed my arm and pulled me up. I could not see who it was, but they held me on the sinking wreckage until Frankie's men rescued me."

Edna didn't comment but gave Tony a worried look.

"The drugs," Tamela said, seeing Edna's glance. "The doctors say he'll be okay. I'm sure it's true because he was flirting with me all the way here."

"I'd be even better if I could have a glass of vodka," Sasha said.

Frankie poured a shot and handed it to him. "Why not?"

"Fog is starting to roll in and two Cuban gunboats are lurking. They sank our security boat when it went out to confront them," Tamela said.

Frankie's reply was terse. "Sasha and you two pissed in their Post Toasties. We're in trouble here."

"What's with all the clothes?" Tony asked.

"We can't risk an international incident," Tamela said. "You'll stay until dark, and then we're going to the masquerade ball."

Chapter 26

Waiting for darkness, they watched a fog-shrouded sun finally sink beneath the Gulf's blue waters. Tamela finished her ginger ale and got up from the couch.

"Time to get dressed. Tony and Sasha, your costumes are in that bedroom," she said, pointing. "Edna, come with me."

They met again later, Tony and Sasha dressed in tuxedos, Tamela, and Edna in party dresses. Edna's face turned red when Tony whistled at her.

"Damn, Edna, I never seen you in a dress before. You got a great set of legs."

"Shut the hell up, or I'll have to deck you."

Edna was practically unrecognizable. Her short, red, low cut dress highlighted every curve of her body, her long hair put up on her head like a supermodel. Draping jewels and deftly applied makeup completed the transformation.

"You both look good," Sasha said, ogling Tamela's long legs sparkling with sequins.

"You like?" she said, doing a pirouette to show off her teal blue gown that matched Edna's, except for the color.

"Ooh la la!" Sasha said.

Tamela was pleased with Sasha's reaction. Edna was mortified, trying to cover her legs, but defeating her purpose by showing extra cleavage whenever she bent over.

"I feel naked," she said.

"You are beautiful," Tamela said. "Relax and enjoy it."

"Can't. This dress makes me feel too vulnerable."

"Then make believe," Tamela said. "Pretend you're a princess going to a ball."

"I feel more like a piece of meat waiting for a pack of wolves. I swear if anybody pinches my ass I'm going to deck them."

"I'll take that chance," Sasha said, running his hand up her leg.

Edna's face turned as red as her dress. She shook her fist at Sasha, but Tamela and Tony were laughing so hard they didn't notice.

"I'm old enough to be your grandmother," Edna finally said.

"I wish my nana looked like you," Sasha said.

The elevator door chimed. Frankie appeared, looking dapper in his tux.

"Okay, here's the game plan," he said. "There's a cigarette boat docked in the marina. We gonna party and mingle. When I give Tamela the signal, you'll go to the boat."

"What about the Cubans?" Sasha asked.

Nothing those damn Cuban's have can keep up with my cigarette. It'll take you up the river to New Orleans."

"What if we get separated?" Tony said.

"Get separated. It'll make you harder to spot," Tamela said. "When the disco ball drops and the strobes start to pulsate, make your way to the lighted star. It's just above the door to the marina. I'll be waiting."

"If you don't speak Spanish, then keep your mouths shut. There'll be agents in the room looking for you," Frankie added.

Feeling better, Sasha was up and walking. Tamela noticed.

"You have remarkable recuperative powers," she said.

"I would be happy to show you some of my other powers," he said.

His words made her blush. She poked him in the ribs without commenting on his other perceived powers.

"Most of the people at the ball are Spanish, so, like Mr. Castalano advised, refrain from speaking English. You never know who you might be talking to."

"Don't know if I can make it without a drink," Tony said.

"I have an idea," Tamela said.

She spent the next thirty minutes applying face paint in various colors. Frankie approved.

"No one will recognize you now," he said.

"I feel like a French Quarter prostitute," Edna said.

"You're beautiful," Tamela said. "You're going to have men all over you."

Edna's eyes crossed. "That's what worries me."

The elevator from Frankie's penthouse suite opened directly into the giant ballroom. With gaudily painted faces covered by Mardi Gras masks, they stepped out of the elevator and began mingling directly with the crowd.

Everyone was in masks and costumes, or tuxedos and ball gowns, and all dripping in jewels. A salsa band was rocking out on the bandstand, but no one seemed to notice.

The resort crew had transformed the ballroom into a tropical island complete with potted palms and grass huts. Colorful decorations, including netting, piñatas, and tropical waterfowl completed the ruse. Lights turned low in the ballroom enhanced the mood of the costumed partiers. Copious quantities of alcoholic beverages contributed to the illusion. Tamela gave the gang the signal to spread out.

"Can I go with you?" Sasha asked.

"If you can keep your mouth shut," Tamela said, grabbing his hand and pulling him into the crowd.

Edna jumped when someone pinched her rear. "I don't like this," she mumbled.

"Relax," Tony said. "These Latinos are all touchy-feely."

"Yeah, well they'll be pulling back a nub."

"I need a drink," Tony said. "Just go with the flow."

Tony didn't wait for a response, pushing through the crowded ballroom to a nearby bar. When he got his scotch, he realized he couldn't drink it without pulling up his mask. Remembering his face was blue, he raised it and took a drink.

Sasha was wearing a blond wig to complete his disguise. Tamela held his hand as she pulled him through the crowd.

"I'm getting a hard-on," he said.

Tamela blushed again, but her mask concealed it. "I said, no more English."

"I speak fluent Spanish, and five other languages."

She jerked him behind a large potted palm and said, "Then no more English, just Spanish."

"Bésame mucho," he said, removing her mask.

They embraced and kissed, long and sensually.

"I think I'm in love," he said in Spanish.

"In lust is more like it. Too bad I'll never see you again after tonight."

"Then let's make the most of the darkness."

"Right here behind the potted plants?"

"Please," he said.

"Forget it, buddy. You're cute, but I'm not losing my job because of you."

"I'd give up my life for you," he said.

"Hopefully not tonight," she said, twisting his ears and kissing him again.

Edna tried to ignore the little man following her through the crowd, but he wouldn't let her.

"Como estas?" he said, catching up to her.

Edna cleared her throat, tapped her chest and pointed toward the bar.

"Si si," the little man said, turning away to get Edna a drink.

"Close one," Edna said beneath her breath as she moved away in the opposite direction.

Her ploy didn't work, the little man somehow spotting her in the crowd. When she bumped into him, she almost knocked the drinks out of his hands.

"Gracias," she said.

The little man did a double take when Edna raised her mask—revealing her bright crimson make-up—and then drained the glass of wine.

"Mi amor," he said, on his tiptoes to kiss her.

It was more than Edna could take and she quickly kneed him in the balls. When he groaned loudly and bent at the waist, she lowered her mask and plunged back into the crowd.

Happy for the moment, Tony had found a buffet laden with gumbo, crawfish and all the fixings of a Cajun bayou fete. He tried not to worry about someone recognizing him as he bit into a spicy ear of corn-on-the-cob. Partaking in the same repast, the people around him didn't seem to notice. He stopped eating when he spotted Edna heading for the bar. He saw someone else he also recognized.

Edna's thigh had started throbbing again. She had the pain pills in her tiny purse but needed something to drink. After looking to see if the little nuisance was following her, she made her way through the crowd toward one of the little grass shack bars.

The salsa band had fired up a spicy Latin favorite, and much of the crowd had formed a conga line snaking through the large ballroom. When she reached the bar, she bent at the waist, grabbing her thigh. Raising her head long enough to point to a bottle of whiskey, she jumped when someone tapped her shoulder.

"It's me," Tony said.

He hushed her when she started to speak, pointing to the person standing beside her. He didn't have to explain. The spider tattoo on his hand with the bloody dagger piercing it said it all. It was Slink in a mask and his black sports coat.

The little makeshift bar was busy, costumed people crowding closer to get drinks. The bartender dressed in white didn't notice Edna taking her drink and backing away without adding cash to his tip jar. Tony motioned with a nod for her to follow.

Waiters and waitresses dressed in colorful calypso costumes moved through the crowd, dispensing drinks. Tony snagged one on their way to a quiet spot between two palms swaying in the artificial trade winds.

"Slink's goons are everywhere. They're checking I.D.s at all the entrances."

"Then we're screwed," Edna said. "We'll never get out the door."

"Unless . . ."

"What's up your sleeve?"

"I picked up a lighter someone left on the bar. If I'm not mistaken, there's a smoke detector above that piñata. If I could light the piñata, it would set off the fire alarm and maybe activate the sprinkler system."

"And cause a distraction until we can get out of here. I like it."

"Problem is, I can't quite reach it."

"I can, if you lift me on your shoulders. This crowd is so crazy, I doubt anyone would notice."

"Slink would," he said. "We need a diversion."

Three men dressed in dark pants, and black sports coats were moving through the crowd toward them.

"What now?" Tony asked.

"Grab a spot in the conga line. When we dance beneath the piñata, I'll climb on your back and light it."

"What if the escape boat's not ready?"

"Guess we jump over the side and swim back to New Orleans."

"Good plan," he said, pushing into the crowd as the raucous conga line passed between them and the approaching Cubans.

Tony and Edna grabbed a spot in the line. So many in the ballroom had joined in, it looked like a giant boa constrictor writhing through the room. The salsa band had gotten into the number, the conga drummer going wild as trumpets, trombones and saxophones rattled the windows.

The rhythm was infectious, both Edna and Tony getting caught up in the beat. Their only problem was they had no control over which way the dancers would go. They had almost reached the piñata when the man leading the drunken procession turned in the opposite direction.

Edna had managed to take the two pain pills before draining her drink. Now, her thigh was thankfully numb. Unfortunately, so were her senses. She giggled when she bumped a man in black as they danced to the solo launched by the conga drummer.

The line finally came close to the piñata. The problem was, three Cubans were also standing near. Tony dropped out of the line and bent down.

"Hop on," he said. "It's now or never."

Chapter 27

Everything began happening fast when Edna crawled on Tony's shoulders. Thinking it was part of the dance, several couples emulated them. The conga line continued, women in gowns and scanty costumes straddled over their partner's shoulders. Edna and Tony didn't notice.

The lighter was almost out of fuel and Edna was about to throw it across the room when a spark ignited the paper piñata. Filled with something flammable, it exploded, belching dark smoke across the ceiling. It didn't end there, other ornaments catching fire and filling the large room with billowing smoke. Edna winced and grabbed her thigh when she jumped down from Tony's shoulders.

"You did it, girl. Now let's get the hell out of here before we get trampled."

Trampled indeed. Sounds of laughter and frivolity quickly changed to ear-piercing screams and frightened shouts. That's when the sprinkler system began spraying water from the ceiling.

Frantic masqueraders jammed up at the main exits, trying to get out. Good for Tony and Edna as they hurried to the obscure door exiting to the marina.

"Hope I didn't kill anybody," Edna said. "Except for maybe Slink and his goons."

A misty wind blew in their faces as they hurried down the metal walkway, trying to find Frankie's getaway boat. They weren't prepared for what they saw.

Dozens of boats lay moored at the marina, some of the super yachts as big as ships complete with landing pads for helicopters. They felt the waves lapping against the boats as they hurried down the walkway in muted darkness lighted only by fluorescent pole lamps. Tony glanced behind them as smoke billowed out of the exit from where they had just come.

"We're in trouble. Slink's goons are following us," he said.

"What now?"

"Hope like hell we find our boat before they catch us."

Chaos had ensued in the smoky ballroom, firefighters and curious onlookers moving toward the scene. Fortunately, the sprinkler system had quickly doused the flames. Frankie's insurance company would have a claim for smoke and water damage. Tony and Edna had other things about which to worry. The cloying mist had suddenly turned to heavy rain, making the steel walkways slippery between the boats. Worse, pistol shots whistled over their heads. Tony bent over to catch his breath.

"I'm gassed," he said. "Go on without me."

"Shut the hell up and come on!" she said, kicking off her high heels and grabbing his wrist.

The docks were a maze of walkways. Edna changed directions, hurrying down a short flight of stairs and then ducking onto a narrow catwalk.

"This way," she said.

"How do you know?"

"Don't, but it's dark. If we can't find the boat, we need a place to hide."

"What about that skiff?" he said.

"Won't give us much cover."

"No, but it has a motor. Let's get out in the water with it."

"You know how to drive a boat?"

"Never driven one that big, but how different can it be?"

"No time to ask," she said, jumping down into the open boat. "Can you start this thing?"

"No key, just a starter button," he said, fumbling with the controls.

Heavy rain continued, their clothes drenched as the engine cranked and Tony maneuvered the boat through the narrow canal leading to open water.

"Waves are tossing out there. Hope this tub can take it," he said.

Edna's fancy hairdo had come undone, and she wiped her face to get it out of her eyes.

"Too late to worry about that."

Once out of the canal, the boat began to rock and yaw.

"I think we're screwed," Tony said as a bullet hit the side of the boat.

"Crank it, Tony. I'd rather drown than die from a Cuban bullet wound."

"You picked your poison," Tony said, cranking the engine and accelerating toward open water.

Conditions continued to deteriorate as he guided the boat in a large circle around the resort. Vision was nil as he slowed to a near stall. They were both trying to cover their heads when a bright spotlight powered through the fog toward them.

"Shit!" Tony said, gunning the engine to avoid almost certain contact with the large boat bearing down on then.

A percussive explosion followed by a large splash off the starboard bow quickly informed them it was a Cuban gunboat. It turned before hitting them, its light disappearing in the fog. Not for long. Piercing the wall of rain, it again pointed in their direction. Another cannon blast landed close enough to rock them in the already swirling water.

"They're tracking us," Edna yelled.

Tony did a one-eighty, heading straight toward the light before making an abrupt right turn. It slid Edna across the floor of the open boat. When she grabbed for a wooden support, she found where the life vests were stored. She quickly strapped one on.

Walking was impossible, so she worked her way on hands and knees to the lone seat behind the helm. Grabbing Tony's arm, she looped a life vest under it, and then wrestled it around his chest. He let go of the wheel long enough to cinch the jacket. When the boat yawed, they saw the light of the Cuban gunboat again. Edna barely had time to yell.

"They're going to hit us!"

Tony grabbed her hand and tugged. "Time to abandon ship!"

With locked hands, they jumped overboard, mere seconds before the collision with the Cuban gunboat. Just in time as the boat burst into a thousand flying pieces.

Saltwater burned Tony's eyes and nostrils as he struggled to reach the surface. Somehow, he managed to retain his grip on Edna's hand. They burst from the roiling water at the same instant, both gasping for breath and coughing up saltwater. Edna was the first to recover.

"You okay?" she said, shouting in his ear.

"Alive," he said. "Now what?"

"Stay that way until the storm passes and hope some friendly fishermen rescue us."

"And hope like hell that sharks don't get us before it happens."

"You could have gone all night without bringing that up," she said.

The storm continued for another hour and then disappeared as abruptly as it had started. Full moonlight shined through the clouds. Best of all, the Cuban gunboat was nowhere in sight. Exhausted, they'd both nodded off when a splash in the water awoke them. It was Sasha.

Beside them, Frankie's cigarette boat danced on gentle waves. Sasha handed them a line and someone began pulling them toward it. Tamela and a man they didn't recognize helped them into the boat.

"We've been worried sick," Tamela said.

"How did you find us?" Edna asked.

"Tracking device sewn into your clothes. We have no armaments to fight the gunboat, so we had to wait until they gave up their search."

"I'm Captain Sweeny," the muscular man with a bronze tan, blond hair and a colorful anchor tattooed on the back of his arm said. "Here's a couple of dry towels."

Tony took one and began drying his face and hair. "They think we drowned?"

"Maybe," Tamela said. "Or else waiting until someone like us starts nosing around. We need to go before they return. There's a cabin below. No shower but you'll find dry clothes."

When Edna and Tony returned from the cabin, the boat was moving at a high rate of speed. Captain Sweeny was at the open helm, Sasha beside him. They joined Tamela on a bench seat near the rear of the boat. A wall and Plexiglas windscreen shielded them from the wind and they could communicate without shouting.

231

"Never gone this fast in a boat," Edna said.

"Probably doing sixty," Tamela said. "Barring more bad weather, we should make it to the mouth of the Mississippi in a few hours."

"Lil's gonna kill me," Tony said.

"You are covered," Sasha said. "She's at the safe house."

"What about . . . ?"

Tamela didn't let him finish. "Your pets are fine. She has them with her."

"No one to worry about me," Edna said.

Tamela touched her hand. "I was. I'm so happy you are both safe."

"So are we."

"Mr. Castalano asked me to implore you to end your investigation," Tamela said.

Tony glanced at Edna. "I can go it alone if this has gotten too much for you."

Her cynical smile could have answered for her. "Before Slink stabbed me I was merely curious. Now, I'm pissed off, and nothing's going to stop me short of a bullet."

"What about Sasha?" Tony said. "What interest does Dr. Mary's murder have to do with the Russians?"

"I know little more than you do," she said.

"Come on," Edna said. "You're Frankie Castalano's trusted assistant. Surely he's confided with you many times."

Tamela hesitated a moment before saying, "Mister Castalano wouldn't confide with his own mother."

"Brutal," Tony said.

"But true. Everything I know I've picked up by keeping my ears open."

"Then at least give us that much," Tony said. "We're on your side here."

The sky was again turning dark, and Tamela glanced up at it. When it began to rain, she reached into a storage bin and handed each of them a hooded slicker. Heavy rain was soon blowing in their faces. Wave action had increased, and Captain Sweeny slowed the boat.

"Well?" Edna said, not letting Tamela off the hook.

"I can't violate Mr. Castalano's trust."

Tony was having none of it. "We wouldn't want you to. We already know the C.I.A., Cuba, the U.S. Public Health Service, the mob, and Russian Special Forces are involved in a cover up of some sort," he said. "Hell, we even know the Krewe of Rex and some obscure satanic sect is somehow connected. We just need to put it all together. Throw us a bone here."

"Please, baby," Edna said. "You know something you can tell us, don't you?"

Tamela cleared her throat. "A while back, I audited some courses at Tulane."

"And?" Edna prompted.

"I did it for a reason. I'm not a complete idiot about who I'm working for. I knew what I was getting into before I took the job."

"The resort seems perfectly legal to me," Tony said.

"It is, but you can't work as closely to Mr. Castalano as I do without hearing what I probably shouldn't hear."

"Like the mobs involvement in the Kennedy assassination?"

Tamela nodded. "It happened long before I was born. I became curious about it as my work with the company evolved."

"And Frankie never told you nothing?" Tony said.

"References to Tulane kept popping up, so I enrolled and took a few history courses. You know, just to nose around."

"And?"

One of my professors seemed to know more than what's written in the books."

"Tell us about him," Tony said.

"A woman, not a man. We became friends, of sorts. She liked to drink. When she did, she'd tell me things."

"Drunk talk?" Edna said.

"Yes, but with a ring of truth, some of it so crazy and disjointed, I never really put it together."

"What's her name?" Edna asked.

"Sinthia Burnwitch."

"You gotta be kidding," Tony said.

Tamela shook her head slowly. "She's as weird as anyone I've ever met."

"What did you learn from her?" Edna asked.

"That there was a complicated conspiracy no sane person would ever believe."

"Does she still teach at Tulane?" Edna asked.

"That's as much as I know," Tamela said with a perfunctory wave of her hand.

The sky had darkened, rain falling increasingly harder. Tamela had pulled her slicker tightly around her head and grown silent. The boat was barely moving in the choppy water lathered with whitecaps. It stopped completely after a metallic thump. Sasha left the helm and joined them.

"Mechanical problems. The boat can go no further and the captain is reporting movement about fifteen clicks south of us. Two boats, probably Cuban."

"Oh, shit!" Tamela said.

"Our boat is without power," he said, shaking his head.

"What then?"

"The captain has an M-60 machine gun and two thousand rounds of ammunition. We fight."

"I know you're a soldier, brother," Tony said. "But they have cannons that'll shoot lots farther than the Captain's popgun."

"You were in military?"

"Army reserve. I trained with the M-60."

"Then you can feed the rounds for me," Sasha said.

"They're gonna blow us out of the water before they get close enough for you to use that peashooter."

"We must fight," Sasha said.

"Hell, man! Didn't they teach you in the Russian army you don't take a pocket knife to a gunfight?"

"I will never surrender."

"No one's surrendering, but we can't just fire blindly into the darkness until our bullets are gone."

"What else can we do?"

"If you don't have a plan to win a war, then you don't fight it."

"What plan?" Sasha asked.

Tony didn't answer, turning to Tamela instead. "See if the captain has some empty jars. Edna, find us some gasoline."

"Molotov Cocktail," Sasha said with a smile.

Tony slapped his shoulder. "Go help Tamela and Edna, and hurry. We don't have much time."

Captain Sweeny was less than cooperative. An ex-marine, he wanted to take control of the situation. Sasha tried to change his mind.

"We have a plan."

"I'm the captain. I'll call the shots," Captain Sweeny said.

"You work for Mr. Castalano," Tamela said. "This is his boat."

"I'm in charge until Mr. Castalano relieves me."

"In his absence, I have the authority to do just that. Consider yourself fired."

Captain Sweeny raised the machine gun and pointed it at them. "This says I'm still captain.

When the Cubans arrive, I'm turning you over to them."

"You sabotaged the boat and sold us out," Tamela said.

"Shut the hell up," he said, waving the gun.

His movement was all the distraction Sasha needed. Launching himself into a fast-spinning pirouette, he kicked the gun out of Captain Sweeny's hands. When it skidded across the deck, Sweeny dived for it.

The ex-marine was fast, Sasha faster. They wrestled no longer than a moment before the Russian got his arms around the larger man's throat. When it broke with a sickening pop, Sasha released his grip, letting the dead captain slump to the deck. Two Cuban gunboats appeared from the mist before anyone could react to Sweeny's abrupt demise. The explosion from the cannon round over the bow sent salt water splashing into their faces. Tony grabbed a bullhorn.

"Don't shoot. We surrender," he said.

Tony's pronouncement caught the Cubans by surprise. There was a pause before they responded on their bullhorn.

"Where is your captain?" someone asked.

"Dead," Tony said.

"You killed him?"

"Accident. He slipped on deck and broke his neck."

"You have weapons?"

"Just this machinegun," Tony said. It splashed in the water when he tossed it over the side. "We're unarmed. We surrender."

"Use your raft and come to our boat."

"Can't," Tony said. "Some of your shrapnel deflated it.

"Then prepare to be boarded," the Spanish man said.

The storm had abated, only a fine mist falling on their faces. One of the gunboats began moving slowly toward them.

"We can only destroy one of the boats," Sasha said. "The other will surely sink us."

Tony ignored his warning. "Light and launch when the boat touches us. When it catches fire, we abandon ship into the dinghy." Instead of the machine gun, he'd thrown two oars and an anchor overboard. The big gun was still at his feet." Hope you're as good as you think you are with old trusty here."

The Cuban gunboat appeared through the mist, several armed men on its bow. Sasha was the first to toss his Molotov cocktail, the others quickly following. Nothing prepared them for the explosion that ensued. Sasha swept the deck with the machine gun before joining the others in the rubber dinghy.

Tony cranked the engine, guiding the tiny craft through the smoke and away from the burning gunboat. Instead of powering in the opposite direction, he moved in a wide arc toward the other Cuban vessel.

"Hold on to your hats," he said. "Wait until I get close before throwing your cocktails. When it catches fire, I'm going to turn and run. Sasha, you empty that thing on them when I do."

They were within a hundred feet of the second gunboat when something unexpected happened. Out of nowhere, a torpedo came whistling through the water. It slammed into the gunboat, the blast from the ensuing explosion knocking them across the dinghy. The boat lit the sky as it exploded into a thousand fiery fragments.

Chapter 28

The gunboat's explosion lighted the horizon as the bow of a submarine broke the water's dark surface.

"Now what?" Tony asked.

Sasha shook his head and said, "U.S. Navy."

"Whose side are they on?" Edna asked.

Sasha's answer was short. "Hopefully, ours."

The hatch opened and a man in a naval uniform climbed out on the deck.

"Ahoy. Everyone okay?"

"Who's asking?" Tony yelled.

"Ensign Drake Anderson, United States Navy."

"Permission to come aboard, sir," Sasha said.

"Granted."

More men appeared on deck to assist the four castaways out of the dinghy. Sasha smiled, saluted, and then gave Ensign Anderson a big hug.

"You owe us one Lieutenant Antakov."

"No way," Sasha said. "We were about to blow that gunboat to hell when you intervened."

"Knowing you, you probably were."

"You two know each other?" Tamela asked.

"Let's just say we've done business on more than one occasion," Ensign Anderson said.

"I did not think you would make it," Sasha

said.

"Always available to assist my Russian brother. Sure you could have handled things on your own?"

"With help from the New Orleans Police Department," Sasha said.

"Pleased to meet you," he said, shaking Edna's hand. "And you are?"

"Edna Callahan. This is Tony Nicosia and Tamela, though I never caught her last name."

"Myles," Tamela said.

"Was that a torpedo that knocked out the Cuban gunboat?" Tony asked.

"It was. Always a rush experiencing it in action."

"That's a fact," Tony said. "Try being on the other end sometime."

Ensign Anderson didn't comment as he led them down a dimly lit corridor in the submarine's interior. Like Tony, Edna, and Tamela, he traversed the passageway easily without mussing his close-cropped brown hair. Several inches taller than six feet, Sasha had to stoop.

"You're on board the battle class U.S.S. Morgan City, specially designed for river running," Ensign Anderson said.

"How so?" Tamela asked, instantly attracted to the handsome, clean-cut young officer.

"This sub is smaller and more maneuverable than your larger, sea-roaming craft. The river at Baton Rouge, for instance, is only fifty feet deep, but we can get there underwater and undetected."

"Or any other river port cities around the world," Sasha said.

"That's classified," Ensign Anderson said with a grin, though he didn't deny the allegation.

"Can you make it all the way to New Orleans?" Edna asked.

"Easily. The river is almost two hundred feet deep opposite the French Quarter. That, in fact, is where I'm taking you."

"That'll cause quite a stir with the tourists," Tamela said.

"Not to worry, ma'am," Ensign Anderson said. "They'll never know we were there."

"Been there before?" Edna asked.

"Many times, ma'am," he said.

"You are very young to have command of a submarine," she said.

"I'm just the acting C.O., filling in while the captain's away. His wife's having a baby."

"Wonderful," Edna said, realizing no one on board was likely older than thirty.

Because of cramped quarters in the control center, Ensign Anderson led them to a tiny commissary near the galley. Tony squeezed in next to Edna, savoring the aroma of freshly brewed coffee.

"Wouldn't mind sharing a cup of java, would you?" he asked.

"Do you one better than that," the ensign said. "How does breakfast sound?"

"Glorious," Edna said. "I'm starving."

A smiling enlisted man nodded when Ensign Anderson introduced him. Like the ensign, he was short and his hair closely cropped.

"Bet those wet clothes aren't very comfortable," he said. "Seaman Jones has dry clothing for you."

They returned to the commissary wearing navy issue coveralls and soft-soled boat shoes.

"That must have helped because you are all smiling," the ensign said. "Now, one of my men will take your order. When you finish eating, there's a bunk where you can get some sleep before we reach our destination."

They were soon feasting on steak and eggs served with hash browns and wheat toast. Shrouded in eerie silence and cut off from sights and sounds of the surface, Tony had lost track of time. It didn't matter as he had a second helping of scrambled eggs along with several cups of coffee. Edna pushed her plate away and sat with crossed arms.

"Don't mean to be nosy, but what exactly is going on here?" she asked.

The ensign's terse reply was evasive. "I'm not sure what you mean."

Edna expected no less, but was persistent. "You just blew up a Cuban gunboat in the Gulf of Mexico. Surely, there'll be repercussions."

"Not my job to worry about," he said. "I just follow orders. How's your thigh?"

"How do you know about that?"

"Let's just say a little birdie told me," he said.

"Starting to throb a bit," she said.

Seaman Jones handed her a vial of pills. "These will help," he said.

Tony and Edna were the only two to opt for sleep. Sasha and Tamela stayed with Ensign Anderson while Seaman Jones led them to cabins. Tony was sitting on the side of his bunk when someone knocked on the door. It was Edna.

"Haven't had a chance to talk with you for a while. Maybe we better take the opportunity now."

"Good idea. Drank too much coffee to sleep anyway."

Edna sat beside him on the bunk. "This whole scenario gets weirder by the hour."

"I hear you," Tony said. "Makes you kinda wonder who is running things in Washington."

"Or anywhere else, for that matter. Lots of odd bedfellows here."

"Got that right," Tony said.

"According to Doc Bruce, Guy Marc Gagnon maimed Dr. Mary purposely. Why didn't he finish the job?"

Tony scratched his chin and shook his head. "You're right. I'd bet money the research facility had a crematorium."

"He could have killed her with that ray gun of his and disposed of her body as easily as cremating one of his dead monkeys. No one would have ever known."

"Then why didn't he?" Tony asked

"Maybe he wanted to send someone a message," Edna said.

"Someone like Angelica Moon?"

She nodded. "Or maybe Louis Hollingsworth."

"Or both, but why?"

"Teach them a lesson maybe?"

"Could be," Tony said.

"The Warren Commission was in town the very day of Dr. Mary's murder. They never got a chance to talk to her."

"Maybe she gave Gagnon reason to believe she was going to tell them something he didn't want them to know."

Edna clasped her hands, the faint metallic ping they kept hearing reminding her they were on a submarine heading for New Orleans.

"He kept her from doing that, and sent a message to anyone else thinking of spilling their guts to the Commission," she said.

"Like Hollingsworth and Moon?"

"Exactly."

Tony awoke on a strange bunk, not immediately remembering where he was. When Edna knocked on the door, it returned to him.

"You awake in there?" she said.

"Barely."

"We're close to our destination. Tamela woke me a few minutes ago to tell me. Thought I'd give you some warning."

"Thanks," he said.

Twenty minutes later, they were standing in a light rain on the deck of the submarine. It was dark and he could see lights of the city in the distance. The sub was near the center of the river as seamen prepared a motorized dinghy.

"The safe house is on the bluff," Ensign Anderson said, pointing.

"Have to trust you on that. My eyes aren't what they used to be," Edna said.

"Hard to see because of all the trees and vegetation. We'll drop you off and someone will be waiting."

"Thanks, young man. We'd be dead now if you hadn't come along."

"You are welcome, ma'am. We'll remain in the vicinity in case you need us," he said.

"How will you know?" Tony asked.

"Sasha and I are in contact. I'll know."

Tamela gazed at the river, toward the lights of the city. "What happens if someone sees you? I'm sure it would cause a stir if a nuclear submarine was spotted in the river a mile from New Orleans."

"Ever seen a flying saucer, or a ghost?"

Tamela shook her head. "No, but I've heard other people say they have."

"Did you believe them?"

"I see your point," she said.

Ignoring decor, Edna hugged the young man as he and Sasha saluted each other. The river was rolling, Tony more than happy he didn't suffer from seasickness as they motored away in the rubber boat.

Borya and Vladimir huddled onshore as a crew member jumped into the water and pulled the dinghy to land. Borya and Sasha embraced.

"You are like a cat," he said. "But you are rapidly using up all of your lives."

"I still have at least one left," Sasha said. "This is Tamela. She works for Mr. Castalano."

"At least I used to," she said. "I'm not supposed to be here."

"I have it on good authority that your job is safe and waiting for you," Sasha said.

"Sure about that?"

Tamela smirked and shook her head when he said, "Would I lie?"

"What is this place?" she asked.

"A simple river camp," he said. "Let me show you around."

Chapter 29

The tall bluff looming above them formed a natural levee on the river. On the cut-bank side of the downriver flow, it rose fifty feet into the air. They soon realized Sasha's river camp was anything but simple.

The camouflaged door in the bluff to which he led them turned out to be an elevator. They were soon on a wooden deck overlooking the river that afforded them a magnificent view.

Lights on the Crescent City Connection, New Orleans' twin bridges, illuminated the hazy river. The Riverwalk and the French Quarter sparkled behind it. For the first time, Tony realized he was no longer in the middle of the Gulf of Mexico. The interior of the cabin was unlike anything he'd imagined.

The place was anything but a cabin. What looked small from the deck was spacious yet cozy. The room seemed like an expensive hunting lodge complete with stone fireplace and a bearskin rug. Colorful Indian blankets and animal trophies mounted on the walls completed the illusion. Mama was waiting when they entered the back door. When she saw them, she rushed to hug Tony.

"I've been worried. Borya wouldn't tell me much, but I sensed you were in danger."

"We're okay," he said. "Sasha told us Lil was here."

"They took her to your mother-in-law's house in Shreveport, along with your puppy dog and kitty cat."

"She okay?"

"Anxious, but once Borya explained the situation, and that you are safe, she understood. You'll need to call her."

"I been worried," he said.

"Worry no more," Borya said. "Anyone attempting to harm her will have to go through the Russian army first."

"Good to know, I guess," Tony said.

"We have to debrief Sasha," Borya said. "Mama is familiar with the safe house and will show you around."

Sasha and Tamela smiled at each other as the Russians disappeared down a hallway.

"And who is this pretty young thing?" Mama asked.

"Tamela works for Frankie Castalano."

"That can't be true. You look too sweet and innocent to be a mobster."

"Don't know anything about that," Tamela said with a smile. "I work for one of Mr. Castalano's legitimate businesses."

"Good." Mama squeezed Edna's hand. "I'm happy everyone is safe."

"Doc Bruce . . . ?

"Not good," Mama said. "He left the safe house."

"Where did he go?" Edna asked.

"Back home. I tried to stop him, but he said he wanted to die in his bed. Vladimir took him."

"That ain't good," Tony said.

"Who is Doc Bruce?" Tamela asked.

246

"A friend," Edna said. "What's the story on this place?"

Mama was quick to respond. "Seems like a quaint hunting lodge, but it's more like a little Russian military base."

They left the pine-scented room, following Mama down a long hallway. The trappings of a hunting lodge quickly disappeared, replaced by unfinished cement walls, and recessed fluorescent lighting.

"This complex tunnels into the bluff. There are barracks for lots of troops that seem to come and go, a large mess hall, and a virtual beehive of computers, sophisticated radio equipment, and intelligence personnel."

"Looks like an old fishing camp from the outside," Tony said.

"Only one road leads in and out, the entrance camouflaged and guarded. There's even a turret on the roof with a machine gun emplaced. This is where their guests stay."

A fire pit centered a circular room complete with T.V.'s, sofas and lounge chairs. Tamela warmed her hands near the open flame.

"Nippy in here," she said.

"This is my room," Mama said, opening one of the doors circling the room. "It's nicer than many five-star hotels I've stayed at."

A tiny terrace, mostly concealed by potted plants and native vegetation, looked out over the river. The sliding door was open, and Mama's three cats wandered inside when they heard her talking. She picked one up and hugged it.

"My kitties miss their backyard and spend most of the time on the terrace. It's beautiful this time of day."

The sun was just beginning to peek through the sky mostly cloaked in cottony clouds. A tanker in the middle of the river seemed motionless,

247

though its wake of muddy water suggested otherwise.

"An American submarine rescued us from a gunboat of angry Cubans. Sasha and the commanding officer seemed thick as thieves," Edna said. "Now we learn they have an army base a few miles from New Orleans. What the hell's going on?"

"I've asked, but haven't gotten any answers," Mama said. "How is your thigh?"

"Still sore but I have pain pills that take the edge off."

Sasha appeared in the doorway. "You are here because there is danger everywhere in the city."

"May be," Tony said. "Edna and I need to go there. Will you take us?"

Sasha crossed his arms. "Do you want to die?"

Edna and Tony were soon sitting in a faded-red pickup truck of unknown vintage. Sasha's elbow protruded from the open window as they headed toward town on River Road.

"This thing got shocks?" Tony asked as they banged through another pothole.

Sasha grinned. "Liliya is old but also almost invisible. Would you rather be in a stretch limo?"

"I get your point," Tony said.

The road was the back way into the French Quarter. Still early, they soon began encountering farm trucks on their way to market laden with fresh produce. The sky was blue for the first time in days and morning sun heated Tony's arm. The scent of magnolia blossoms, wafting in a humid breeze, filled the cab with gentle perfume. It wasn't the only wonderful aroma floating in the air.

"Pull over when you reach Café du Monde," Tony said. "The coffee and beignets I smell are making me hungry."

"I cannot just stop in the middle of the road," Sasha said. "It will attract attention."

"Please, I'll only be a minute."

Tony got out of the truck before they came to a complete stop. Sasha was tapping the steering wheel when he returned with coffee and beignets in paper sacks.

"You took almost ten minutes," he said.

"Quit your bitching. We made it, didn't we?"

Sasha's mood changed when Edna handed him strong Creole coffee in a steaming paper cup and a sugary beignet in a napkin.

"This is why I love this city," he said, pouring vodka into his coffee from the flask he kept beside him.

"I'll take a shot," Edna said.

"Me too," Tony said.

Sasha steered with one hand, avoiding tourists already crowding the streets around Jackson Square. The throng of people surrounding a young woman singing folk songs almost blocked the colorful art lining the fence.

"Another hot as hell day," Tony said as they turned on Canal, barely missing a streetcar heading for the cemeteries. "Where did you learn to drive? Afghanistan?"

"Funny," Sasha said as he swerved to miss a couple wearing straw hats and dark sunglasses.

Tony's post office was off the beaten tourist path. Rather than a modern building complete with electronic doors and stamp machines, this one was granite and steel surviving from decades past. Sasha hung back on the sidewalk as Edna and Tony climbed the wide stairway. Once they'd entered the building, he followed.

The place reeked of must and age. Deserted, except for themselves, their heels clicked on the marble floor. Tony remembered going there as a boy with his father and wondered if the wanted posters on the bulletin board were still the same ones. A single manila folder waited as he opened his box. Tony quickly tore into it, removing the document inside it.

"Thank you, Tommy," he said.

"Well?" Edna said.

"It's the coroner's report. It says Dr. Mary died from the piercing of her heart by a knife-like object."

"We already knew that," she said.

"But we didn't know this."

"Didn't know what?"

"The identity of the doctor that signed the report."

"Don't keep me in suspense, Tony."

"Our very own Doc Bruce performed Dr. Mary's autopsy."

Edna glanced down the empty corridor. "You have to be kidding. Why didn't he tell us?"

"I think we need to ask him and find out," Tony said, stuffing the report back into the manila folder.

Tony's legs were short, but Edna had a hard time keeping up as he hurried around the corner to the front door. Sasha was waiting.

"Well?" he said.

"You know the way to Doc Bruce's house?"

"Of course I do."

"Then give me a shot of your vodka and take us there," Tony said.

Sasha wasn't happy about depleting his stash of vodka but handed it to him. Tony took a swig and then gave it to Edna. The flask was empty when she returned it to Sasha.

"You two drink like Russians," he said. "I like that, but I do not like being out of vodka."

Edna and Tony waited in the truck as Sasha went into a strip center liquor store. He returned with a smile, a large bottle of Russian vodka and flasks for Edna and Tony.

"Enough for each of us. No more sharing."

"Thanks," Tony said. "I hate doing detective work with a clear head."

"Amen to that," Edna said.

"Don't know how I stayed with the N.O.P.D. as long as I did."

"If God had meant for us to be sober he wouldn't have invented vodka," Sasha said.

"Amen to that," Tony said. "How far to Doc Bruce's?"

"Not far. He lives in the Garden District."

Sasha turned off St. Charles Avenue in front of a rumbling streetcar, his screeching tires startling the pigeons an old man on a park bench was feeding. Tony wasn't familiar with the houses on the street, but something about the passing addresses jogged his memory. He fumbled for his P.I. badge.

"Damn it!" he said as Sasha pulled in front of an old Victorian mansion. "Must have lost my badge."

"Don't worry," Edna said. "When we get out of this mess I'll buy you another."

"That's not the point. I think this is the address I jotted down as being Angelica Moon's. It was in the leather flap where I kept my badge."

"That would be a twist. Sure about that?" Edna asked.

"Only that this address seems familiar."

"Who is Angelica Moon?" Sasha asked.

"The lesbian lover of the person whose murder we're investigating," Edna said. "She grew up in a Garden District house. Maybe this very one."

Sasha glanced at the beautiful but run-down antebellum mansion with teal blue shutters.

"She knew Doc Bruce?" he said.

"They knew each other," Tony said. "Let's talk to him about it."

A woman answered the door. When she saw them standing there, she looked as if she were about to slam it in their face. Tony didn't give her a chance.

"Ma'am, we're here to see Doc Bruce. We're friends of his."

"He did not tell me that anyone was coming by," she said with a clipped accent.

The woman was almost as tall as Tony was and glared at him with faded blue eyes. She rubbed a hand through her painfully short hair and looked to be in her forties or early fifties. She wore flip flops, men's gym shorts and an armless muscle shirt that showed off her bony body and braless chest.

"I'm Tony. This is Edna and Sasha. And you are?"

"I did not say," she said.

"Look, ma'am, if you tell Doc Bruce that Tony, Edna and Sasha are here to see him I'm sure he'll tell you we're friendly and to let us in."

You wait here," she said.

The woman held the door open when she returned, beckoning them to enter.

"I am Sinthia Burnwitch. Please follow me."

Tony and Edna exchanged glances as they followed the woman down a darkened hallway lighted only by candles. She led them to a bedroom on the first floor. When Tony's eyes adjusted to the room's dimness, he saw Doc Bruce lying in an antique four-poster bed.

"Sin," he said. "Please help me."

Doc Bruce looked as though he'd aged twenty years since the last time Tony had seen him. His unkempt hair had gone completely white. Sinthia put her arms beneath his and lifted him into a sitting position as easily as if he were a child.

Edna's hand went to her mouth when she saw how much weight he'd lost. His pallid skin pulled tightly around jaws and forehead. Severely thin lips made his teeth look oversized and his head almost like a living skull.

"Thank God you're alive. I thought you were dead."

"We've dodged a few bullets," Tony said, sitting beside him on the bed.

Edna joined them. "Why don't you come with us to the compound? We can take care of you there."

Doc Bruce laughed and it drew into a hacking cough that resonated deep from within his hollow chest. His baby blue pajama tops were unbuttoned and revealed his skeletal frame. Shadows created by the flickering candles scattered around the room highlighted the illusion.

"Most of my adult life was spent in this house, much of it in this very bed. Love, hate, anger, sex; you name it. Now I'm gonna die in it."

Edna squeezed his hand. "We need your help. You didn't tell us the truth, did you?"

When Doc Bruce grinned, his glinting teeth and sunken eyes caused him to appear even more like a living skeleton.

"I told you I was there the night Dr. Mary died."

"Were you complicit in the attack?" Tony asked.

"Please," Edna said. "We need to know."

Sinthia ripped Doc Bruce's hand away from Edna's. Her wiry arms encircled him as she moved him against the backboard.

"Leave him alone. Can't you see how weak he is?"

"It's okay, Sin. There's something I need to get off my chest." Sinthia released her grasp but continued clutching his arm. "I did lie to you. I was in the lab the night Guy Marc burned her. When he

253

finished, I helped move her from the research lab to her apartment."

"She was still alive?"

Doc Bruce nodded. "Mary was one tough bird. Her arm was missing, much of her body severely burned. She had no eyelids or lips left but she wasn't dead. She just kept staring at us with angry eyes, even though unable to move or speak."

She was deadweight, and it took four of us, me, Slink, Jesus Molina and Tex to lift her up the stairs. She slipped out of our arms and we dropped her before getting her to the bed. Tex told us to leave her on the floor. He began going through her drawers, looking for something with which to start a fire. I'd seen lots of shit as a doctor but nothing like this. I threw up in a corner."

By now, tears were pouring down Doc Bruce's sunken cheeks. Sinthia hugged him again and began to groan.

"Please stop it!" she said. "None of this matters anymore."

Doc Bruce managed to extricate himself from her grasp. "It's okay, Sin. I have to finish this story and I need to do it now while I still have the strength."

Before Doc Bruce could continue, a black kitten with a white star on its chest pushed through the cracked door into the shadowy room. Jumping on the bed, it arched its back, demanding attention. Doc Bruce smiled for the first time.

"Such a beautiful animal," Edna said. What's its name?"

"Haven't named him yet but he's one of a kind," he said. "He sings to me when I'm feeling blue. He's a star and has one on his chest to prove it."

As if on cue, the kitten began to meow, making Edna laugh. "He is singing," she said.

Sinthia stroked him. "Bruce found him when he was just a kitten. He was pawing through our trash and looked as if he hadn't eaten in a week."

"He's still skinny, but not like he was," Doc Bruce said.

When Edna gave the creature a pat on the head, he rubbed against her hand, demanding more.

"He's beautiful," she said.

Sinthia's frown disappeared. "If you are cat people, you can't be all that sinister. I'd get you something to drink but all we have is water."

Tony grabbed his flask. "We got plenty of Russian vodka. Anyone want a pull?"

Sinthia took the flask and held it to Doc Bruce's lips until he began to cough. After wiping his mouth with the back of her hand, she drank from the flask, closed her eyes a moment and then drank some more. Tony had another swig before returning the flask to his pocket.

"Am I mistaken or is this Angelica Moon's house?" he asked.

"It was hers," Doc Bruce said.

"Then what are you doing here?"

Sinthia answered for him. "Bruce and Angelica were secretly married. She inherited this house when her mother and father died. For obvious reasons they kept their marriage a secret. Bruce loved Angelica and she loved him."

"Did you kill Dr. Mary because of jealousy?" Edna asked.

"I didn't kill her but if you'll give me one more sip from the flask I'll tell you who did."

"You got it," Tony said.

Candles flickered as Doc Bruce braced himself against the headboard. "We left Mary on the floor while Tex tried to light the pile of clothes on the bed. It barely flamed, mostly just smoldering. We turned when we heard a key rattling in the door.

255

"It was Angelica. When she saw Mary, she stared in disbelief. Then she lost it, throwing herself on top of her. She was wailing so loudly I was sure someone would call the police."

"But no one did," Edna said when Doc Bruce's pause turned into a lengthy gap.

Doc Bruce began crying again. "She sprang off the floor, shouting at us to do something. Tex laughed and kicked Dr. Mary. Angelica tore into him, trying to scratch his eyes out. He knocked her across the room, then grabbed her blouse and backhanded her so hard it broke her nose. Blood was spurting out of her nostrils. He just kept hitting her. Until . . ."

"What?" Tony asked.

"Someone else followcd her through the door. It was Hollingsworth and the ASH. Tex was strong but the ASH stronger. He squeezed Tex's jugular until he passed out, and then pushed him against the wall."

Edna grabbed her flask and took a drink. "Dr. Louis Hollingsworth was in Dr. Mary's apartment the night of the murder?"

The frail doctor nodded. "He came in with Gagnon and was terrified. ASH pushed him to the floor, grabbed his collar and forced his face into Dr. Mary's.

"Blood still gushed from Angelica's nose, her face swollen and beginning to bruise. She was hysterical, begging someone to help Dr. Mary. I'll never forget the way she looked at me."

"Have another hit," Edna said when his hacking cough returned.

Doc Bruce's eyes rolled as he drank from the flask. "The ASH had brought a surgical scalpel. He handed it to Angelica. 'You know what to do with this,' he said. Taking the instrument, she plunged it into Dr. Mary's heart."

"Angelica killed Dr. Mary?" Edna said.

Doc Bruce nodded. "She was bloodied, hurt and angry. She had long fingernails and turned them on the ASH. He wore a gold medallion, engraved with the symbol of the cult he headed. He backhanded Angelica when she ripped the medallion off his neck."

Tony wasn't paying attention. He winked when he glanced at Edna. "So Angelica killed Dr. Mary."

Doc Bruce lowered his head and closed his eyes. "A mercy killing. She couldn't bear to see Mary suffer another second. She held the scalpel, but the ASH truly murdered her. He also murdered Angelica, but not with his own hands."

"Who, then?" Edna asked.

"Gagnon yanked Angelica off the floor by her long hair and exposed her gorgeous neck. He put the scalpel in Hollingsworth's hand and ordered him to kill her. Hollingsworth refused. By now, Tex had recovered from his pummeling. He and Slink took Hollingsworth's arms. While Gagnon held Angelica's head, Tex grasped Louis's hand and then forced him to cut her throat."

Doc Bruce slumped forward and Sinthia supported him with her bony arms.

"Stop it now! You're killing him," she said.

Tony ignored her plea. "How did they dispose of Angelica's body?"

"Cremated it at the research lab."

Edna was shaking her head. "Something doesn't make sense. Why didn't they leave Angelica beside Dr. Mary's body with the knife in her hand?"

"Because Gagnon had other plans."

"Why didn't he kill Hollingsworth?"

"ASH was furious with Mary, Angelica and Louis. His anger resulted in Mary and Angelica's deaths, but he needed Louis."

"Why?"

257

"Because of his influence with conservative power brokers and politicos from Central and South America. Mary knew too much about the Kennedy assassination and she needed to disappear. She and Angelica were expendable; Louis wasn't."

The black kitty with the star on his chest jumped back on the bed and Edna stroked it.

"Hollingsworth is long dead but ASH, Slink and Tex are all still alive. How do you explain it?"

"The experiments with the monkeys and mice yielded lots of medical secrets. Immortality was one of those secrets."

Sasha had ignored most of the conversation, smoking a cigarette in the hallway outside the door. When Doc Bruce mentioned immortality, he suddenly became interested.

"Then why aren't you immortal?" he asked.

"Because I embrace mortality."

Sasha opened his flask and handed it to Doc Bruce. "Who controls this secret of immortality?"

"Tonight is the full moon. A ceremony is pending at ASH's plantation on River Road. The answers to all your questions reside in that mansion. Go there at your own peril."

Chapter 30

Mingo slowed his old car when we reached the river. Eddie and Lucy waited for me to tell them what I had, Eddie the first to speak.

"You've stalled long enough. What was in the hole?" he said.

"The NOFF office was just a front. The real business took place in the secret room beneath the floor."

"What business?"

"Don't know but I found this," I said, showing them the information crumpled in my hand.

"What is it?"

"Page two of a decrypted report. Whoever received it must have left in a hurry because I couldn't find page one."

Eddie ripped the report out of my hand, Lucy jostling for space so she could get a look.

"An old C.I.A. transmission," he said.

"How do you know?"

"Because I've seen dozens just like it. It's C.I.A., and was sent by a high-ranking authority, maybe even the president."

"What's in it?" Lucy asked.

"Like Wyatt said, it's a continuation of page one. Page two says 'dismantle lab with all due

259

haste'. The last sentence is in caps."

Though impossible to know who had authorized the order, the final sentence of the communication made its intent very clear.

DESTROY ALL RECORDS PERTAINING TO HUMAN RESEARCH.

"Is there a date on the transmission?" Lucy asked.

"The same day Dr. Mary died," Eddie said.

Lucy was astounded. "Whoa! Think page one was an order to terminate her?"

Neither Eddie nor I had an answer.

"Where is this lab?" Eddie finally asked.

"I was hoping you knew," I said.

Mingo spoke up. "I know where it is."

"Where is it and how do you know?" Lucy asked.

"A secret facility in the Medical District. Unless you were an illegal alien you probably never heard of it."

"Because?"

"Evil things went on there. Experiments on monkeys and humans."

"You're saying a government organization was running a secret lab here in the city and performing experiments not just on monkeys but also on human aliens?"

Mingo nodded. "It is true."

"Can you tell us how you know this while you take us there?" I said.

Mingo cranked the car and pulled away from the curb. "I moved to New Orleans with my parents when I was young. They followed my uncle who'd lived here for years. He had a job at the research hospital long before I was born."

"That explains your excellent English," I said. "Your uncle told you about the lab?"

Mingo nodded. "He took care of the monkeys and mice. He worked odd hours and saw things he was not supposed to see. Horrible things."

Talk of the secret medical facility had affected Mingo's normal joviality. He grew silent, withdrawing into himself as we splashed through puddles on our way to the Medical District. The area was mostly well-lighted except for Charity Hospital, the thirteen story edifice abandoned following Katrina. Like Charity, the building where Mingo took us loomed in darkness. Eddie began searching maps on his cell phone.

"It's the U.S. Public Health Service Hospital," he said. "Makes sense as Guy Marc Gagnon was the head honcho of the U.S.P.H.S."

Lucy was still on point. "Anything else?"

Eddie's fingers worked feverishly as he switched from item to item. "Nothing official but there are several articles about it. Like Mingo said, they were doing primate research. The program was discontinued years ago."

Rain had moved on. Hazy clouds filled the sky above us, a nearly-full moon casting moving shadows on the old facility.

"Couldn't tell it by looking. The grass is cut and shrubbery trimmed," I said. "Now I remember this place."

"You've been here?" Lucy asked.

"No, but an older cousin told me about attending a function with my parents at an adjacent complex. I didn't believe him when he claimed to have seen armed Marines patroling the grounds, and that there was a machine gun turret on the roof. When I asked my dad about it, he told me to mind my own business."

"Too bad your dad's not still around. Sounds as if he knew more than he let on," Eddie said.

"He was lots of things. Loose lipped wasn't one of them."

"The place is empty," Mingo said. "It's been unoccupied for many years."

"Decades," Eddie added.

"I sense there's something in there," I said. "Something very important."

"How do you know?" Lucy asked.

"Detective's hunch. Anyone coming with me?"

Mingo replied in Spanish. "Los fantasmas y los espíritus."

"What?" Eddie said.

"He says the place is filled with ghosts and spirits."

"My little keychain light won't be much help," Eddie said.

Mingo handed Eddie a flashlight. "I keep one in the taxi," he said. "I'm coming with you. There are many things I have not told you."

Lightning continued flashing above the live oaks surrounding the U.S. Public Health Service Hospital as we approached its darkened entrance. A wrought iron fence encircled the facility and Lucy, Eddie and Mingo stared at the front gate.

"Now what?" Eddie said.

"It's open," I said, holding the door while the three disbelievers entered the compound.

"How'd you do that so fast?" Eddie asked as the big metal door clanked behind us.

"Wasn't locked," I said.

The front door to the hospital was also unlocked. Eddie's light cut a bright swath through the large room with polished wood floors. We weren't alone, the sound of inhuman moans coming from behind a closed door. Domingo crossed himself.

"The room behind that door is where they kept the poor animals," he said

"How do you know that?" I asked.

"When the hospital closed, they never changed the locks. Uncle Jorge brought me here one night. It is a visit I will never forget."

Eddie opened the door and shined the light around the room. "No animals in here."

The noise had only grown louder as Lucy grabbed me, burying her fingernails into my wrist.

"What's making that sound?" she said.

"Ghosts and spirits," Mingo said.

Lucy's hand went to her mouth. "They sound so forsaken."

"Doctors and assistants that worked here performed horrible experiments on them," Mingo said. "They hated humans and had to be sedated with dartguns before anyone could touch them."

Eddie was searching his phone again. "The few that survived were moved to a primate facility near Shreveport. Mingo is right. Even now, they'll allow no human interaction."

Haunted moans and wails followed us as Mingo led us back into the open room, empty except for a few overturned trashcans.

"May I?" he asked, reaching for the flashlight. He pointed it at the ceiling.

"This is where they had the instrument my Uncle Jorge called the ray gun. It was enormous, shaped like a cigar and one end of it stretched all the way to the top of the ceiling. Where we are standing was once a laboratory surrounded by concrete walls. Because of the radiation, you had to follow a maze to get inside. That is where they did all the experiments with the ray gun."

"Was the instrument so dangerous that it had to be surrounded by concrete?" I asked.

Mingo flashed the light across the floor. Marred wood revealed where the walls surrounding the lab had once stood. Gazing up at the rafters, I could almost imagine the large tube extending into the top of the room.

"Uncle Jorge was not supposed to know what went on inside the concrete maze. He'd been told never to go in there for any reason. He did know what the monkeys looked like when they returned to their cages."

"And the experiments on humans?"

"There were rumors. Uncle Jorge took over the job from another Mexican who had to quit after having a nervous breakdown. He had told my uncle about seeing gurneys with humans going in and out of the concrete room. He was horrified. At first, Uncle Jorge did not believe him."

"But he saw something to change his mind?" I said.

Mingo nodded. "He was working late when a commotion disturbed him. He peeked through the window to see staffers wheeling a man into the ray gun lab. The man was struggling but was strapped down, unable to rise off the gurney. He was grunting loudly but couldn't speak because of a rag stuffed in his mouth. When the staffers left without the gurney, locking up the hospital for the night and leaving, Uncle Jorge drew courage enough to enter the lab."

Lucy clutched Mingo's hand. "I know this is difficult. Please tell us."

"The man's body, what was left of it, was still on the gurney. His head, arms and legs were missing, his body split open like a watermelon."

Lucy's hand went to her mouth. "Oh my God!"

"What happened to the body?" Eddie asked.

"There is a crematory in the building. It is where they disposed of the bodies of the dead animals."

"You think it's still here?" I asked.

"It was in the basement. Follow me."

A short flight of stone stairs led to the basement below the main floor of the hospital. With no windows, the open room was even darker than the one we came from. The place reeked of dust and what I imagined was the stench of death. Mingo shined the light at a large metal oven and opened the door.

"Uncle Jorge was responsible for burning the bodies. He came here often." Mingo grasped a rack on roller's and pulled it toward us. "He would load the bodies on the rack, close the door and start the natural gas flames. When the timer sounded, the bodies would be cremated."

"Nothing left?" I asked.

"There's always something left," Mingo said. "Bone and ash."

"Metal?"

Mingo nodded. "Joints, braces and all manner of medical apparatus remaining from experiments performed on the monkeys."

A thick layer of ash covered the bottom of the oven. "Mind if I have a look?" I asked, taking the flashlight from him.

As they watched in revulsion, I swept my free hand through the ash. A flash of metal glinting in the dusty beam of light revealed I'd found something. I pulled it out of the oven and flipped it in my hand.

"What the hell is it?" Eddie asked.

"Looks like a gold medallion," I said, dusting ash off of it with the back of my hand. "Have a look."

"It's the same satanic symbol as the one on your doubloon."

"Check the inscription on back," I said.

When Eddie flipped the coin, Lucy drew closer so she could also see.

"Holy crap! It says ASH Guy Marc Gagnon. What's it doing in the crematory?" she said.

"And why didn't it melt?" Eddie asked.

"Apparently the crematory doesn't get hot enough to melt gold. What it was doing in there, I have no idea."

With the medallion clutched tightly in my palm, I followed Mingo back upstairs. Eddie stopped when we reached the top.

"Anything else we need to see?" he said.

"Maybe," I said, picking something off the floor I'd stepped over.

"What is it?" Lucy asked.

"Tony was here."

"How do you know?"

"This is his wallet. It's where he keeps his detective's badge. There's an address scribbled on one of his business cards. It's in the Garden District."

Chapter 31

Eddie's cell phone rang as we left the Hospital District. I could only hear his side of the conversation but quickly got the gist.

"You're not going to believe who's here with me," he said. "Wyatt and the newscaster Lucy Diamond. We aren't far away. We'll pick you up in front of the bar."

"Who are we picking up?" I asked.

"Rafael Romanov. He was in Bertram's last night and asked about you. Can you swing by Bertram's, Mingo?"

"You bet," Mingo said.

"Hope you didn't just make a horrible mistake," I said.

"What?"

"If someone's monitoring your phone, you just gave them our location," Lucy said.

"My phone's secure. I work for the government. Remember?"

Lucy was skeptical. "You better be right, Eddie. I'd hate to have to kick your ass."

Lucy's comment brought a big grin to Eddie's face. "I'd love it. Can we make a date?"

"If you're wrong, we won't be around to keep it," she said.

"I'm not wrong."

"Sure about that?" I asked.

"As sure as I know the rain will never stop falling in the Big Easy," he said.

Rafael was waiting on the sidewalk in front of Bertram's. He had to bend his long frame to get into the front seat. When he did, he gave Lucy a hug.

"Madeline and I have been so worried about you and Wyatt," he said. "I can't tell you how happy I am to see you."

"Us too," Lucy said. "The last couple of days have been a real nightmare."

"I can imagine. What the hell's going on?"

"Working on a cold case. We just left a secret research lab in the Hospital District. Tony's working the case with me and was apparently there before us. I found his badge wallet and it had a card with a Garden District address."

"And you're on your way to check it out?"

"You got it."

"Mind if I tag along?"

"Why the hell not?" Eddie said.

Thunder rocked St. Charles Avenue as Mingo turned into the Garden District. Lightning laced the sky, illuminating the live oaks lining both sides of the street. We found the neighborhood deserted as we pulled in front of an elegant Garden District mansion.

"This is it," I said. "Don't see any lights."

"The front door is open and blowing in the breeze," Eddie said.

"I'll park down the street and keep watch," Mingo said.

Thunder shook the veranda as we reached the front door. Eddie waited for us to catch up.

"What do you think?" he asked.

"We're here. Let's go in," I said.

The house was dark but not vacant. Someone inside was weeping. Eddie flinched when Rafael bumped into him.

"You can wait in the car if this is disturbing to you," he said.

"You kidding me? Wouldn't miss this for the world and it sounds like someone needs me."

I stopped just inside the door and raised my voice. "Anyone home?"

"In here," a female voice answered.

We found a bedroom door ajar at the end of a dark hallway, dim light of a single candle the only illumination. A frail-looking man lay on the bed with a weeping woman draped over him. Rafael rushed inside and put a finger to the man's neck. When the woman looked up at him, he opened his arms, crushing her in a Romanian bear hug.

"Your husband?" he asked.

She shook her head. "We've lived together for years but were never married."

"He's your husband in the eyes of God," Rafael said. "How long has he been dead?"

"Minutes," she said.

"What's your name?"

"Sinthia."

"I'm a priest. Would you like me to perform the last rites?"

As Rafael spoke, the woman seemed to deflate from the stress entangling her. "Oh, Padre, you are an angel. God himself must have sent you."

"Yes he did," he said.

As Rafael began performing the last rites, the woman named Sinthia noticed Lucy, Eddie and me for the first time.

"I thought it was the Russian, and the two detectives returning," she said.

"Two detectives?" I said.

"Tony and Edna. They're cat people, and Bruce was telling them about Dr. Mary's murder."

"Your husband knew who killed her?" Lucy asked.

At the mention of the man's name, Sinthia began to cry again. "Yes. He'd kept it secret all these years. Even I didn't know."

Lucy gave me a quick glance. "Who killed her?"

"Bruce just died. Please give me a moment?"

Rafael had finished the rite. After covering the dead man's face with the bed covers, he grasped Sinthia's shoulders and began rocking her like a baby.

"Your husband is in the arms of God," he said.

A black kitten with a white star on his chest jumped on the bed. When he stepped into Sinthia's lap, she began crying again.

"I can't believe he's gone," she said, stroking the cat.

"He's in a better place," Rafael said. "Looking down on us and smiling."

Sinthia wiped her eyes and rubbed her nose on Rafael's shoulder.

"Bruce's wife Angelica killed Dr. Mary," she said.

"Bruce had another wife?" I said.

"Yes."

"The same Angelica that was the lover of Dr. Mary Taggert?" Lucy asked.

"Yes."

"Dr. Mary's lover was your husband's wife?" I said.

Sinthia nodded. "This is complicated.

"What was Angelica's last name?" Lucy asked.

"Moon."

Lucy's eyes darted. "Was she related to Tiana Moon?"

"Tiana's mother and Bruce's daughter."

"We heard that Dr. Louis Hollingsworth was her grandfather," I said.

A wry smile crossed Sinthia's face. "He thought he was her father. He told Tiana he was her grandfather because he was so much older than Angelica."

"Hollingsworth thought he was Tiana's father?" Lucy said.

Sinthia's smile returned. "I imagine many men did. Bruce was Tiana's real father, though she doesn't know it."

"Then Dr. Mary was killed in a lesbian lover's quarrel," Lucy said.

The candle flame flickered as thunder rocked a crystal chandelier. Sinthia paused until the distant rumbles died away.

"Angelica killed her but it was a mercy killing," she said.

"How do you know all this?" I asked.

"Because Bruce was there the night she died."

Her admission caught me by surprise. "Was he complicit in the murder?"

Her vigorous headshake answered my question before she spoke.

"He was not there of his accord. They trapped him into witnessing a murder that he could do nothing about."

"Who trapped him?"

"Slink, Tex and Guy Marc Gagnon. Bruce kept it secret all these years. He wanted to get it off his chest before he died."

"How did you become involved with Bruce?' Eddie asked.

"I was having an affair with Angelica. One night, we did a three-way with Bruce. I was hooked from then on," she said.

"A three-way?"

"Angelica swung in many directions."

Sinthia grew silent when I said, "And you?"

Lucy must have seen something in Sinthia's eyes that Eddie and I missed. Sitting beside her on

271

the bed, she put her arms around her. Sinthia closed her eyes and rested her chin on Lucy's shoulder.

"It's a night for making confessions," she said. "For years, I've been someone I'm not."

"Please explain," I said.

"I was born in Cuba, my mother a Cuban, my father a Russian. I was little more than a girl when Cuba sent me here as an agent."

"Who were you sent to spy on?" Eddie asked.

"Cuban ex-patriots conspiring to overthrow Castro. New Orleans and Miami are hot beds of anti-Castro activity. Cuba provided me with stellar credentials. I got a job at Tulane.

"You taught at Tulane?"

"I was a teaching assistant. I mostly drank and hung out with the expats rampant in the area."

"And that's how you met Bruce and Angelica?" Lucy asked.

"Yes and many others. I have another secret."

Rafael patted her shoulder. "I'm here for you," he said.

"I'm a double agent. My allegiance is to Russia."

Eddie's interest was immediately piqued.

"What do Russians have to do with New Orleans?"

"Western Hemisphere intelligence. What better place is there to keep tabs on U.S. interests in Central and South America?"

Eddie's expression was that of a skeptic. "There are other Russian spies in New Orleans?" he asked.

"There was a Russian Army officer here earlier with your friends Tony and Edna."

Eddie had moved closer so he could see Sinthia's face. "I'm finding your story hard to believe," he said.

Sinthia shook her head slowly. "The love of my life is gone. I have no reason left to live. I'm telling the truth for the first time in twenty years."

We'd left the front door ajar. The storm had returned, rain pouring through the open window and thunder rocking the house. The lone candle continued to flicker until Rafael shut the window.

"Who are the men responsible for Dr. Mary's death?" I asked.

Sinthia's smile was bittersweet. "You asked me earlier if Bruce was complicit in her murder. He wasn't but many others were. Perhaps even your government."

"That's impossible," Eddie said. "I would have heard about it."

"Did you know about the secret research facility where they were experimenting on living humans?"

"Not until tonight," he said. "Who authorized the installation?"

"Your government. The man they chose to head it had his ambitions. He still does."

"Guy Marc Gagnon?" Eddie said.

"He was given the green light to perform Nazi-like medical experiments."

"Dr. Mary worked there," Lucy said. "The Warren Commission was in town to interview her the day she died. Is there a Kennedy assassination connection as conspiracy theorists say?"

"Like I said, it's complicated."

"Was the Mafia involved?" I asked.

"Kennedy had Mafia connections and was close friends with several mob bosses. Under his orders, the C.I.A. trained Cuban expats for a Castro overthrow attempt."

"He was trying to halt Russian intervention in the Western Hemisphere," Eddie said.

"You think? When Castro took over Cuba, he kicked out the mobsters from their exclusive travel and gambling Mecca. Organized crime lost untold fortunes. They had reason to hate Castro, and Kennedy tried to help them get it back."

"Preposterous!" Eddie said. "He wanted to rid Cuba of nuclear weapons aimed at the United States."

"Good story but completely false," Sinthia said. "The C.I.A., Texas oil millionaires, and the mob have been long accused of Kennedy's death. They weren't involved."

"Then who was?" Lucy asked.

"Fidel Castro."

Lucy wasn't convinced. "That's nuts."

Sinthia dismissed Lucy with a wave of her hand.

"You think an American crazy who'd spent time in Russia and had a Russian wife killed him with a single-shot, inaccurate, W.W.I. rifle? Don't you find it ironic that Oswald had Russian army ties?"

"He also had ties to New Orleans, the C.I.A., and the mob," I said.

"Exactly. The very reason Castro and his operatives framed Oswald for a crime he didn't commit. The assassination was so perfectly planned it implicated every one of Cuba's enemies."

"Sounds improbable to me," Eddie said.

"Think about it," Sinthia said. "The Cuban Army had elite soldiers that trained dissidents all over the world, from Africa to Granada. Castro was pissed when the Russians pulled out of Cuba. He also hated Kennedy because of his support for the Bay of Pigs invasion."

"So you're saying . . ."

"What I'm saying is true and makes perfect sense. Castro's operatives assassinated Kennedy and made it look like enemies of Cuba, including Russia, conspired to do the killing."

"The government says Oswald killed Kennedy all by himself," Eddie said.

"Your intelligence community is much too sophisticated to believe that claptrap," Sinthia said. "They know many bullets were fired and that he was killed by multiple assassins."

"If that's true, then why do we continue to perpetrate a cover-up?"

"Because people in your government had no idea who was responsible. Did LBJ give the order? Was it the C.I.A., or maybe J. Edgar Hoover? Was it Russia, your primary Cold War nemesis? Everyone suspected everyone else, but no one knew."

"So they perpetrated a cover up?" I said.

"Yes."

"You say you're a double spy. Why would you betray Cuba for Russia?" I asked.

"Because the Cuban government is oppressive. They torture citizens who oppose their views. There is no freedom of speech in Cuba. There is no freedom at all in Cuba."

"You sound bitter," Lucy said.

"I am. They treated my mother worse than shit because my father was Russian. The Castro regime needs to be ousted."

Another question rattled around in my brain. I let it simmer a moment before asking it.

"The secret research facility was shut down the day Dr. Mary died. Do you have any idea how this might have found its way into the crematory there?"

I pulled the medallion from my pocket and handed it to Sinthia. Recognition filled her eyes as she turned it in her hand.

"Gagnon's medallion. He never removed it from his neck. Angelica ripped it off before he had Hollingsworth cut her throat. It must have been in her hand when they cremated her."

"Hollingsworth killed Angelica?" Lucy said.

275

"Forced to kill her by Gagnon, and with Tex and Slink holding his wrists and controlling the stroke," Sinthia said.

"But why?" I asked.

"Control. Gagnon needed Hollingsworth and used the killing to blackmail him and get what he wanted."

"I can understand why he doesn't want Lucy poking around," I said. "Why is he so intent on killing me?"

"Maybe you have something he wants."

"Like this?" I said, showing her the gold Mardi Gras doubloon.

"I don't know where you got Gagnon's prized doubloon, but it sealed your fate the moment you touched it."

It was Sinthia's final words.

Chapter 32

Intent on Sinthia's story, none of us heard three men enter the open door behind us. A single pistol shot pierced the silence, exploding our concentration. The bullet struck Sinthia between the eyes and she fell dead on the bed beside her beloved husband.

"Die, Russian bitch," the man who'd pulled the trigger said.

The men stood at the door, one in khakis and black sports coats. He pointed his automatic weapon directly at us. The other two men seemed even more menacing.

"You two, up against the wall," the man with the pistol said.

"Who are you?" I asked.

The person who'd killed Sinthia was short, wiry, and had a shaved head that reflected light from the flickering candle. He also had an ominous tattoo on the back of his hand. My question made him smirk.

"I'm Slink. My friend here is Tex, and this is my Cuban amigo Jesus. Looks like you got something that belongs to our boss."

Tex was as short as Slink but with a broken grin, and faded brown hair poking out from beneath his Panama hat. He took the doubloon from me, tossing it to Slink.

"Jesus, tie the priest and the other man. These two are coming with us."

"You're messing with the wrong person," Eddie said. "I'm a U.S. District Attorney."

Jesus's face sported a jagged scar that looked as if it had encountered the working end of a dull knife. His black Pancho Villa mustache twitched as he listened to Eddie's hollow threat.

"Yeah, and I'm a black belt in karate. Don't need it because I got this," he said, knocking Eddie backward with the butt of the automatic weapon.

Slink laughed. "Damn, Jesus! I was going to thank him for giving us directions."

Jesus wasn't listening. After tossing the weapon to Tex, he pulled twine from his coat pocket and tied up Rafael. Out cold, Eddie didn't need it.

"You almost caused us to miss tonight's ceremony," Slink said. "Good thing you didn't because it would have really pissed me off."

"Why are you doing this?" I said. "We've done nothing to you."

"Oh, but you have. Now you must pay the consequences. Get the cat and take it with us, Jesus. We can use it."

The Cuban reached under the bed, grabbing the black kitten by the scruff of his neck. The frightened feline swiped a hunk of flesh off Jesus's arm, angering the Cuban. To alleviate his ire, he backhanded Lucy as he returned for his weapon.

With their weapons pointed, they herded us outside, rain drenching our clothes. A faded step van waited on the curb and they pushed us into it, slamming the sliding door behind us. Solid metal separated us from the driver's compartment and we couldn't hear the three men. As the engine started, we pulled away from the curb with a rough jolt.

"You okay?" I asked.

"Nothing a little ice on my busted lip wouldn't help," Lucy said. "I hope they didn't kill Rafael and Eddie."

"Or Mingo," I said.

"Where are they taking us?"

"Don't know, but I'm betting Gagnon's plantation on River Road."

There were no regular windows, only two portholes through which to peer. Lucy banged on the door, trying to open it. Finally giving up, she sat on the floor. I continued looking through one of the portholes until the lights of the city finally disappeared.

"We're on River Road. Full moon beneath the cloud cover, and just in time for a party," I said.

"Wyatt, I'm scared."

I sat beside her on the floor. "Me too."

"What now?"

"They didn't kill Eddie. He won't let us die. I trust him to figure something out."

"And if he doesn't?"

"Then Rafael can perform our last rites."

My words made her smile and we were both soon laughing. Lucy's laughter turned to tears, and she rested her head against my shoulder.

"At least they can't eat us," I said.

She smiled again and said, "Don't bet on it."

The storm continued as flashes of lightning lighted the back of the van. Except for the gravity of our circumstances, heavy rain pounding the metal roof would have soothed my jangled nerves. Tonight, it had little effect.

"At least we accomplished a couple of things," Lucy finally said.

"Like what?"

"You found out who killed your client's mother, and I found out who killed Kennedy."

"If you believe Sinthia's story."

"Sounded plausible to me."

"Doesn't matter," I said. "Nobody would believe us."

"But don't you have a deep sense of personal satisfaction?"

"Right now, the only sense I have is that of desperation."

"I know. I'm sorry I was so mean to you the past few days. You're not a bad person."

"Thanks, at least I think. You're pretty special yourself."

"This city is another thing altogether. How can you live in a place with heat and humidity so high, at least when it's not raining."

"Look at the bright side. We have lots of roaches and mosquitoes."

"Funny! You should have been a comedian."

"Some of my legal clients used to think I was."

"Are you married?" she asked.

"Once, but not now. You?"

"A sorry little prick who's probably screwing his mousy secretary instead of grieving for me."

"Then what's the purpose?"

"He's my agent. I married him to advance my career."

"You don't love him?"

"Not now and never did," she said.

"Sounds like you need to move on down the road."

She began to weep softly again. "You know what's ironic?"

"Tell me."

"There's another female anchor at the station in line for my job. She's ten years younger; a former Miss Arizona. She probably already has my job. I can almost see her catty smirk when she reads about my demise on the air."

"Then let's not give her the satisfaction," I said.

"Wyatt, would you have made love to me at Bertram's cabin if I had let you?"

"You kidding? You're a beautiful woman."

"That's not an answer."

"I'm a man, aren't I?"

Lucy sat up straight and banged my shoulder with her fist.

"Wyatt Thomas, you're the most exasperating person I've ever met. Can't you even answer a direct question?"

"Sorry," I said. "Legal training seems to stick around even though I'm years removed from practice. Of course, I would have made love to you, probably even if I'd known you are married."

"Probably?"

"Stop fishing; that's the best you're going to get. Right now we need to stop thinking about sex and start devising a plan to get us out of this mess."

"Any bright ideas?" she said.

"Maybe we can get the drop on one of them, and then run like hell."

"That's it?" she said.

"Nothing else comes to mind. If that doesn't work, we'll have to go to plan B."

"Which is?"

"Survey the terrain and play it by ear."

"Is that what you used to tell your clients as you walked into the courtroom?"

"Yes, come to think of it. Maybe that's part of the reason I got disbarred."

"Lord help us," she said, resting her head on my shoulder again.

"By the way, I wasn't a divorce lawyer though it sounds like you need one."

She squeezed my arm. "And a punch in the nose for that little bitch after my job."

When the vehicle slowed, and the road got bumpy, I peered out the porthole.

"We're here," I said. "It's the River Road plantation home I remember from when I was a boy. From the cars in the parking lot, I'd say we're running late."

Even in the dark, I could tell the plantation was magnificent. The two and a half story structure featured a wrap-around porch reached from the ground by an ornate stairway. Seven gables topped the steep roof. It would be a show place if ever opened to the public. That possibility seemed remote.

Limos, Ferrari's, Rolls Royce's and other expensive vehicles filled the makeshift parking lot on the side of the house. Our van almost sideswiped a new Bugatti as we made our way to the back of the plantation home. It made me wonder if I would recognize any of the guests. As Armand had said, they were probably judges, prominent business people and other local celebrities. Whatever, they were all there to witness a show that likely included Lucy and me. The van stopped and we waited as the sliding door opened.

"End of the line," Tex said in his deeply southern accent. "Get out of there."

Tex directed us up the backstairs and into a storage area. Cages filled with various animals littered the room. Sinthia's black kitten with the blaze of white on its chest was in a cage, pacing nervously. We weren't there long until Slink and Jesus arrived.

"Almost show time. Won't be long now," he said.

With only a tiny flashlight to guide them, they directed us down a dank stairway into a rock walled basement below the plantation. I had the sense that something was intensely wrong. There was an under smell I couldn't quite identify. Lucy squeezed my hand.

Something was taking place above us, and we could hear muted chants, the drumming of African tom-toms and occasional cries of terror usually followed by shouts and applause. While Slink watched, Tex and Jesus locked our legs and arms in irons attached to the rock wall. Slink had a large, hypodermic syringe.

"A little something to relax you," he said as he injected us with the syringe.

Lucy exhaled once we were alone. "I'm feeling woozy."

"So am I."

"What now?"

"Don't think I could run even if I wanted to," I said.

"That should scare the hell out of me. It doesn't. Whatever drug they gave us has taken away all my anxiety."

"My eyes are so unfocused I couldn't see the far wall even if it wasn't pitch dark in here."

"Then maybe we won't feel it when they kill us," she said.

"Not exactly what I had in mind."

Darkness began filling the crevasses of my thoughts. It must have been the same for Lucy because she'd grown silent, her eyes closed and head cocked toward the floor. I was ephemerally aware of the ceremony going on above us, but didn't really care. All I wanted to do was sleep. I fought with every breath of my strength to stay awake, though it mattered little in the room's darkness.

Hours seemed to have passed when a flash of outside light heralded the opening of the door, and a beam of light moved down the stairs. It was

Jesus returning to unlock our shackles. He herded us to an elevator that had a floor of white marble. He didn't join us.

When he pushed the up button, the lift began rising slowly. The ceiling above us opened and we emerged onto a marble stage. The crowd below us numbered a hundred or more, all dressed in identical black monk-like garments.

Cowls cloaked their heads, hiding both their genders and their identities. A murmur pulsed through the throng as we appeared, the floor closing slowly beneath us. A woman dressed in a translucent sheath of white silk, and nothing else other than the white tignon on her head, approached us with another hypodermic needle.

The audience roared its approval as she injected Lucy and me with yet another drug. It began working quickly. I was soon wide-awake and sated with a feeling of elation and well-being. I knew we needed to run, or at least do something. I just couldn't will my legs to move.

The ballroom of the antebellum plantation was large, the ceilings high. Gagnon had converted it into a cathedral of death. Animal bodies littered the marble floor. A person sat high above the stage on a gilded throne covered with plates of gold, diamonds and red velvet. A hooded robe masked his identity. Except for one thing: he was wearing my client's Rex Doubloon on a gold chain around his neck. It had to be Guy Marc Gagnon.

Near the front of the stage sat a bloodstained sacrificial table. Above the table, a huge, cylindrical machine extended into the rafters. It was the medical instrument that had maimed Dr. Mary and the vehicle of death that would likely end our lives.

Chanting and drumbeats continued as another woman appeared from behind a curtain and walked out on the stage beside us. Though I was mentally incapacitated, I recognized her as the person that had received the lave tet we'd witnessed while at the White Dove compound.

Behind us, a large, marble tub filled with steaming water exuded the sweet odor of crushed rose petals. Two more White Doves joined the woman who had injected us and began removing our clothes.

The three all but naked Doves led us into the warm water and began cleansing us with soft sponges. Though the women were real, their touches titillating, I felt as if I were floating through the experience in a waking dream.

The audience rumbled their approval as the Doves finished bathing us. Leading us out of the water, they curtsied to the person on the throne before presenting us to the satanic congregation.

Lucy and I were physically and mentally incapable of running. Not that it mattered because the Doves locked our ankles and wrists in timbered cross braces that seemed the antithesis of a Christian cross. The crosses were on wheels and they rolled us out on stage. As the tempo of the drums increased, I awaited with dull interest for what was to happen next.

Shackled and naked in front of the congregation, I watched as overhead lights began to dim. A Dove lighted candles, all black and set in silver candelabras. Torches and flickering candles soon filled the auditorium with an eerie light.

Someone played a trumpet solo behind the curtains. When the music ceased, a cold mist began filling the stage. A person in a black robe stepped through it, stopping to bow to the man sitting on the throne. When he nodded and waved his hand, the person stepped to the front of the stage and dropped her robe. It was Tiana Moon.

A gasp and then a titter flowed and ebbed through the rapt audience. Tiana was naked except for a chain of gold around her waist and the Rex broach on a chain around her neck. Flickering candle light and the drugs in my veins had mesmerized me, and I found her incredibly beautiful. A White Dove handed her a silver chalice and she drank from it until wine trickled down between her breasts. The auditorium became deathly quiet as she produced a sheet of paper and began to read.

"In Nomine Dei Nostri Satanas, Luciferi Excelsi," she said, her words echoing through the satanic temple. "In the name of Satan, Ruler of the earth, true god, almighty and ineffable, who hast created man to reflect in thine own image and likeness, I invite the Forces of Darkness to bestow their infernal power upon me. Open the gates of hell to come forth to greet me as your sister and friend."

"Amen," the congregation chanted.

A bell rang from somewhere in the darkness. A Dove refilled her chalice. She had a silver receptacle in her hands. Tiana placed the paper into it, lighting it with a spark straight from her palms. When the flame died away, she drank more wine from the silver chalice.

As the audience watched with rapt attention, Tiana raised her arms toward the ceiling. Two Doves led a naked young woman to her. It was the woman initiate from compound on Carondelet.

The two Doves led her to the table and then handed Tiana a hypodermic syringe. She inserted it into the artery behind the young woman's left ear. As she did, the linear accelerator began moving, the tip halting above the woman's head.

When a single burst of electronic light issued from the accelerator, the woman groaned loudly. Tiana removed the syringe from her neck, spurting a shot of blood into her mouth. She dispensed the rest into her chalice, handed it to Gagnon and then prostrated herself in front of him. As I watched, he removed the cowl over his head and began to transform as he drank from the chalice.

"Hail Satan," someone called from the audience.

It was Satan. Gagnon's features grew coarse, his skin the color of Tandoori chicken, his eyes an unearthly yellow. Descending from his throne, he kicked Tiana aside and moved to the table where the young woman lay.

Gagnon took control of the linear accelerator, using it to torture the young woman. She finally died a screaming death. Members of the audience went crazy as he lifted the burned body in his arms, raising it above his head for all to see. When Gagnon dropped the body in the front row, the satanic faithful began pouring toward the stage to touch it.

Even under the influence of the drugs in my veins, I could see Lucy was horrified.

When the Doves came to release her shackles, I said. "Take me first."

Chapter 33

After hearing of Bruce's dire condition, Mama Mulate insisted that Sasha take her to the doctor's Garden District mansion so she could see him before he died. Though ready for a breather, Tony and Edna went with her, and so did Tamela.

The day's massive storm had dissipated, only gentle rain falling when they reached the house. They found the front door open and wafting in a rainy breeze. Sensing something amiss, Tony rushed to the bedroom. He encountered a scene he hadn't anticipated.

Eddie was lying on the floor, his eyes closed. Mingo crouched over him. Rafael was sitting against the wall, gagged and bound. Doc Bruce and Sinthia were lying dead on the bed. Tony dived on Mingo, wrestling him to the floor and holding him there until Sasha put a pistol to his head.

"Don't shoot," Mingo said. "I am just the taxi driver. I brought these people here. Rafael will tell you."

Edna was already removing the gag from Rafael's mouth.

"He's telling the truth," he said.

"Mama went searching for a bathroom, returning with a damp rag with which she used to revive Eddie.

"What the hell happened?" Tony asked.

Eddie groaned as he rubbed his head. "Slink, Tex, and a Cuban creep named Jesus ambushed us. They killed Sinthia and kidnapped Lucy and Wyatt."

After a moment spent massaging his wrists, Rafael checked on Sinthia. After performing the last rites, he handed something to Tony he'd found in her hand.

"Wyatt said you were working with him on an investigation. He found this in the crematory of some secret medical lab."

Tony flipped the gold medallion. "What is it?" he asked.

"According to Sinthia, a woman named Angelica Moon ripped it from a man's neck just before he had her killed."

"What man?"

"His name is engraved on the medallion."

"Check this, Edna. Here's the medallion Angelica yanked off Guy Marc Gagnon's neck. Wyatt and Lucy must have visited the research facility."

"I was with them," Eddie said. "We found your wallet with this address on the back of one of your business cards."

Eddie handed it to Tony. "I never expected to see this again. Know where they took Wyatt and Lucy?"

"A plantation on River Road. Are you going to introduce me to this gorgeous woman?" Eddie said, smiling at Tamela.

"I'm Tamela," she said.

"Eddie. Pleased to meet you."

Rafael stepped forward. "And I'm Rafael. Sorry to be so obnoxious but Eddie and I are both single."

Tamela shook his hand. "Always happy to meet handsome single men."

Edna hadn't noticed the amorous exchange. "Tony, we have to do something," she said.

Sensing Edna's anxiety, Mama said, "How much danger are they in?"

"Big time danger. There's a satanic ceremony happening tonight and Wyatt and Lucy may be the main attraction."

"Devil worshippers," Mama said.

"The Forces of Darkness," Rafael said.

Mama's hand went to her mouth. "Oh no!"

"Bad?" Rafael asked.

Mama nodded. "Couldn't be any worse. It's a full moon tonight and evil's afoot."

Sasha checked his pistol. "Time is short. I am going to the plantation."

"I'm coming with you," Tony said.

"So am I," Edna said.

Sasha embraced them. "You are both warriors. I have more weapons in the car. Mama, you will have to find another ride to the compound."

"My cab is outside," Mingo said. "I will take her."

"That's not where I'm going," Mama said.

Sasha shook his head. "You cannot come with us. You have no training and would just get yourself killed."

"There are other ways to combat satanic evil. I'm going to Madam Aja's."

Sasha embraced her. "I have seen your magic, and it is powerful. Lucy and Wyatt are in grave danger, maybe already dead. Are you ready, comrades?"

"If you're not moving forward, then you're backing up," Tony said.

"What about Sinthia and Bruce?" Rafael asked.

Edna and Sasha were already out the door. "Leave them," Tony said. "They ain't going no place."

"Then Godspeed," Rafael called to them.

"Amen to that," Mama said. Turning to Mingo, she shook his hand. "I'm Mama Mulate, a voodoo mambo. Do you believe in spirits?"

"Yes, pretty señorita," he said.

"Well, if you go with me, you are guaranteed to encounter a few."

"I cannot see into the future, but I feel I am safe with you," he said.

They didn't bother shutting the front door of the Garden District mansion as they returned outside to drizzling darkness. Sasha's car was already gone as Mama gave Mingo directions to Madam Aja's.

"What do you have in mind, Mama?" Tamela asked.

"My religion practices two types of magic: good and dark. I have only practiced the former. Tonight, we need the latter."

"Everyone in New Orleans has heard of Madam Aja," Mingo said. "She is a legend, though I did not know she truly exists."

"She is ancient but very much alive," Mama said. "An old-style, French Quarter hoodoo priestess that can cast spells and perform black magic. Right now, we need her powers desperately."

"What about the police?" Tamela asked.

"They are in on this up to their necks," Eddie said. "We'd probably all end up in jail."

"I'll call Mr. Castalano," Tamela said. "He'll know what to do."

"Frankie Castalano?" Eddie asked.

"I work for him."

"Tell him Fast Eddie says hi."

Tamela quickly connected with Frankie Castalano, their conversation short but concise.

"Well?" Eddie said.

"He has a connection with the state police and is calling in some chits. He had another idea he didn't share with me."

"If anyone can pull a rabbit out of the hat, it's Frankie," Eddie said.

"I just hope we're not too late," Mama said.

Though it was long past dark when Mingo parked on the street in front of Madam Aja's cottage, they found Senora and the old woman sitting on the covered porch. Mama hurried out of the rain. Madam Aja left her wheelchair to hug her.

"Child, I been so worried."

"Madam Aja refused to go to bed tonight," Senora said. "She told me you were coming."

"I sense Wyatt is in grave danger," the old woman said.

Mama squeezed her hand. "Yes, and so is the woman with him."

"The television anchor?" Senora asked.

"They are captives of the Forces of Darkness. We may already be too late."

Madam Aja sat back in her wheelchair. "Senora," she said. "Take me to the altar."

They followed Senora as she pushed Madam Aja into the house. Dark curtains blacked out all light. After situating Madam Aja at a table, Senora began lighting candles. When their eyes had adjusted to the dim light, they saw the room was almost empty except for the table, a few chairs, and a voodoo altar. Mingo crossed himself.

"Now tell me as much as you can," the old woman said.

Eddie glanced first at Mama Mulate before speaking. "There is a powerful man named Guy

Marc Gagnon. He is the head of the Forces of Darkness."

"I know Eddie. Who are your other friends, baby?"

"This pretty woman is Tamela. The tall, dark and handsome one with the tiny goatee is Rafael. His mother is a witch. Mingo is my new friend that brought us here."

Madam Aja grasped their hands. "You must help me. I'll need every one of you. I must take a spirit walk, and I need help to enter the trance."

Senora began shaking her head. "No, Madam Aja. You are too weak. It almost killed you last time. I won't allow it."

She put her hand on Senora's shoulder. "No one can save Wyatt except me. I'm an old woman. Long past ready to die. It's a chance I'll have to take. Mama, you know what to do."

Mama grabbed Madam Aja's hand and began to chant.

"Nina nguvu. Sisi niwenye nguvu. Kutusoudia mungu. Uniokoe sasa."

Mama clutched Tamela's hand and she Rafael's. They soon formed an unbroken circle.

"Help me," Mama said. "Follow my words and repeat the chant after me."

Senora produced a small tom-tom and beat it as Mama chanted, Mingo, Tamela, Eddie and Rafael repeating her words. As the song became ever more intense, Madam Aja's eyes closed and her head began to roll on her neck. The little room filled with ancient sound, flames of the candles first orange, then yellow and finally royal blue.

Spittle began dripping from Madam Aja's lips, along with an unearthly drone that vibrated the walls. As the drumming and chants became ever more intense, she raised her arms to the ceiling and began speaking in a language so ancient that even Mama didn't know what she was saying. After

293

what seemed an eternity, her gyrations ended with a piercing scream as she collapsed on the tabletop.

Mama stopped her chant. Senora ran from the room, returning with a bottle of Old Crow. Tipping it into the old woman's mouth, she held it there until Madam Aja swallowed some. In a moment, her eyes popped open, and she was instantly alert.

"We must hurry. We have little time. Senora, bring me the crucible and a doll."

Senora hurried away, returning with what every tourist to the Big Easy would recognize as a voodoo doll. Along with it, she brought several long needles, and a crucible carved from stone. Madam Aja smiled and nodded, then took a big swig from the whiskey bottle. Finally, she spoke.

"A man walks tonight in the body of the devil. One of you has something that belongs to him."

Mama, Tamela, Eddie, Mingo and Rafael exchanged glances.

"It is I," Rafael said, handing her Gagnon's medallion.

Madam Aja's body shook when she took it from Rafael.

"This object has seen the fires of hell. Tonight, only hellfire can save Wyatt."

She dropped the medallion into the crucible and picked up the doll. Light from the flickering candles dimmed. Thunder rocked the frame cottage as she used the needle to pierce the left eye of the doll.

"Help me now. Sisi niwenye nguvu," she chanted, the others repeating after her.

Madam Aja's attention focused on the medallion in the crucible. Everyone had joined hands again, their repeated words growing ever louder.

As the candles dimmed further, the medallion began to glow, soon turning blood red as the gold started to bubble, and then melt. The pulsating liquid caught fire, issuing a scorching flame that shot to the ceiling. Finally, it exploded, knocking them out of their chairs and onto the floor. Mama was the first to recover, helping Madam Aja back into her wheelchair.

"Are you all right?" she asked.

"I'm alive, child. Let's pray Wyatt still is."

The flame was gone, as was the medallion. Not even a trace of soot remained, only a wisp of black smoke that slowly turned white as it rose to the ceiling.

Chapter 34

Sasha broke every existing speed limit as he raced down River Road. Edna and Tony held on tightly, afraid to speak. He pulled to the side of the blacktop and stopped when they neared the plantation.

"The weapon I have issued you is an MP-443 Grach, a high-capacity double-action, short-recoil semi-automatic pistol. Are either of you afraid to shoot someone at close range?"

"I'm good with it," Tony said.

"Me too," Edna said.

"We do not want to advertise our presence. We go in wearing no bulletproof vests or other military paraphernalia."

"Can't you call some of your men to back us up?" Tony asked.

"And have everyone in America learn we have a Russian Army detachment stationed in New Orleans?"

"I see your problem," Tony said.

"Not to worry. We got your back, Sasha," Edna said.

"Good. You each have only eighteen rounds. Make every shot count."

Tony hefted the finely crafted weapon. "What if we encounter a platoon of Cuban crazies?"

"As you said on the boat in the Gulf, we improvise."

Rain continued to fall as Sasha drove past the parking lot. Because of the weather, they encountered no attendants, guards or otherwise. Sasha didn't worry about the ruts he created in the lawn as he pulled behind the back porch of the plantation.

"All the activity is toward the front of the building. We go in through the back."

They found the door unlocked and made their way down a hall to a room filled with animal cages, most of them empty. A lone man had his hands and arms in a cage, trying to catch an unhappy cat. Edna recognized the man as Tex. The black kitten with the star on its chest looked like the one she'd seen on the bed at Doc Bruce's.

Reacting immediately, she grabbed Tex around the neck and wrestled him to the floor. Tony jumped into the fray, attempting to help. Both he and Edna were soon bleeding from the knife Tex quickly produced. Sasha put his knife to Tex's throat, killing him instantly.

Edna and Tony pulled themselves out of the bloody pile, only to face an angry Sasha.

"I thought you were professionals," he said. "Wait for me in the car. I will take care of this alone."

"No way," Tony said.

"We're sorry, Sasha," Edna said. "I just lost it when I saw that low-life abusing the kitten."

"You could have gotten us all killed and caused our mission to fail. I will not work with amateurs."

"Cut us a break," Tony said. "That's one of the men that branded Edna's significant other. You would have acted the same."

"No, I would not have. I will accept your explanations because I need you. Next time, go for the kill. There is no room for sentiment in the game we are playing."

"Duly chastised," Edna said.

"What now?" Tony asked.

"You are both bleeding."

"Mine's just a scratch," Edna said.

"Most of it is Tex's blood," Tony said.

"There is a bathroom. Clean it up. Some people can smell blood, you know."

Sasha was peering out the door when Tony and Edna returned.

"The ceremony is in progress somewhere near the center of this building. We spread out, establish strategic positions, and prepare for a possible crossfire." Sasha pointed. "That is north. Your post, Tony. Edna's will be one hundred twenty degrees west of yours. Mine is one hundred twenty degrees east of Edna's. Hold your fire until you hear my first shot. Is everyone on board?"

Sasha grinned when Tony said, "You got it. When we hear your pistol, then Katy bar the door."

"Lots of black cloaks on hangers," Edna said. "Should we go in disguise?"

"I need no cloak," Sasha said.

"I'm putting one on," Edna said.

"Me too," Tony said.

"As you like," Sasha said.

Once he had disappeared out the door, Edna winked at Tony.

"Hardheaded turkey," she said.

"He's just a kid," Tony said. "When he gets as old as you and me, he'll learn you can't do everything by the book."

"If he lives that long," Edna said.

Once the dark cloak covered his head, Tony exited the room to find his post. Before Edna could follow, something brushed against her leg. It was Doc Bruce's kitten.

"How you doing, baby?" Edna said, reaching down to pet the cat.

Seeing how frightened it was, she picked it up and stroked it. The kitty closed its eyes and fell asleep in her arms.

"Okay, you're coming with me," she said.

After stuffing the kitten into the pocket of her cloak, she opened the door to see two men in black sports coats exit from a doorway. Before the door shut behind them, she heard a muffled shout that sounded like Sasha. She followed them down the hall to see where they were going.

When they entered a room through a metal door, she observed the building's command center, complete with viewing screens for the plantation's security cameras. Checking first on the kitten still asleep in her pocket, and then the Russian pistol, she retraced her steps down the hallway.

She found the door from where the two men had exited unlocked, and carefully opened it. The stairway was dark, only a muted glow coming from the basement. Dressed in the black cloak, she knew she was almost invisible. The guard sitting on the steps didn't hear her creeping down the stairs. He wheeled around when the kitten woke up and emitted a terrified howl.

Edna nailed the man with the barrel of her pistol. He tumbled down the stairs and didn't get up.

"It's okay, kitty," she said, giving the feline an assuring stroke. "Are you in here, Sasha?"

"Over here," he called, his voice echoing off bare walls.

"I can't see a thing," she said.

"There's a lantern on the floor in front of me. I saw it when they brought me down."

Edna groped in the darkness, moving toward the sound of Sasha's voice. When she reached the wall, she touched something sticky that caused her to recoil.

"Sasha, where are you?"

"Here," he said.

She found the lantern, kicking it as she moved toward his voice. The batteries were fresh, and the lantern powered up when she fumbled for the switch. The basement was suddenly awash in dim light and dark shadows.

Skeletons and decaying bodies clasped in wrist and leg irons hung from the walls. That wasn't all. Medieval torture devices filled the dank basement. Edna realized what she had smelled when she'd opened the door. Death!

"Oh my God!" she said. "We're in a torture chamber."

"The guard has keys," Sasha said.

Edna found them in the unconscious man's hand.

"Why did you not kill him?" he said.

"Would have made too much noise. Now stop criticizing me. I have the keys and you're hung up like a Thanksgiving turkey."

Sasha spent a moment rubbing his wrists once Edna had released him from his chains.

"Give me your gun," he said. "You stay behind, and I will join Tony."

He gave her a dirty look when she said, "I have a better idea."

"And what would that be?"

"The command center for this little piece of heaven is down the hall. Let's take it, and then we'll have control."

"Show me," he said.

When they reached the metal door, Sasha raised his pistol to shoot the lock. Edna touched his hand and shook her head.

"Let me," she said.

Sasha watched as she tapped on the door. When it opened a crack, and a man peered out, she grabbed a hank of his dark hair and yanked him into the hall. As he fell forward, she kneed him in the chin, dropping him to the floor. Sasha started for the door, but Edna stopped him.

"I said, let me."

With the door ajar, she whistled. In a moment, she whistled again. When a second man poked his head out the door, she grabbed his hair and yanked him into the hall.

"There are two more men in there," she said.

"I will take them out," Sasha said.

Edna shook her head. "Too much electronic equipment we don't want to destroy. Give me the pistol and I'll take care of the two men."

Sasha handed it to her. "Then do it," he said.

Two men sat at computer screens when Edna entered the command facility. They turned when she spoke, finding themselves staring into the muzzle of her pistol.

"What's for dinner?"

Sasha dragged the two men in the hall into the room and shut the metal door after them. Their prisoners were all soon disarmed and locked in a closet. The main screen focused on the ongoing ceremony in the main auditorium. Sasha and Edna stared at the screen as Gagnon first tortured and then killed a young woman. Sasha began studying the control panel.

"Good thing I am an engineer," he said.

"What are you doing?" Edna asked.

"We cannot help Tony in the auditorium. There must be another way to save Lucy and Wyatt."

Edna watched with interest. "Better you than me. I don't even own a computer."

The closet where they had locked the Cubans was mostly soundproof. All they could hear were kicks against the steel door and muffled shouts.

"That is Tony standing against the wall," Sasha said. "I glimpsed his face. He will be in grave danger if my plan is successful."

"I'm going to get him," Edna said.

"And then get out of the building and as far away as you can run."

"What do you intend to do?"

"Blow this God forsaken building straight to hell."

"What about Lucy and Wyatt?"

"If my plan works, they will be safe."

"How will you free them from their chains?"

Sasha paused, glanced at the ceiling and tapped on the keyboard with his fingers. "I do not know."

"Tony and I can do it," she said.

"I will cause a diversion. When I do, rush the stage, free them, and then get out of the building."

"You don't sound very confident."

"I will continue working on the plan," he said.

"You're not planning on getting yourself blown up, are you?"

Sasha grinned. "I am a Russian soldier, not a suicide bomber."

"Sure about that?"

Sasha didn't answer, asking instead, "Do you have any vodka left?"

Edna fished inside the robe until she found her silver flask. She handed it to him. He took a drink and then gave it back to her.

"May God go with you," he said.

"No, may God go with us. Keep the hooch. You're gonna need it," she said, winking as she placed the flask beside the keyboard.

Tony had realized the futility of Sasha's plan before he'd ever entered the dimly lit auditorium. There was no way of getting the participants of the ongoing ceremony into a three-point crossfire. Even if they could, gunfire would result in mass mayhem. Backing against the wall, he watched the spectacle occurring on the stage.

He'd heard Doc Bruce's description of the linac. When he finally saw it, he wasn't prepared for how large and intimidating it was. The giant medical instrument pointed at a table on the stage, its other end stretching into the rafters. What else Tony saw disturbed him even more.

Lucy and Wyatt were on the stage, naked and spread-eagled, and chained to twin crosses. A cloaked person sat on a golden throne, observing the audience and the stage. Tony had little doubt that it was Guy Marc Gagnon.

Another thought struck him as he glanced around the auditorium. How would he recognize Edna and Sasha? The plan seemed to have fallen apart, and he mulled what he should do when mortal danger faced Lucy and Wyatt. The event seemed imminent when two women escorted another woman to the table.

Tony watched the scene unfold, wondering if he should rush the stage, open fire and try to kill Gagnon. He had almost resigned himself to do just that when someone tapped his shoulder.

Chapter 35

I was hoping for a miracle when two Doves led me to the table and strapped me down. The creature staring at me was so close I could smell his rotten breath. It was truly Satan himself, I thought, and not Gagnon.

Tiana Moon had recovered and appeared with a giant hypodermic needle. The hulking monster took it from her. Spittle dropped from his lips onto my bare chest as he positioned the needle behind my left ear. Something happened before he penetrated the skin.

The monster's red, lumpy face began to pulsate as if something were in his skull trying to escape. The sound coming from his throat became an unearthly growl as the hypo flipped in his hands, the needle pointing at his eye.

The veins in his neck began to swell, his yellow eyes growing larger as he struggled with the needle that suddenly seemed to have a life of its own. Muscles in his arms bulged as he strained to keep the needle from plunging into him. He screamed when his muscles failed and the needle pierced his eyeball.

As I watched, his fingers began to smoke, and then to burn. The flames caused the hypo to explode and spew liquid and broken glass in all directions. The creature's hair caught fire in a burst of flames.

The audience was aghast, motionless and silent as Gagnon's embodiment of the devil ignited into total flame. The monster's face began flickering between Gagnon and the devil's, though it was Gagnon screaming bloody murder. A Russian voice started giving orders through the building's sound system.

"Get out of the building. There is a bomb set to explode. Evacuate now!"

Gagnon's scorched body continued to smolder as mass hysteria spread across the stage and auditorium. Tiana Moon and the remaining Doves exited the stage, fighting along with the people in the audience to get out the door. Everyone was in panic mode. Almost everyone.

Slink and Jesus appeared from behind the dark stage curtain.

"Take care of those two," Slink said. "I'm going for the Russian."

Jesus approached us with a knife as Slink vaulted off the stage and disappeared through a side door. Strapped to the sacrificial table, I closed my eyes, preparing to feel the blade in my heart. A single shot rang out, causing me to reopen them.

Two people in black robes watched as Jesus clutched his chest and dropped to his knees. When they removed their cowls, I saw it was Edna and Tony.

"You look like hell, Cowboy," Tony said as he unstrapped me from the table.

He gave me his robe as Edna released Lucy from the cross by pulling a lever. Removing her robe she pulled it over Lucy's head, then grabbed her wrist and led her to the edge of the stage. Edna jumped, and then helped Lucy to the floor.

No one remained in the auditorium except Tony and I. "Is there a bomb?" I asked.

"Don't know, but if that silly Russian said there is, then let's not take any chances. Follow Edna and Lucy and get the hell out of here!"

"What about you?"

Tony vaulted off the stage, following Slink through the side door. "I got one more card to play before cashing in my chips."

Sasha had released the prisoners from the closet and told them to run for cover if they wanted to live. He was alone when Slink appeared through the open door. The wiry ex-C.I.A. man gave him no time to reach for his weapon as he attacked him with his knife. Only Sasha's strength and training saved him.

Lifting Slink off the floor, he slammed him into the wall, repeating the action until he managed to free himself from the death grip. He turned as he received a cut across the chest.

"You're paying for this you worthless sack of Russian wolf shit," Slink said.

Sasha did a three-sixty, dropping his attacker with a well-aimed kick to his chin. The knife flew out of his hand, and they both dived for it. Though Slink was smaller than Sasha, he seemed to have super-human strength.

He was soon on top of him the knife clasped in both his hands as he attempted to plunge it into Sasha's throat. Sweat beaded off Sasha's face as he held on to Slink's wrists, fighting to prevent the inevitable. The inevitable never came, a bullet penetrating Slink's brain. It came from Tony's weapon.

Sasha sprang from the floor when Tony kicked the dying man off him and then proceeded to empty his remaining sixteen rounds into the twitching body.

"That felt good," he said.

"You will never make a soldier," Sasha said. "What if we meet resistance?"

"You're welcome," Tony said. "What now?"

Sasha glanced at the clock on the wall. "We have less than a minute to get out of the building."

"We'll never make it," Tony said.

Sasha pulled him toward the door. "We have one chance."

Chaos ensnared the area outside the building. I exited the old plantation home, unprepared for the unfolding scene. Helicopters filled the sky, their spotlights trained on people in dark robes scurrying around, trying to elude the regiment of Louisiana State Police surrounding the area.

"Wyatt," someone called. "Over here."

It was Edna, hiding in the shadows amid the plantation's live oaks. She had a kitten in her arms.

"Where's Lucy?" I said.

"Fox News. I managed to get away before they started asking too many questions. Don't know who alerted them, but they're here in force, along with every other news agency you can name. State police are rounding up the Satanists, so you better ditch that robe."

"No can do," I said. "I'm naked beneath it, remember?"

Edna grinned. "You looked pretty good, even for a man."

"Thanks, I think."

"Where's Tony?"

"Still in the building," I said.

"Hard headed fool," she said.

Helicopters with shining spotlights filled the sky with light and noise. Reporters and men with cameras were everywhere. The police, their sirens blaring and horns honking, were rounding up the Satanists.

We both glanced at the sky as a fiery object coming from the river began a downward spiral toward the plantation. It exploded into a giant firebomb when it connected. Everyone stared in awe as the explosion rocked the site. Flames lighted the area, illuminating police, news people and Satanists trying to flee the scene.

"Oh, shit!" Edna said.

"Nothing we can do," I said. "There's a little bar not far from here. I need a drink in the worst way."

Edna was speechless as I led her to the road, the kitten asleep in her arm. Miles of cars had backed up, honking their horns. Fire trucks, news helicopters, and more law enforcement officers flooded the area as we hiked the short distance to the Satan's Bend Bar. There were no cars in the parking lot. We found Red and Trey glued to the big screen T.V. behind the bar.

"Red and Trey, this is Edna. Get her what she wants. I need a shot of straight whiskey."

"Pleased to meet you, Miss Edna," Red said. He didn't comment about my black cloak. He just said, "Thought you were a teetotaler."

"Right now, I intend to get drunk as a skunk. With the drugs floating around in my system, it won't take much."

"Wild Turkey for me," Edna said. "I lost two close friends tonight, and I have a heavy heart."

"You got it, Miss Edna," Trey said.

River Road and South Louisiana were soon national news, Lucy reporting live while still dressed in Edna's black satanic robe. A customer entered the door and threw a hundred dollar bill on the bar.

"Drinks are on me till this runs out," he said.

"Lots of traffic out there?" Red asked.

"You bet. Can't believe people aren't pouring in here."

The door opened as he spoke, the first gawker of many trying to get a firsthand glimpse of the ongoing story. Before long, Red and Trey could barely keep up with business.

Lucy was in her element as cameras panned the chaotic scene. As Edna and I watched from stools at the bar, she told me about the Russian soldier and filled me in on what had occurred at the plantation on River Road.

Her kitten never moved far away from her. After lapping up the bowl of milk Red had brought him, he fell asleep in her arms.

"The little rascal saved my life," she said.

"You taking him to the pound?" Red asked.

"Elvis will never see the inside of a pound," she said. "He's coming home with me."

"Elvis?" I said.

"Why not? He's a star, and never quit singing to me through the entire ordeal."

With all the drugs and alcohol in my system, I closed my eyes and fell asleep with my head on the bar. I awoke when Edna poked me and pointed to the big screen. It was Lucy, still going strong as her camera operator panned the smoldering ruins.

"Firemen are bringing someone out of the rubble of the destroyed plantation. I believe it is two men. They are singed and covered in soot, but they are walking on their own."

Edna's eyes grew wide. "Oh my God, it's Tony and Sasha. They're alive!"

My heart skipped a beat as Trey brought me a glass of lemonade.

"Think you're gonna need this," he said.

It was the best lemonade I'd ever tasted, and things only got better. Most of the crowd had gone home, Red's bar empty except for Edna and me. That changed when Bertram Picou walked through the door. Tony and the Russian soldier I'd never met were with him.

"Thought I'd find you here," he said, locking me in a Cajun bear hug. "I brung Tony and Sasha with me."

"Bertram helped us slip away before the authorities even learned our names," Sasha said.

Edna and Tony embraced. "I thought you were dead."

"Would have been if Sasha hadn't got us to the basement. That was one hell of an explosion."

"Ensign Anderson and the U.S.S. Morgan City?" she asked.

Tony nodded. "Don't tell nobody, though."

"Hundreds of people saw it happen in person," Edna said. "Millions more watching on television."

"Sometimes you cannot believe your own eyes," Sasha said. "A missile fired from an American submarine hiding in the middle of the Mississippi River, a mile or so from New Orleans? No one will ever believe it."

They laughed when I said, "I think I missed something."

Chapter 36

A month had passed since the plantation on River Road had exploded for the entire world to see. I sat on a stool in Bertram's bar, Eddie, and Rafael on either side of me, Bertram holding court across the counter.

"That Miss Lucy is one looker," Bertram said.

"Too bad she dropped you like a hot potato," Eddie said.

"It's okay," Rafael said. "I lied to you. I never got to first base with her either."

"Okay, boys, cut me some slack. Our time together wasn't about sex."

"You'd think she'd at the very least send you a thank you card," Eddie said. "After her exclusive on Dr. Mary's murder, her career has soared."

"She wouldn't have gotten that exclusive without you," Rafael said.

"I'll never understand how a woman thinks," Bertram said. "I can't believe she hasn't called you."

I gave them a noncommittal look. "How do you know she hasn't?"

"You've talked with Lucy Diamond since the explosion?" Rafael asked.

"Nope, but I got this in the mail today," I said, pulling a letter from the pocket of my sports coat.

"Dear John?" Bertram said.

"No, it's not a dear John letter," I said.

"Then read it to us," Eddie said.

"It's private."

"Not if you let us in on it," Rafael said.

"Come on, Cowboy," Bertram prodded.

I pulled the letter from the envelope that hinted of expensive perfume.

"Does this smell like a rejection letter?" I asked, waving the envelope so they all could get a whiff.

"Read it, damn it," Eddie said.

I had their rapt attention as I began to read. "Dear Wyatt. So sorry we never had a chance to say goodbye. I haven't called because my job in New York has kept me busy. The first thing I did when I got home was divorce my asshole husband. You were right. I've never felt so empowered. I wish I were telling you this in person, but I detest New Orleans. It is either too hot or too wet."

"That little gal didn't get a chance to see the best side of the Big Easy," Bertram said.

"Sorry she stiffed you, Wyatt," Rafael said.

"At least she wrote," Eddie added.

The letter was still in my hand. "You didn't let me finish."

"Did she give you the dagger in her final sentence?" Rafael asked.

"Tell us, good buddy," Eddie said. "We're on your side."

"No time," I said. "Gotta pack."

"Going somewhere?" Bertram said.

"Tomorrow, for a week. Can you take care of my cat while I'm gone?"

"Okay, I'll bite. Where you going?" Eddie asked.

I held an airline ticket in the air as I headed toward the stairway to my apartment upstairs.

"Jamaica," I said. "Fun on the beach, Blue Mountain coffee, a little reggae music and hopefully, a lot of Lucy Diamond. Boys, wish me luck."

As I picked up my cat Kisses and stepped out onto the balcony, it began to rain. I drew a deep breath, remembering what the great playwright Tennessee Williams had said about rainy days in the French Quarter:

"Don't you just love those long rainy afternoons in New Orleans when an hour isn't just an hour—but a little piece of eternity dropped into your hands—and who knows what to do with it?"

His words rang true, and it was one of those days.

END

About the Author

Born on a Louisiana bayou, Halloween night, beneath a full moon, Eric Wilder grew up escaping snakes and alligators, and listening to his grandmothers' tales of ghosts, voodoo, and political corruption. Author of nine novels, four cookbooks and many short stories, he now lives in Oklahoma, about a mile from historic Route 66, with his four dogs, one coyote, and cat, but not a single alligator. If you liked *River Road*, please check out the French Quarter Mystery Series, and all of Eric's books.